FAULTY BONES

J. M. FRASER

FAULTY BONES

Copyright © 2016 by Joseph Fraser

Cover art by Elle J Rossi
Interior formatting by Author E.M.S.

Published in the United States of America by Natalyn Press
ISBN-13: 978-1-946464-00-2

This story is dedicated to Mia Jo Celeste.

She kick-started my slumbering pen.

CHAPTER ONE

HEY, WAIT UP.

See that guy walking past the cemetery? The one who looks like a Bradley Cooper type, only with darker hair? Or a young Tom Hanks with lighter hair?

The guy with a strong-chinned, leading-man look, even though he's homeless?

Hold on. Don't roll up your window or turn away. Go ahead and make eye contact. Mike doesn't *define* himself as housing challenged, so why should anyone else? He's going through a phase, that's all.

And oh, what a ride this phase will become!

Within the next few hours, Mike will be squeezed for money, propositioned by a grifter, swindled by *another* con artist in a poker game, and then sent tumbling backward through time, as in his tomorrow will be our yesterday, in a crazy sequence of events where the effect happens before the cause. Like when he gets banged in the knee by an angry hellcat before a deeper fall into the past creates the situation that makes her go postal.

But we're getting ahead of ourselves.

For now, I'm here to tell you that Mike will soon sit down at a poker game where most of the players at the table aren't what they seem and *every one* of them matters a whole lot. So pay

1

attention, even if you don't play cards or give a hoot about gambling or understand anything about the game of Texas Hold 'em. None of that's important, but the players will be.

What's that? Who am I to express an opinion?

I'm the Many-Named Goddess, that's who. A folk hero, thief, and a liar.

A *celebrity.*

So, of course you'll listen. Who wouldn't?

Anyway, more about me later. For now, let's get into Mike's head and see everything through his eyes at the start of what can only be described as a very bad day.

VOICES RISE FROM ACROSS the cemetery wall, spiraling up from the crosses, stone vases, towering angels, and plump baby nymphs keeping guard. The loudest words hitch a ride on shimmers of southern heat, floating over to find me walking on the other side.

Why does the mule cross the French Quarter, Mike?

Stop it, Billy, you don't exist. Never did. Except in my head, and that doesn't count.

I needed to find a better way, so… I sought help, got meds, chased my hallucinations, neglected the meds, seemed fine, quit the meds altogether, still seemed fine—*for eight years*—and now you're lobbing chicken jokes at me out of graveyards?

Crossing the street, rounding a corner, and quickening my pace do no good. His imaginary voice chases me down.

To bray like a donkey on the other side.

Ha ha. I'm on a bad run, Billy, that's all. No need to call me a dufus.

And I'm speaking to him, because…?

Shouldn't be. Fugue states and conversations with shadows need to stay locked away in the crypts of my addled mind where they belong.

Watch where you're stepping, he whispers.

Geez, Billy, you've got that right. A single misstep onto one of these sidewalk cracks could mean I'll lose today. Superstitions die hard.

So I ease across the next crack but almost onto a gob of gum. That wouldn't have been cool. Not on a sweltering late morning like this one, when everything and everyone melts into paste.

This is the problem with shortsighted strategies. They can boomerang. Like back when I was the teenage Mikey willing to sell my soul to kiss the pretty girl, only to get pounded by her big brother. Even now after I've growth-spurted into Mike and toughened up, the girl has blossomed too, into the fickle Lady Luck. Play poker for a living? Should have taken into account the up-and-down nature of the game. Now the sidewalk cracks threaten to swallow me whole and spit me out as Michael, just another stiff with too thin a resume and the pedestrian hope for a desk job somewhere.

No sweat. I'll get past this. First step is to shut Billy out, along with whatever cynicism he might try throwing at me from the darker corners of my mind. Confidence breeds success, especially for a poker player.

So forget *him*. I'm training my sights on the immediate prize instead—a big enough win for a night in an actual hotel room rather than one more toss and turn on the backseat of my car.

No, the hell with thinking small. I'm all in for the larger dream. A step up the ladder from the antebellum charm of New Orleans to the flashy decadence of Vegas, with its promise of ESPN final-table fame and fortune.

I round another corner and almost run into Stan. He's one of those preppy types who tuck their shirts in and spend too much time combing their hair—like more than three seconds a day. I'm reaching for my wallet before he can speak. Forking over forty bucks.

Stan looks down at the offering in his hand like I spat on it. "That's it?"

"Catch you tomorrow, man," and I move on.

Oh, those sidewalk cracks. I've got a massive amount of

bankroll rebuilding to do. Not to mention repayment of small loans from friends who weren't savvy enough to run the other way when they saw me coming. They've turned into stalkers now who hit me up for a twenty here, a fifty there, and that's before the seedier types who've been pressing for a pound of flesh. Stan's okay, though. Just a little whiney.

So here I am, staggering along the same tired streets of New Orleans. A lot of guys might have skipped town by now, but I'd never bolt before paying back every dime. Besides, there's the bankroll to reconstruct before I go anywhere.

Hard to do for a donkey, Billy. But I'll try.

A few hundred steps and at least as many unsettled thoughts later, the shade of neglected housing dulls the sunlight. Sounds of commerce have faded farther into the distance than they should be, and they lack their usual bustle. In fact, the elbow-to-elbow, touristy streets of the French Quarter are nowhere in sight. Thanks to all brooding and no navigation, I must have turned the wrong corner somewhere past the cemetery. I've wandered off the grid and into the slummy patch of no-man's land big cities are famous for.

Everything in my immediate surroundings hints at ruin. Wrought-iron balconies bend toward inevitable collapse. Paint peels from crumbly brick walls. Discarded party beads litter the gutter. A sour breeze offers no respite from the heat.

Somebody angles toward me from across the street. Jeans and a muscle shirt, average height, close-cropped hair. Stocky. Maybe thirty or so. He slows, takes a drag from a cigarette, eyes me, and keeps on coming.

Ex-military, judging by the crew cut. A panhandler now, or a drunk. I'll always spare a few bucks for either, no matter how thin my bankroll might be. I could find myself in the same spot one day. Halfway there already. And anyway, these down-on-their-luck types do need help from *somebody,* rich or poor—more often than not, simply in the form of eyes able to see them; or an ear willing to listen.

But this man's smirk paints him as a grifter. Or maybe a street thug looking to mix it up—for money, for sport, or for no better reason than he got up on the wrong side of the bed. I shove fists into pockets to grab the makeshift weaponry otherwise known as car keys with one hand and protect my wallet with the other.

Fight or flight? No need to get hasty. Anybody could peer at us from out of a window or on a balcony. A patrolling squad car might round the corner. If this guy's goal is a mugging, he needs to find a spot with deeper shadows.

Our paths intersect, and we come face-to-face. A bead of sweat itches the bridge of my nose, but I'm ready. Electric.

"Name's Runbad," the man says, without a hint of booze on his breath.

"Runbad?"

"Don't lift your brows like that, son. Never mock the weary." He offers his hand.

"Don't call me son." Let's rule out drunk and place the bet on annoying grifter. Still, I do extract a hand from a pocket and shake his with a firm grip. For all I know, he could be planning to do me a solid, bent on some unfathomable pay-it-forward mission of goodwill. Either way, I can handle this guy. "Mike," I say.

"The game," he replies.

That doesn't register. None of this does.

"The game." He nods toward a connecting street so narrow it might as well be an alley. Halfway down, a red canopy announces *Casino* in faded black letters.

Huh. I'll need to check that dive out for action, but not today. "*My* game's at Snake Eyes," I say.

"Your loss, kid." He shifts to let me pass. Then, speaking loudly at my back, "The right kind of action could be your ticket west."

But I forget Runbad and head south toward downtown. I'm a good distance away, lost in the crowd and well on my way to Snakes, before I wonder how he knows what I'm looking for. *West* equals Vegas and all the glitz that comes with it. As opposed to east... south... north.

He nailed it.

For now, I'm walking elsewhere. Nine blocks this way, three the next. Through the entrance to Snake Eyes, on past the slot machines begging for my wallet with their clangs and their flashing lights, into the poker room, and up to a Texas Hold 'em table just getting started.

I grab a seat, buy in, rub my hands together, and get settled, only to do nothing but fold each two-card delivery landing on my doorstep. The dealer button shifts from player to player, hand after hand, and my dead cards threaten to bury what's left of my bankroll if I even think about playing them. King-five... nine-seven... seven-six. Wait. That one's suited!

Yeah? Good luck playing such garbage. High cards rule in this game.

Meanwhile, chips whir in hurried clicks not just here but at a half-dozen other tables in a frenzy of no-limit Hold 'em. The stakes aren't terribly high—just one-dollar, three-dollar blinds and a three hundred dollar maximum buy-in—but hundreds, if not thousands of dollars can be won or lost at these tables.

I'm itching to play, and that's dangerous. Boredom leads to all kinds of rash behavior, such as me throwing a two-dollar bet into the pot without looking at my hole cards. For better luck. For action.

A gal who just sat at the table pounces on my idiotic play by raising to eight dollars. She's got a girl-next-door, redhead look to die for, but we're in a poker game, and the opportunity to exploit a move even worse than my no-look bet is screaming my name. Her sizing is weak, relative to the standard ten- or twelve-dollar raise in this situation. Soft moves like this one often signify a Bambi-like willingness to fold against a sudden show of aggression.

So... I sneak a peek at my hole cards.

Ace-nine unsuited. Wonderful. A hand this junky oughta be tossed in the muck against any kind of raise, even a weak one.

Except... oh, hell, I pump the bet up to thirty. My cards won't matter if I can chase her out.

But...

Uh-oh.

Instead of mucking quicker than the wind, she's stare, stare, staring straight into my soul.

Numbers and I have always been tight. So here's the breakdown. Out of one hundred sixty-nine possible two-card combinations, ace-nine unsuited ranks twenty-fifth in strength.

Not bad, right?

Wrong.

The pixie across the table—definitely not a Bambi anymore—is almost certainly holding something in the top ten. Or else she would have folded by now. Bad read on my part. Terrible read. Most of her possible hands dominate me if we play this thing out. Ace-king, ace-queen, jack-jack... the list goes on and on.

But she doesn't know how weak I am. That's why she's staring me down, as opposed to re-raising my ass out of the pot. She needs information.

I gaze at a point in the middle of her forehead and dig deep for a stoic expression. Otherwise, weakness could crash right out of my eyeballs in this game of chicken, causing one too many blinks, an uncontrollable twitch, a watering...

Toughest thing about the current situation is how cute those bangs on her forehead are. My body could go turncoat on me at any time, throwing off some unconscious tic of attraction—a nervous finger-comb here, the slightest hint of a grin there—which she could misread as indications my hand is in trouble.

Which, obviously, it is.

So what can a guy do?

Take my soul out of the equation, that's what. I'll turn the emotional side of my brain off by going all analytic on her. Like maybe spelling the alphabet backward in my head. Let's see now... Z, Y, X, W... U?

No.

V.

Sadly, the gray-green eyes of my nemesis burn no less hot, threatening to scorch the truth out of me sooner or later.

Such power for one so young. Would the grifter in the

Quarter call *her* a kid, too? At twenty-six, give or take, we're almost the same age as him, I'm sure.

Son, Runbad called me. The slightest hint at superiority never fails to rankle. That's why I ruled out a day job ages ago.

Damn. I should have stuck with the alphabet. Now, I've gotten myself irritated for no good reason, and she might mistakenly read the puffs of steam coming out of my ears as a signal of weakness. Anything's a sign. Gotta hold still here and think about nothing.

Why didn't I wait for the two seat to raise some hand and go after him, instead? This Old Man Coffee sitting to the left of my pixie is all grizzled face and tattooed arms. He doesn't pose the slightest challenge. I'll know the guy's moves before he makes them.

The pixie discovers a couple black chips in her pile, a two hundred dollar raise if tossed into the pot. She tumbles them from finger to finger in her right hand with practiced dexterity.

I'm done for. Can't watch.

The two hoodies side by side in seats three and four look like the type who cut their teeth on the Internet in fast, multi-table action, playing six, ten, twelve tables at a time like chess masters. Hopping from table to table, folding again and again, then winning somebody's stack with a well-timed, craftily sized raise before moving on. They play tight but pounce with extreme prejudice when they hit something.

I crush this type by out-betting them.

But not Bambi-On-Steroids.

Am I slumping in my chair a tad? Gotta hold steady.

The woman in seat five, just to my right, the one with big hair and loopy earrings. She's thrown a couple smiles my way as if she knows me. Maybe we've played together before.

Same with the middle-aged Asian player wearing a Guns N' Roses T-shirt in seat eight.

Odd. I can't remember either of—

"Fold," Bambi declares.

Whew. But that was a hell of a struggle for an eight-dollar

win. Nobody rises to Vegas by recklessly stealing small pots with oversized bets.

My surrendered opponent motions toward the empty seat to my immediate left, glances at the dealer, and when he nods, comes around the table to sit down in a new chair, right next to mine.

The dealer shoves a half stack of red chips, a green, and some whites from the now vacant, unlucky seat to the one on my immediate left where the pretty redhead pitches a new camp. Two hundred ninety-two bucks, including the two blacks still in her palm.

Math and observation. What else is there in life? Hope. This gal just went out of her way to sit next to me.

"Tell me you didn't have something stupid like ace-nine off-suit," she says.

"Right." The incredulity surely shows in my face.

"I'm a sucker for dark-haired strangers," she adds. "Why not let guys like you win a pot now and then?"

"Thanks, Mom."

She doesn't answer, except for her hair, which throws off an enticing strawberry scent.

Mental note. Offer to buy lunch if the slightest opportunity presents itself. But do not try raising her ever again.

At least for a little while.

After we both fold the next round of cards, she slides her two black chips up against my stacks of red. "Change please?" She bats her eyes outrageously enough to amuse even herself, to the point she shows more than a mere grin. Dimples.

This kind of barter occurs time and again in every casino. Players prefer having plenty of reds, so they don't have to slow the action by asking the dealer for change in the middle of a hand.

Or am I party to something more? She could have asked the dealer to cash her blacks, but she hit on me instead. I'm never sure about the poker gods, but whatever gods bestow their graces on guys without girlfriends might be smiling today. Trading my reds for her blacks carries plenty of promise. "Lucky chips," I say and slide them over.

"I doubt that," she retorts. "You're one of those guys who live out of their cars while chasing the dream. Vegas, the World Series of Poker, and so on. What's so lucky about a wasted life?" Her sudden meanness comes low and fast as she peeks at two new hole cards and flings them into the muck with a well-practiced flick.

A shadow worries my soul. One in a thousand she'd guess my hand the way she just did. Not the poker hand, my life hand. My donk of an existence and hopeless Vegas dream. What can I do but make a lame joke? "It's a nice car," I say. "The backseat's comfy."

She scowls.

How has innocent banter careened off course so badly? She's trying to get into my head, that's how. We're playing no-limit poker. Did I seriously think she sidled over to flirt? "I didn't mean that the way it sounded," I offer.

She peers at and folds another hand.

The action around us flows with determined silence. Poker players in casinos sometimes talk a lot but mostly not at all. With the exception of yours truly and the now icy gal sitting beside me, we're at a quiet table. Small measures of wealth shift soundlessly from one player's stack to another, then another, and another again.

She reaches behind her head, undoes a band, and her previously ponytailed hair cascades across lightly freckled shoulders. Did I mention she's wearing one of those longish summer dresses with spaghetti straps? Probably not. This is a poker game. Fashion commentary can wait for the garden party to start.

The sight of red hair brushing against pale flesh reawakens the misplaced longing I thought she'd squelched when she started to mind fuck me. But then...

"Like you'd ever find anything but trash in your backseat," she says.

I choose to ignore her crack and focus on the current hand.

"I'm Amy," she offers anyway.

"Mike," I growl.

Her cell phone bursts into song—two quick beeps and a kapow, like a cartoon gun going off. I've heard that before... the getaway sound for Bugs Bunny on the run. No, the roadrunner beating feet to leave Wile E. Coyote in the dust.

She takes the call, listens... listens some more and, "I kicked you out of my life once already. Don't make me do it again." End of call.

This Amy makes friends wherever she goes.

Beep-beep... kapow. There goes the phone again. She doesn't answer right away. Squints at the caller ID as if she can't make sense of what she's seeing. Finally, "Hello?"

She listens. And her jaw drops. She turns to me, wide-eyed. Listens some more. "No. I can't go anywhere near them." Then she shoves the phone in her pocket. "Keep grinding, Mike." Amy racks her chips, pushes back from the table, and takes off.

"It's on you," the dealer says.

"Sorry." But mostly I'm woozy. Too strange a morning for me. I try to stick around, but after a few more cold hands, I'm done. So, I rack my chips for a lunch break and head to the cage.

"Hey, Sally." We're on a first-name basis, the cashier and me. I've been coming here far too long. Let's face it. Vegas is farther away than Mars.

Sally nods and smiles, stacks my reds, separates the two blacks, then reaches for a wand to wave over them. That's a new rule in this house. Anything bigger than a five-dollar chip gets swiped for verification.

Motion catches my eye. Amy and Old Man Coffee hurry toward the exit, heads down, in a manner that can best be described as...

Sally's handheld chimes an off note.

I swivel back to her.

"Where'd you come up with these blacks, Mike?"

Hold on. Don't tell me. Amy scammed me with counterfeit chips? Who does this? Even the players of a game based on lies

11

are supposed to follow the established protocols of honor among thieves.

What can I do but shrug? The gal who just hustled me out of two hundred bucks is a fellow traveler, adversary or not.

The cashier eyeballs me with anything but love in her expression. "Pete!"

A uniformed security guy rises from a stool in a corner of the cage and…

Is my mouth gaping open?

I know this guy.

In a casual sort of way.

A weirdly coincidental, casual sort of way.

Runbad.

Chapter Two

THE BURNING SUN STINGS the back of my neck and slithers down my spine in a shiver of heat. I surrender to a bench on the Riverwalk.

A barge floats downriver. With any kind of luck, my hangover will kill me before this lazy show of commerce drifts out of sight.

Wait. When was I drinking? I'm drawing the wrong conclusion here. Runbad and his cronies probably dragged me to the casino basement and beat the hell out of me for trying to pass counterfeit chips. I could be concussed.

Honestly? I don't remember what happened between point A at the casino cage and point B here by the river. Physically, I feel fine.

A quick feel of my head proves to be a lump-free journey through sweaty hair.

No, we are *not* talking blackout. Those days are long over and never to be considered again by us solid-minded, reality-facing types who dropped their fugue episodes years ago. The most likely culprit is a beating, followed a distant second by one too many hurricanes at the bar and grill down the sidewalk. My mouth tastes like olive, onions, garlic—muffaletta, the specialty of the house. I could have stopped in, eaten a half sandwich, and downed a few drinks to wash it down. Rum can hit hard on a hot day.

God. That place isn't cheap. What was my zombie mind thinking? I grab the wallet from my pocket. One, two, three crispy hundreds and a few worn singles.

Whew. A buy-in for the next card game still itches for action from within the folds of worn leather. Down to my last few hundred, I've been teetering on the edge for the past few weeks. Pawned my watch already. Sold my smartphone. Yeah, I know, but I needed the cash. Besides, living off the grid means never having to say LOL.

At least the bad run did plateau recently, leaving me stuck at the point where I win just enough to eat a little and gas up my car, skipping only the occasional meal here and there. Overpriced hurricanes aren't in my budget, but better days have got to lie ahead.

Bad runs always turn into good ones, sooner or later. At times like this, what can a guy do but cling to that timeworn maxim? Mathematics, good reads on weak players, and the occasional smile of fortune are the life support of any good player.

But what if I'm not good?

I'm off the bench, on my feet, and I've been that way for a while now, or I wouldn't have wandered all the way into the French Quarter. These inexplicable on-again-off-again zig-zags of my brain get me into fist-clenching mode until Dixieland music wafting out of a storefront provides enough rhythm for me to breathe.

The jazz ends all too soon, replaced by high-pitched laughter from a few girls across the street. They're looking up at a balcony where a couple guys holding drinks throw strings of beads down with their free hands. Anyone who ever roamed this part of town after dark knows the transaction going down. But these girls are barely legal. I hurry on just as one of them starts pulling her T-shirt up over her head.

After dark? How did that happen? I left Snakes in the early afternoon.

Concussed. No other explanation.

And back in no-man's land once again.

We've seen this movie before. The sudden quiet. The crew-cut con man angling toward me from down the sidewalk. Only he's no grifter. This man works security at Snakes. Sure, he's lost the suit and gone back to jeans and muscle garb, but this isn't Superman, who can hide his identity by changing his shirt.

Runbad stops in front of me, drops a worn-out cigarette, and grinds it into the sidewalk with the sole of his shoe. "Still Mike? Your name keeps changing."

"No it doesn't." Nothing this guy says ever makes sense. Nor do the circumstances. Running into any stranger twice, let alone three times in one day goes well beyond coincidence. "Did *your* name change to something real yet, *Runbad?*"

"You'll figure out who I am soon enough. Meanwhile, I've got a decent stake for you if you want some action." He motions down a familiar street, the one barely more than an alley, to the red-canopied dive still announcing *Casino* in tired lettering.

"Not interested. Let's get to the point here. What's your angle in stalking me?"

"My angle?" He fishes a fresh cigarette out of his back pocket, gets it going with a flick of his lighter, and leans against an imitation gas lamp planted at the edge of the sidewalk to give a run-down area some antebellum charm. But it's not like tourists are flocking down this street to soak in the atmosphere. Runbad and I are the only ones present.

A car speeds by and splashes water out of a puddle. Smoothie smooth, he steps out of the way. "Let's skip the needle to a different groove."

Good old Runbad, always speaking Greek. "How about instead, you tell me what happened at the cage? Somebody clubbed me from behind, didn't they? Security guards work in teams." A tic-like insistence compels me to feel the back of my head for damage again. Still no dice.

Runbad guffaws.

Good. I hope he chokes on his cigarette.

Quick as a fox, he reaches a hand behind my ear and pulls out two black Snake Eyes poker chips like a street magician, then holds them up for the audience to gaze at in wonder. "Nothing happened at the cage," he says. "I palmed these bad chips, switched them for good ones, told Sally to wand them again, and presto! You're a free man. She let you fly away like the bird you are."

"Uh-huh."

"Hey, man, you were there, remember?"

I won't ask him any of the dozen questions coming to mind. The thing about these scam artists—and casino employee or not, this guy falls dead square into that category—the thing is, if I start asking, he'll spin some tale with the objective of my money slipping into *his* wallet. Or if not ready cash, then whatever he's after. "I'm out of here. Have a good one."

"Hang on there, Mike. I have a few favors to ask."

Who didn't know *that* was coming?

"I'll stake you if you handle them for me," he adds.

"I'm walking." And it's true. I've turned my back on him and taken the first few steps.

"You're saying no to a lot more cash than you think. We're talking the World Series of Poker main event. Vegas, baby."

I should move on, but people have been guessing my goals with alarming precision lately. Time for an about-face.

Runbad stands there with a bankroll big enough to choke a horse in one hand and those two stupid Snakes chips in the other. He's holding either or both of them out for the taking. "Vegas," he says.

"I heard you the first time." The thought of walking away from that much money doesn't come easily. He's flashing what truly could be the entire ten-grand buy-in, but... "Sorry, I've never been a team player." Saying no to ten large dries my mouth, but without convictions, what does a guy have? If I win... no... *when* I win big in Vegas, it'll be on my terms with my bankroll and no sleazy backer who wants seventy percent of the take.

"These favors I'm asking, they're things you'll wanna do."

"Is that a threat?" A fight could be just what I need to shake the cobwebs. So what if he's got a few inches of height and fifty pounds on me? I'll go down swinging if it gets this goof out of my face.

But he's all smiles and counterfeit chips. "You've got it all wrong," he says.

"Some other time, Runbad."

And I'm out of there. As far as I can tell, he doesn't follow. Good.

About a dozen blocks later—at the outdoor lot where I've been keeping my car—lights beam down like a triangle, not a square, from standards at the corners. The fourth pole went dark a couple weeks ago, and the owners still haven't fixed it. I've been grabbing the best spot I could find in the shadows ever since, settling into the backseat and getting in some z's almost every night without being hassled. Better yet, a truck stop with showers and cheap food is ready and waiting for my morning self only half a mile down the road.

But when I get in the backseat and recline this time, the mysteries keep me awake. What happened to me at Snakes? Why am I simultaneously half-drunk and hung-over? Who is Runbad and why is he stalking me?

The hell with all that. I'll never doze off if I obsess over questions with no ready answers. Time to think about nothing at all and let the atmosphere do its thing. This part of the lot is dark enough. And quiet. My seat is soft. That's the best thing about old cars. So easy to lie the length of it, just bending my legs a little… close my eyes… breathe in… breathe out.

"Huh!" I lurch away from a flashlight beam in my face and into some woman scrunched tight between me and the seatback—nude, cuddly, and all curves.

"Who?" She jerks up, nearly knocking me off my measly share of the seat.

Who—that's a great question. If I got lucky last night, I sure don't remember. How long do these damned concussions last, anyway?

And who is this second woman glaring down at me from outside the car, her red hair accenting the fury in her eyes? The door's wide open, like she barged in on us. And with a vengeance, judging by a flashlight she's now wielding like a weapon. "Damn you, Ricky!"

"Who?" We're wearing the question out, but how did I become Ricky? And where's a pair of pants when a guy needs one? I'm naked as the day I was born. First instinct? Straighten to vertical and cover the merchandise with both hands.

Wait a minute. I know the maniac taking aim with the flashlight. What was her name again? The gal who got in my head after I won eight bucks from her at Snake Eyes today. Or yesterday?

It's on the tip of my tongue.

Alice?

Christy?

Amy!

Why is *she* here? This can't be happening.

No. I can't think that way. *Shouldn't* be happening.

Even *that* has bad implications.

"We're done, asshole," she snarls. "Next time we meet, I don't know you."

"Wait! What are you talking about? I don't—"

"Bastard!" She lets the flashlight fly for all she's worth.

"What the—" I shift hands from my crotch to her true target a couple beats too late. "Fuck!"

This hellcat is real, at least. My aching knee can attest to *that* little reassurance of my sanity.

Amy storms away, but I'm not alone. The better woman—warm, soft, and not insane—the one who'd been sleeping beside me, scrambles up to nuzzle my neck and whisper in my ear. "I could kiss it and make it better, Ricky." She's drop-dead gorgeous, even in the pale, early-morning light. A blonde with all the right curves. And her sexy whisper would make anything better, even before she starts doing what she's doing to my earlobe.

"Wait. My name isn't—"

Her nibbling stops.

Damn. I should have kept my mouth shut and saved the small talk for later. She isn't all over me anymore. Nice job, *Ricky.*

"Who the hell are you?" I ask.

"Cynthia." Still sidled beside me but no longer in girlfriend mode, she reaches to the floor for a wad of discarded clothing. "From the casino in the Quarter? He said you looked kinda shaky when you left the game, so I followed you here and one thing sort of led to another."

"Slow down. What game?"

Cynthia gets out of the car and turns to me bare breasted, but she's already working a blouse back on.

"Somebody told you to follow me?" I have trouble lobbing the question over my thick tongue.

Blouse half-buttoned, Cynthia slithers into jeans, leaving her lithe, bare legs either a fading memory or one fine hallucination.

I wouldn't mind another taste, one I might remember this time, whoever she is.

But she eludes my grasp.

"He wants those favors," she says.

"Who?" But I'm already guessing it's an answer I don't want to hear.

"Runbad."

Yeah. That one.

CHAPTER THREE

CALL ME AMY.

And no, I wasn't a hellcat when I bashed Mike with the flashlight a year ago. Nor was I crazy. It's a long story, so bear with me.

First, let's get rid of the eight-hundred-pound gorilla in the room. We poker players do lie for a living, but *I* leave the fibs at the poker table. You can take the things I say to the bank, as long as you don't hear them in the middle of a game.

Can we trust Mike's version of events, too? Uh-huh. He tells things as they are from his perspective. Always has.

I suppose a shrink might have a field day with him. Is he brain damaged? An amnesiac? A sufferer of severe trauma earlier in his life? He often gets confused about the simplest things, he blacks out at times, and he might even have an imaginary friend.

All this is part of why I love him so much. He's Mike, and he's the most interesting man in the whole wide world.

A shrink wouldn't figure him out in a million years.

I sure didn't.

After everything went south, Peter told me about Mike's fugue-ridden, backward tumble through time and all the other weird stuff. Imagine the confusion time-travel might cause. And the reaction. Like a flashlight to the knee, for starters. We'll get to that eventually.

Peter? He's not important till later. We'll get to him, too.

Anyway, my tale begins a little over a year ago, just a few days before I first met Mike. Back then, I was absorbed in my own misadventures and totally oblivious to the extra dimension or two clinging to him like so many shadows. Think of me as overly blonde for a redhead. Starting with the ridiculous notion that a little more money might buy happiness.

So here we go:

One day, running on empty and down to my last few dollars, I run into a friend of a friend who introduces me to another friend, who tells me about Hal, who knows some guy named Philippe. A French guy. Philippe has a scam going. Counterfeit chips.

Enter Philippe. We're at his joke of an apartment, and I'm sitting across from him at an ancient Formica table with wobbly legs, in a kitchen so old the appliances are colored yellow and green. Not white or stainless steel like the kind I'd buy if I could ever build up a bankroll large enough to cover anything more than a poker buy-in and the next meal. We're talking hard times all around, and that shouldn't make any sense to me, given the fact Philippe is supposed to be a successful counterfeiter and all.

But I'm a little too desperate for cash to worry about that. Besides this man's nationality has captured my entire focus, distracting me from all else, cuz for a poker player, there's nothing more important than the initial read. Ironic, huh?

Anyway, Philippe isn't French. He's an everyday, balding, older guy with tattoos all over the muscled arms bulging out of his dirty T-shirt. He looks like another Joe or Bob or Hank. A former seaman or retired cop who let himself go in his declining years. Until he opens his mouth to speak.

"What can I help choo weef and how much woudchoo pay me?"

Yep, he's Russian through and through, not only based on his accent, which I won't try to pathetically imitate anymore, but also the *give something to get something* attitude, especially the way he emphasizes the word *pay,* dragging it out slowly, the same way he'd undoubtedly prolong my torture if I fail to return every penny I'll ever owe him, notwithstanding the fact I'm a woman, and a pretty one at that. Uh-huh, that's a brag, but I work long and hard at taking good care of myself. We're talking six miles of roadwork a day, minimum. I eat the right foods, barely any at all, and thanks to the unfailing wisdom of my late mom, I brush my hair to a shine at least once a day. She always said what a man finds the most appealing in a woman at first glance sits north of her forehead. My mom insisted on that, so don't believe anyone who claims they're a tits man or a legs man. That all comes after the initial impression.

I know all about reads, believe me.

I gaze into Philippe's eyes, cool as can be, and I silently count to twelve before answering, just to convey how unintimidating I find his subtle menace and the overall dire situation I may be getting sucked into. Who in their right mind goes to a man who isn't only Russian but undoubtedly mobbed up, to get involved as a mule for his dastardly counterfeiting enterprise? Yes, my right knee is beginning to tremble in its hiding place under the table and out of view, but I command it to hold steady. *Not one inch of my body* can even hint at the absolute terror causing my heart to pump a thousand miles per hour.

Otherwise, I'm sunk with a guy like this. He'll have me for breakfast if that half-empty bottle of vodka at his elbow hasn't satisfied his appetite already.

"I don't like the feel of you," I say in a steady voice, "so let's just say I came for a visit, and I choked down a nice glass of vodka with you, but now I'll be on my way."

That's what's known as a bluff, folks.

I start to rise from my chair, but quick as an eyeblink, he has me by the wrist with a powerful hand. Anyone... *anyone* would scream at this point, but I've commanded all body parts, including my throat, to behave, so I merely whimper, and then I bust out crying.

Not that he notices or even cares. More likely than not, he's deriving great pleasure from my ridiculous breakdown. So while I'm trying to gather myself into something if not approaching an Amazon, at least not resembling Little Orphan Annie anymore, he's half out of *his* chair and shouting in my face. "I'll sell you to a road crew if you try to outsmart me, bitch!"

His threat is so full of holes I'd normally laugh, but the ferocity of his expression has euphemism written all over it. He's not talking about me baking in the sun with my wrist cuffed to one of those reversible *stop-slow* signs. It's gotta be worse than that. Maybe he meant he'd sell me to the gypsies, like in *Heidi*. And why is that a Christmas movie, anyway?

Honestly, I don't know *what* he means, but I cry all the harder with terrible racking sobs.

He softens, releases my throbbing wrist, and settles back into his chair.

Tears work. Not that I planned it this way. But who am I not to smile at good fortune?

He grabs a box of tissue from atop a stool and hands it over. The guy's a good planner. Gotta admire that.

I dab my eyes and begin to wonder whether I'm cut out for anything remotely resembling criminality. Why do I have this deep, burning hunger for cold, hard cash? The same shrink who wouldn't have a clue about Mike would probably size me up with professional ease. Dad ran off when I was little. Mom waitressed to make ends meet. And when she got fired for supposedly shortchanging the register, she turned to whatever scam she could get away with, and not always with great success. Mom and I actually lived out of a cardboard box near a truck stop for a whole summer.

So yes, my heart gets all fluttery when I see a twenty-dollar bill. Imagine what a hundred does to me.

I'm greedy. Does my end goal have to be saintly? I've taken good care of Mike. I try to be his everything. Give me points for that, even though he hasn't entered my story quite yet.

We do have compatible aspirations, Mike and I. Money.

Fame. Neither one of us *needs* the latter, but celebrities always seem overly pampered, don't they? I'd take a little of that.

Meanwhile, Philippe has been talking, and astonishingly, I haven't been paying close attention. My game's way off today. I did get the gist of it, though. He has a rack of black Snake Eyes chips he wants me to move. It's already on the table between us. Clear plastic holder containing five rows of bones—chip slang my ex-boyfriend loved to use in his typical stab at panache, the conniving bastard. Twenty per row, and since they're black hundreds, we're looking at ten grand in cash money. My mouth is watering. "What was that last thing you said?" I ask. "About the five thousand?"

He smirks and reaches for my wrist again.

I fight the urge to shrink away. We're doing business now, and I have to be strong.

"You give me five thousand *real monies,* and I give you these chips. We each make five dimes that way. See?"

"Whoa. That's not the deal I came here for." Naively, I thought he'd just consign the chips to me with no up-front cash required. Instead, we're talking straight purchase, COD, so that yours truly has all the risk of investment. Like I said before, overly blonde.

I begin rising from my chair, then remember the road crew threat. Was he thinking about crating me off to Russia, where random, sassy redheads perhaps *can* be bought and sold for summer construction work? *Or winter?* I slink back down, saving face by maintaining an unwavering gaze at his unrelenting eyes. I even manage to wriggle my wrist out of his grip and move it to the relative safety of my lap. "I don't have five thousand, Philippe."

The Russian is beside himself with laughter, ever so natural, not at all forced, cuz this whole thing is an obvious set-up. I'm already mentally placing the friend who referred me here on my blacklist, plus his friend, and Hal, and whoever else helped string the spider strands together to tangle me into this man's web.

"Of course you don't have the money," Philippe says, "but I have a friend who will lend it to you."

"Look, don't take this the wrong way, but is he... Russian?"

"You got a problem with that?"

That's the deal. Say no more. I'm to borrow five thousand dollars from a Russian loan shark and invest it with a Russian counterfeiting mobster who may or may not have come up with bones good enough to pass Snakes security screen. They've started wanding all of the high-value chips over there. Not only that, I'll be turning my back on the idea of simply winning the money fair and square in legitimate poker games just because I've hit a little bad streak that has lasted, oh, eleven consecutive months or so.

And I'm starving. Or soon will be. Mike would certainly help me out if he had the cash, which he almost never does, except at this point in my story, I haven't even met him yet.

So what can I do but sell my soul to a Russian devil?

I'll stall, that's what. And think it over. "Snakes won't work, Philippe. Getting counterfeit chips through their security is next to impossible."

"And yet here you are, coming to see me today."

"Fine, I'm a risk junkie, but I still need to know this'll pan out."

Philippe grabs the vodka bottle and takes what's got to be a mind-numbing swig, draining a scary amount of the stuff in big gulps. He comes up smiling. "I know a guy at the factory where they make the chips. It's all handled. Wand away, honey."

"A guy?"

"A friend of a friend," he says.

Philippe and I must be truly blessed, having so many friends. "How about a trial run, first, Philippe?"

He arches his brows, crinkling his pockmarked forehead in the process. "Trial run?"

I reach across the table for the rack and daintily extract a single black chip from its ninety-nine brothers and sisters. "Let me take just this one to the cage and see whether they cash it. If not, I'll shrug my shoulders and say I found it on the sidewalk. Silly me."

"Fine. Give it a whirl."

"Okay then." I push from the table. "Back in a flash with the cash, Philippe."

"Call me Igor. Extra name or two is good in this business. You'll be moving from place to place."

"No, I won't. Snakes is the only decent casino here, and I like my name."

He's laughing again. "Don't think small. We have friends in Vegas."

The midday crowd at Snake Eyes is as touristy as usual, with most patrons foregoing fashion statements to dress like merchants at a flea market. Blouses, T-shirts, some sandals, shorts. That's a mistake. These people are newbies. Casinos are always on the cold side to keep everyone awake, and this one is chilly enough to bring goosebumps to my arms. Or maybe I'm just nervous.

I walk past the clattering slot machines—the wildly popular lifeblood of any casino, even though they produce bland paper receipts now rather than coins like they did back in the day, according to my mom. She's the one who taught me to play poker, but how good a learner was I if my occupation is coming to this?

I almost skip the cage and head to the cardroom for one last crack at it. Who couldn't beat a bunch of tourists sprinkled with only a few decent players here and there? Some of the visitors are so stupid they wear sunglasses in a room where making out the numbers and suits in the dim lighting is hard enough already, and a simple mistake can cost hundreds, even thousands of dollars.

I couldn't beat them, that's who. I mean, I could, but for some crazy reason, I can't. Not lately. Not in like… almost a year.

The woman at the cage smiles.

I set the black chip on the counter and slide it forward.

"Should I break it down to reds for you?"

Not sure whether to trust my voice, I shake my head.

"Cashing out, then?"

"Uh-huh."

"A big bill?"

She's killing me. My knees almost buckle as she reaches for the wand.

CHAPTER FOUR

I'M WELL PAST THE intersection of French Quarter elegance and creeping neglect where I last found Runbad—this time so deep into no-man's land the clamor of civilization is less than a distant whisper. Why, I don't know. I woke up with cuddly Cynthia in the backseat of my car. Angel-of-death Amy banged the hell out of my knee with her flashlight. And... I don't have the slightest idea what happened between then and now.

Blackout from a concussion? I am *not* going crazy again.

"Your head's fine." Runbad steps out of the late-day shadow cast by a thick old tree dripping with vines.

My crew cut pal arrives in dress-down mode today, his Snake Eyes stint a one-time gig in my bruised-brain misadventures. The larger question is his uncanny ability to pick thoughts out of my head—the lifeblood, I suppose, of fortune tellers and con men everywhere. "Did I say something?"

"It's all over your face, Mike, or should I say Ricky?"

"Why would you?" The words are barely out of my mouth before I realize how inexplicable his name drop truly is. Cynthia and Amy called me Ricky at the lot this morning for no apparent reason other than an insane case of mistaken identity, but Runbad wouldn't know. Setting aside the possibility of paranormal, mind-reading abilities—I've always been a down-to-earth kind of guy, and sorry, I've never noticed any flying saucers, either—the most logical explanation is that I *am* experiencing blackouts. "Am I joining this conversation midstream?"

"We're just getting started." He offers a cigarette from his pack.

"I don't smoke."

"Except secondhand?" He takes a drag, puffs a cloud at me. "Gambling houses reek of it."

I'd turn away, but the impossible notion I'll see an old casino again, on a different street from where it was yesterday, holds me steady. Can't afford any more cracks in an already shaky mental foundation. I'd be searching the Internet for my old shrink by now if I hadn't sold my smartphone. "Well, as long as I'm fully engaged, you might as well tell me your con."

"You mean my deal?"

"Whatever."

Runbad uses the glowing tip of his cigarette to stab three points of an invisible triangle in the air. "I'd like a few favors from you."

"Why me?"

"You're in a unique situation."

"Not gonna happen."

He sighs like I'm the dumbest kid in the classroom. "Every deal has a give-and-take. You do a few things for me, and I'll stake you to the World Series of Poker main event in Vegas. Airfare and accommodations included."

I'd ask why, but that'd be a floor for him to tap dance on. I could drill down on the favors, but I don't want to know. "How much would your percentage be?"

"Optimistic of you to think that matters."

"Who enters a tournament thinking they'll finish out of the money?"

"Confidence is a must in your line of work, isn't it?"

"Yours, too," I counter.

The streetlights flicker on. Another day has passed without

me noticing. I shove hands into pockets and hang on to my sanity for dear life.

"I don't want a percentage," Runbad says. "Just a few favors, beginning with a simple one tonight. Whether I come through with the Vegas stake or not, you shouldn't have a problem with this first thing I'm asking."

How long do concussions last? Days? Weeks? A random stranger offers me a WSOP stake with no strings except some easy errands. I could be hallucinating this entire scene.

Yet would my mind conjure these surroundings in such intricate detail? An imaginary friend or miscellaneous fugue state in the past was one thing. We're talking full-stage choreography here. The atmosphere has a genuine flavor to it, combining Runbad's smoke, the yeasty aroma of a local brewery, and the dampness in the air. One of the streetlamps blinks at spastic intervals. His cigarette has burned down to the stub.

This is no fantasy. More a case of concussion victim in this corner and grifter in the other.

Runbad extracts a thick roll of hundreds from his pocket. "I do have the stake," he says.

I can't help swallowing at the sight of the wad. Last time he flashed it, my reluctance to enter a percentage deal kept me from grabbing the cash then and there. That and my pride. I should build up a Vegas stake on my own, using mad poker-playing skills.

But how well have the games been running lately?

He's wearing me down.

The record skips, scene changes a smidge. Runbad's two counterfeit chips from yesterday now rest in my palm. I've been missing things, entire moments of my life.

"I want you to call yourself Ricky tonight and get rid of those bones for me," he says.

I don't trust my voice enough to spit out a complete sentence. Only, "Why? Where?"

"One too many questions," he says. "Pick what I'm most likely to answer."

No Mensa is needed for that one. My addled mind will do just fine. "Where then?"

"Down the block."

Should I bother to look where he's pointing? Maybe just a peek for verification. Yep. "I don't get it. That old casino wasn't anywhere near here yesterday."

"It's a gypsy operation," he says. "Bad license. They pay off the local foot patrol for as long as they can. Then they pull up roots and shift to another site."

A reasonable enough explanation, but so is my rapidly intensifying lunacy. Am I to believe the owners moved the entire façade—red canopy included, and faded casino lettering, the whole nine yards—overnight, from wherever it was before to wherever we are now?

"The good news is they take Snakes currency." He stuffs the wad of money back into his pocket. Apparently, my only stake tonight will be the two black chips I'm supposed to lose. "Hell, kid, they'll take anything worth money, and at full price—not eighty cents on the dollar like some street player might offer for those blacks. In fact, I hear the Russians pay less than that."

"What Russians?"

"Let's not get sidetracked. Are you in or not?"

"Yeah, for now." I'm totally doubtful Runbad will keep his end of the Vegas bargain after only a few favors—and I should've asked how many—but I have a scheme of my own. He didn't spell out any instructions. I don't need to *lose* these two chips, just get rid of them. Either cash them in, or break them down into reds at a craps table or... play a little poker.

The canopy entranceway leaks a drop of water from an earlier shower. It chills the back of my neck—a bad omen if ever there was one—as I pass a few loitering lowlifes on my way through the doorway. Once inside, we're looking at the kind of whorehouse motif usually reserved for old riverboats, complete with frescos of plump nymphs on the ceiling, deep red wallpaper, and worn carpeting. The buzz of customers sounds more resigned than electric. A clatter of slot machines echoes throughout, but payoff bells aren't ringing. And the haze... Don't get me started about indoor smoking.

Blue neon signs hanging down through the fog point out various attractions: *roulette, craps, blackjack, poker.* That last notice includes an arrow pointing to a staircase just behind the bar, where a dark-haired, blue-sequined singer belts "Cry Me a River." A snort and a listen would suit me fine, especially since the worst thing to happen in this place would be the drunken loss of my *counterfeit* chips. This wobbly fool needs a bracer.

"Dirty martini, Ketel One."

I'm on a barstool soaking in the singer's sultry voice. My drink arrives halfway through the last stanza, and the first sip tells me all I need to know. Yeah, I can taste some olive juice, but just barely. The rest of my oversized glass is pure vodka.

This dive wants its customers to get plastered.

Four or five gulps later, a blonde on the adjacent stool talking to some guy on the next one laughs at his joke so hard she almost falls. She gropes a hand behind her and catches my knee for balance.

"Sorry," she slurs.

I get a good look at her face.

Man, what a small world. I've found my sexy pillow from last night. "Cynthia? It's me, Mike. Wait, I mean Ricky." The fact she knows me by that name makes her Runbad's partner by default. My mom didn't raise a stupid child. But I'm following the script regardless. Since the con man did give me two nice black chips, I might as well play by his rules.

"Can't decide on your own name?" She chortles again and turns to the man next to her. "Meet Ricky."

"Friend of yours?" the guy asks.

"No, we never met."

"Sure we did." At what point did my world turn squirrely? I really should close my eyes and reconstruct what's been going—

Cynthia is off the stool and grabbing my arm. "Come on, stranger, let's you and me play some cards."

Normally, I'd shrug her off, but we have a halfway decent history, if only I could remember it. Also, she doesn't seem sober enough to walk without support. Nor am I. After draining only half my drink, I feel no pain. So we climb the stairway to the second floor, arm in swaying arm.

Upstairs, a half-hearted poker room beckons. Just three tables in action out of six. The one nearest the stairway has a couple open seats.

The floorman motions us to that table. "Chips?"

Somehow, my half-polluted mind manages to remember the plan. "Nah," I say. "I'll buy them from the players." Counterfeit chips can be exchanged at a table without the swipe of a verification wand, unlike at the cage. That's how Amy managed to pass these to me in the first—

No.

This can't be possible.

The counterfeit queen herself is sitting at the table behind a decent-sized triangle of reds, staring at me with eyes that, if broadswords, could cleave any man's soul in half.

I grab an empty seat, and Cynthia takes the one next to me. She settles a warm hand high up my leg. "Play nice now, baby," she says.

With a dealer change underway, the other players have nothing better to do than watch this smoking blonde all over me. And the angry adversary across from us? Let's not even go there.

What can a guy do to cut the tension? "Hey, Amy, small world."

"It's *Rebecca*." She's out of her chair like a rocket, slamming her stacks of reds into racks with extreme prejudice.

Rebecca, my ass. No way is this a case of mistaken identity. *Amy* and I have met twice already. She's crazy, all right, but also pissed about something I must have said in the game at Snakes. Or maybe she imagined some slight. Hey, I can almost relate. My mind could use a tune-up, too. Stupidly, I slide my two blacks across the table like a ridiculous peace offering.

"Seriously? Are you mocking me?" She takes the blacks anyway and shoves two stacks of reds my way. "What, may I ask, is *your* name today?"

"Um. Ricky?"

She grabs a fistful of chips. *Every eye* in the room is on us, and who wouldn't be rooting for this redheaded hellcat to throw the chips at me? Poker's a boring game for the most part. Any kind of action is always appreciated.

"You *told me* you were a one-woman guy," she says, "and I *believed* you. Now you walk in here with some whore on your arm and refer to yourself by the very name you coined the first day we met?" Each of these sentences rises twenty decibels higher than the one before.

How did I sleep through the entire movie she's talking about?

"Who are you calling a whore, bitch?" Cynthia lurches out of her seat, spilling a drink all over the table in the process.

An air horn goes off. No lie.

Two hulking gorillas hustle over, grab me by the arms, and pull me out of my chair.

"You're kidding me, right? You clowns wanna toss *me* out of here?"

I suppose I could have worded that more politely.

As they drag me down the stairs, Amy's shrieks ring in my ears. "I'm gonna kick your butt, you loser!"

Cheers. And laughter. From *everyone*. This isn't a whole lot of fun.

The bouncers hurry me through the casino and out the door, where lowlifes still linger. I've joined the club.

"Don't come back, asshole!"

Who would?

Well, at least I moved Runbad's chips for him.

Mission accomplished.

But if this *simple favor* is any indication of the trouble I'm in for, his Vegas promise better be real.

CHAPTER FIVE

IT'S ME AGAIN. AMY.

Enter Eugene. He's the loan shark Philippe mentioned earlier. The man is as balding, old, and muscle-bound as his buddy, with similar hand-me-down taste in clothing. Main difference between the two is that Philippe had a bottle of vodka on his table and Eugene nurses a glass of milk. I'm guessing ulcer. The business of lending money and breaking legs undoubtedly takes a toll.

We're at Eugene's moldy apartment, sitting across an even older and scummier Formica table than Philippe's. As I look around, I seriously consider a new career as a home decorator for Russian mobsters. They've got a ton of cash without the foggiest notion what to do with it. A wide-screen TV could fit on that wall over there. Range/microwave combo against the wall to the right. Fridge—

"Collateral!" He pounds his fist on the table, almost spilling the glass of milk he's been sipping.

I almost spill, as well.

One deep breath and I'm fully upright again, but completely at a loss what to say. If he's looking for something of value to secure a five-thousand-dollar loan, all I have is my word. Philippe surely told him I'm a poker player, so how much could my word possibly be worth?

Have I mentioned my self-esteem issues? This is still a day before I first met Mike, and the carnage of earlier relationships did little to build me up. Not to mention my eleven-month losing streak and the lack of an actual job despite a college degree. So at the moment, I can't string three words together, let alone the couple sentences, minimum, required for a well-reasoned rebuttal. "Collateral?" I ask.

He grins. Not a dastardly one but not fatherly, either. A loan-shark grin. "I'll give you the money if you give me the chips to hold."

"No, see, that's not how this works. I need the chips to—"

"Not all of them you don't need! I'll take eight thousand."

He's speaking in more of a bark than anything resembling a heavily-accented conversational tone, and I'm recoiling to the point I've almost fallen to the floor, but mostly because what he wants is ridiculous. "No way," I retort.

"What did you say?" Now he's half out of his chair, and the glass of milk actually does spill, flowing sideways between us and down to the linoleum, where a big brown mutt with short ears arrives seemingly out of nowhere to lap it up.

If I were a cop, I'd be calling for backup.

"Are you arguing with me?" His eyes bulge, and he's reaching both hands across the table toward my throat.

I will not cry. I will not cry. I—

Eugene bursts into laughter and settles back down in his seat, reaching for a box of tissue in the process—these mobsters are *amazingly* well prepared—and sliding it over to me.

I dab my eyes and give myself a silent kudo for shedding only a few tears this time, as opposed to the all-out blubbering fit at Philippe's. But I *am* shaking, and I mostly just want to go home. Sadly, though, there's no turning back. Philippe's ten thousand in chips, minus the single black I successfully cashed at Snakes, is already in my possession, resting on my lap, inside the Coach purse I bought during better times.

The deal has been struck. I am to return in an hour with the five thousand for Philippe or he's going to send somebody after me with a meat cleaver.

Should I gamble that the counterfeiter's threat is a bluff? No, cuz he handed the meat cleaver to a Middle-Eastern-looking guy in a hoody, and that particular somebody is waiting outside this apartment in the hallway as we speak. I caught a glimpse of another hooded thug in the living room of this creepy place when I came in. To tell them apart, let's call Philippe's guy Thing One and Eugene's thug Thing Two, cuz they're interchangeable and also out of respect for the late Dr. Seuss, whose books delighted me as a child. I see hoodies sitting at poker tables all the time. Those types are typically harmless, and the timid ones are exploitable in a card game, but not the dudes wielding meat cleavers.

Am I babbling? I do that when I'm mortified. But I've summoned enough courage to speak without stuttering. "I mean no disrespect, Eugene. It's just that I don't understand why you would ask for eight-thousand dollars in chips as collateral for a five-thousand-dollar loan."

"My money is real. Yours is... chips."

His dog snarls.

"Sell the other two," he adds, "bring the money back to me, and I'll give you two more. Come back with that, and I'll give the rest of it to you. Five thousand."

"You mean six?" I do know my arithmetic.

"Not after interest." Eugene's smile is borderline dastardly now.

There it is. I started out going after ten thousand in counterfeit chips, thinking maybe I could give the seller a twenty-percent cut, since I'd be the one taking risks in moving them—such as being banned from a casino, which is my livelihood during times when I'm not losing for eleven consecutive months. But instead, I'll be giving fifty percent to the seller, and ten percent to the money man, leaving me with a mere forty percent, just *four thousand*, and *all the risk,* including the added threat that Thing One will come after me with a meat cleaver should anything go wrong. Perhaps now my low self-esteem is more understandable. I got myself into this mess.

Still, Philippe mentioned Vegas earlier, which implies he has plenty more chips for me to move, at many different casinos. Forty percent of *that* might be awesome.

But at how much more risk?

Eugene pulls a thick wad of hundreds out of his pocket and starts counting them out on the table, pausing to look up at me. "The chips?"

I open my purse, pull out the plastic rack of blacks, and go to work, stacking eighty of them—eight thousand dollars—on the table between us. My hands don't shake. They're too numb with worry. If possible, I'd click my ruby slippers and go back to Kansas, even though I'm originally from Missouri and those two states were at odds just before the Civil War. The argument was over slavery. How fitting. What am I now, until I move enough chips to get out from under the thumbs of two Russians?

Eugene slides the money to me with one hand and scoops the bones closer to him with the other. "Yosef!" he calls.

Thing Two comes bounding in from the living room, hoodie open enough for me to see the thick, dark, wavy hair just above his brooding eyes. He hasn't spoken, so I'll have to profile him based on looks. Not Russian. Looks more like Thing One. Unkind expression, and that's being generous. If looks could kill...

The term *bloody Kansas* sticks in my head. I'm thankful this particular Thing isn't holding a razor-sharp weapon like his counterpart in the hall.

"Yosef will accompany you back to Philippe's for protection," Eugene says.

"No thanks, I'll be fine." I'm scooping the money into my purse without counting it, the quicker the better. "I've walked through this neighborhood a hundred—"

Eugene laughs, slaps his hands on the table, and pushes away to tower over me. "Yosef will protect my money. A pretty girl should just behave and stay pretty, no?"

That's the nicest thing anyone has said to me in the past two days, which sums up how swimmingly things have been going.

I head for the door, as fast as my pretty-girl legs can carry me.

Thing Two falls lockstep behind me, and without a word, Thing One joins the parade once we're in the hallway. We march out the building and down three ruined blocks. Birds don't chirp. The sun hides behind clouds. If I had a loan shark or counterfeiter's income, I'd pick the Marigny neighborhood near the river, or Uptown with all of those quaint shops and restaurants. But what do I know?

Wiping sweat from my brow and glancing back, I wonder how the two Things picked New Orleans as the best place to live. The wet heat here can be stifling, even in mid-May. Especially on a day like this when the breeze isn't blowing. Chicago might suit them better, or Minneapolis. They've got to be overly warm here in those hoodies.

Since misery loves company, the opportunity shrieks for me to bond with them. Something resembling friendship, or at least a nod-in-the-hallway acquaintanceship, might come in handy at some point down the road.

I slow and let them catch up with me. "Hot one today. Sticky."

Neither says a word.

"I'm Amy, by the way."

"No, you aren't," Thing One declares. "You're Iris. Every day a different name."

"Words of wisdom from your boss?"

He flashes an actual smile. "Something like that."

"I appreciate that you left the meat cleaver behind at Eugene's place."

Thing One's grin broadens. "It's a loan from Philippe to Eugene. Why else would I walk around with such a thing?"

"Can't imagine," I say.

"Eugene is butchering a goat for his daughter's wedding tomorrow."

"Say no more."

Thing Two, Eugene's thug, drapes an insufficiently deodorized arm across my shoulders. "Hans and I can help you move those blacks at the casino."

Hans? Oh, *Thing One.* I have no intention of letting a single chip out of my sight until it's laundered, by *me*, but we're in full bonding mode at the moment. Also, we need to be in a nice, safe, public place, such as the hallowed halls of Snake Eyes, before I say anything that might be construed as disagreeable. "Really, guys? That's great."

Once we arrive, nothing spectacular happens at Philippe's. I drop off the cash, he thanks me and pats my ass—ugh—and Thing One peels away from the follow-Amy detail to stay with him.

Out the door and back on the sidewalk, I turn to Thing Two. "Later," I say.

"No, we'll help you move the chips now. Let me get Hans."

"That's tomorrow." Since he's already leaning toward the building to run back in and get his buddy, I'm able to spin away, take two steps to the curb, and open the door of the Uber car waiting for me. Amy, I mean *Iris*, always plans ahead.

Next morning, the charming brick façade of Snakes does little to slow my beating heart. It never did. In the past, the prospect of a good poker game always got me going. If I happened to awaken an hour early, I wouldn't have gotten back to sleep. Most gambling addicts share this quality, whereas few professionals do, so maybe it's time to face my real problem.

Or later? Right now, my heart is racing. My purse holds nineteen black chips created on the sly by some Russian, and I'm about to commit the crime of my life. I'll soon be changing these faulty bones into greens and reds at poker games, craps tables, roulette, and maybe even the wheel of fortune, using stops at various cages throughout the casino to cash them in from time to time. I'll need to make an entire day out of this, lingering at this game and that, or the security watchers peering through their eyes in the sky will become suspicious.

My original plan, before a bloodthirsty loan shark got his hooks in me, was to take my time over a period of days or even weeks. I'd move a black chip here, another there, transforming my small daily losses into wins. This would ease the pressure of earning enough to eat so I can focus on getting my confidence back. I'm a self-help kind of gal.

My new plan is full of holes. I haven't frequented table games in the past, only the poker room. If casino customers play under constant surveillance, red flags will go up when the watchers notice my change in habit. Also, I've never walked in with black chips before. I always buy chips first and then play, not the other way around. That'll arouse suspicions, too.

A partner to help me move all these bones would sure be nice.

But not Things One and… Oh, God, I thought about them and here they are. Dressed in their perpetual hoodies, they're waiting for me just inside the entrance door—unless they dropped in to gamble, which I highly doubt. I skirt around to the side way in, eliminating the immediate crisis but clueless how to evade those two clowns *all day long.*

A man holds the door for me, then staggers back as if he's seen a ghost. "Wow. If we keep getting thrown together like this, you'll think I'm stalking you."

Do I know him? He's probably some random guy from a poker table. I run into them far too often, and they usually stop me for no better reason than to leer at my breasts. I have a thing for low-cut sundresses. Not that *this man* is ogling. He looks past me, as if eager to get away.

But how could I forget such a memorable character? Twentysomething, which is always a plus—since I am, too— he's got dark, curly hair, deep blue eyes, and a baby face to die for. This guy could model men's underwear, and he isn't stuck in my head? "Sorry, have we met?"

"I'm fine pretending we didn't."

"Well, in that case, call me Iris." It's yesterday's name, according to Thing One, but I've been too wired this morning to think of a new one. Besides, nobody heard me say Iris before, so yesterday doesn't count.

"Honestly?" Like he knows I made it up.

"For now," I add.

We've been blocking the doorway. He shifts sideways to let an older couple inside. The clang of slot machines fills the airwaves, then quiets as the door closes behind them.

"Okay, Iris, I could go with Mike *or* Ricky today. Pick whichever one doesn't make you go postal."

"Why would either? But if you're giving me a choice, let's try Ricky. Mike has too much of an assembly-line flavor, or grease monkey."

"Great."

So his name's Mike. I blew that one. "Let's make a game of it. We'll call ourselves someone different each day we meet."

"Sounds like a plan, Iris." He leads me through the door.

Out of the bright light and into artificial, I pause for a moment to let my eyes adjust.

Ricky lingers. An intriguing mix of friendliness and skittishness shows in his half smile. "Promise you won't bang me with a flashlight this time. My knee's still sore."

How interesting! He truly has mistaken me for somebody else. Before I can think of a response—

"Carol!" One of the hoodies waves at me from the bowels of the casino. He and his partner in crime hurry in my direction.

Mike/Ricky arches his brows. "I was hoping the name thing would be a private game between the two of us. We got off on the wrong foot before, and I'd like to set it right."

"Okay, Ricky."

"Call me Bob."

Thing One arrives at my elbow. In an inexplicable fit of mad infatuation, I grab ten blacks out of my purse, hand them over to my Thing, and follow Bob toward the poker room.

CHAPTER SIX

I'M CLEARHEADED FOR A change after a decent night's sleep in the finest accommodations available, the backseat of my car. Then a shower and breakfast at the truck stop, long stroll to the Riverwalk, and I'm ready for action.

The day offers promise. A refreshing breeze carries a tolerable, almost appetizing scent of fish. The seagulls dive-bomb the lazy waters like there's no tomorrow. *Squa, squa, squa.* And the sun smiles down from a clear blue sky.

"The walrus is dead."

The speaker's gravelly voice betrays his identity before he comes around my bench to face me. Runbad is all dolled up in summer suit and deck shoes, like he fell straight off the pages of an L.L. Bean catalogue. Even his crew cut has yachtsman written all over it.

"Hot date?" I ask.

"Appointment with somebody way above my pay grade." He snatches a well-read newspaper out of the way and grabs a seat beside me.

The con man's random appearances have evolved from surprising to customary, but the notion he kowtows to a boss and grovels like any other working stiff, *that's* tough to wrap the old noodle around. Bigger issue is what I'm gonna do with this guy.

Last night's incident at the gypsy casino doesn't inspire any eagerness for the next assignment.

The hope of a Vegas stake is fading fast. I just don't buy it and never did. Besides, with Snakes a short walk away, offering a new start and a ton of auspicious morning promise, my three-hundred-dollar stake could be all I need. Last night's Amy fiasco cost me two counterfeit chips—the bouncers failed to let me grab the stacks of reds she gave me—but not one real buck out of my wallet.

Damn, Amy's a looker when angry. Her eyes were *blazing.* And the low-cut dress she had on—

Okay, that's exactly the type of random thought to derail the sanity train. Time to focus on the here and now. Runbad has been unusually quiet next to me, nose buried in the torn sports section of a ragged newspaper. Why is he here?

"What's this about a walrus?" I ask.

"Huge story fifty years ago. Paul McCartney's fans thought he died in a car crash."

"Did he?"

He sets the paper aside. "Man, you kids don't know your rock-and-roll legends. Quick! Tell me what happened to Buddy Holly."

I shouldn't let myself get drawn in, but this guy has a genius for pushing my buttons. "Tell *me* something, smartass. How are you qualified to call me a kid? What do you have, three years on me?"

"A single day would punch the ticket."

I get off the bench. "I've got some poker to play, with my own money."

"What about Bellagio and the favors I need?"

"Find some other sucker."

I'm thirty paces down the sidewalk, almost out of earshot but not quite. "Those McCartney fans," he shouts, "they heard Paul was dead when they played one of the Beatles songs backwards."

Uh-huh. I've been dealing with a lunatic. Only a bad run of

cards could have caused my guard to fall so low. Otherwise, who in their right mind would have gotten involved with such a manipulative nutcase?

A few blocks later, I'm just outside the side entrance of Snake Eyes, at the point where the sleepy morning of a southern city collides with the frantic insomnia of a modern casino. The glass door serves as a window between these two worlds. The partial reflection of a woman in a sundress approaching from behind mixes with the flashing lights inside.

I'll always do the gentlemanly thing in this spot. Hold the door. Show a smile. Say good morning, good afternoon, or whatever. Does acting out of habit make me insincere? Sometimes. After all, I'm a poker player by trade. But most random strangers turn out to be likeable once I get to know them, so why not start out—

Good God, not again. Normally, the smiling face of a pretty redhead with a smoking tan is a great reward for my gallantry, but not when she's *Amy*. "Wow," I say, "if we keep getting thrown together like this, you'll think I'm stalking you."

I can expect many possible reactions from her, none of them good, but she tosses a curveball, the surreal stare of non-recognition. How to interpret? The last two times our paths crossed, Amy at least seemed to know me, but she came across like I'd spurned her, treating me to the ugly endgame of the girlfriend experience. Our first meeting at Snakes started with questionable recognition on her part and finished almost as badly. So we're batting zero for three, regardless of how each story opened, meaning I need to focus on my exit strategy. I look past her for the next random stranger who might need a door holder. Where's a babe with less baggage when you need one?

But how can I give up on such a memorable character? Twentysomething, which is always a plus—since I am, too—she's got the red hair thing going for her, moody bluish eyes, and dimples when she smiles. Not to mention she's completely insane, and I'm drawn to that like a moth to a stomping foot.

"Sorry, have we met?" she asks.

"I'm fine pretending we didn't."

"Well, in that case, call me Iris."

"Honestly?"

Where's my notepad? This gal goes by more names than I'll ever remember without documentation.

"For now," she adds and brushes a bang from her forehead. That's not on the list of poker tells, so Amy/Rebecca/Iris maintains her enigma status.

We've been blocking the doorway. I shift sideways to let an older couple inside. As the door opens and the cacophony of a gambling house leaks out, Amy's eyes brighten a bit, only to dim as it closes. So she's more of an addict than a pro. Something inside this casino gets her heart pumping. What could it be but action?

Where were we? Oh, yeah, names. She's heard a couple of mine. "Okay, Iris, I could go with Mike *or* Ricky today. Pick whichever one doesn't make you go postal."

I've thrown her off again. She gazes at me for a beat and a half. "Why would either? But if you're giving me a choice, let's try Ricky. Mike has too much of an assembly-line flavor, or a grease monkey."

"Great." Do I really look like a grease monkey? I've always leaned more toward bartender.

She's got something resembling sympathy in her eyes for the poor widdle monkey. "Let's make a game of it. We'll call ourselves someone different each time we meet."

"Sounds like a plan, Iris." I lead her through the door.

Out of the bright light and into artificial, I pause for a moment to let my eyes adjust.

So does Amy. She's lingering. An intriguing mix of friendliness and skittishness shows in her half smile. But if this is going somewhere, I've gotta lay down the ground rules. "Promise you won't bang me with a flashlight this time. My knee's still sore."

There's the confusion again. The squinting eyes, crinkled forehead.

"Carol!" Some random hoodie waves from deeper in the casino. He and a hooded buddy hurry in our direction.

How can I possibly be experiencing a pang of jealousy over this? Even if I had a thing for this woman and the approaching nerds were rivals, she'd run them off with a flashlight to the knees soon enough. Still, "I was hoping the name thing would be a private game between the two of us. We got off on the wrong foot before, and I'd like to set it right." Geez, I sound like somebody's English professor. Dress me in a tweed suit and wrinkled shirt.

But she smiles. "Okay, Ricky."

And I smile right back. "Call me Bob."

Let the name games begin!

Nerd One arrives at her elbow. He turns out to be a muscular type, but I'll stick with computer geek. Nerd Two follows close behind. He's kinda big, too. I might need a different label for these guys. Amazing Hulks?

She must know them. I'll give her some space and head into the poker room.

Ball's in her court.

CHAPTER SEVEN

HALFWAY TO THE POKER room, a truckload of sanity spills its goods across my lost highway of a brain. Why am I following some good-looking stranger who pretends he knows me? Did I actually let a simple flirtation distract me to the point I coughed up ten blacks to Thing One?

The two hoodies are probably long gone. I don't see them.

Maybe down here by the craps tables?

Uh-uh.

Roulette?

Nope.

I'm walking fast now. Turning my head this way and that like it's on a loose swivel.

This is on Ricky for using his handsomeness and charm to lead me astray. I mean Mike. No, he's Bob today. Whatever his name is.

He and the Things must have tag-teamed me. Oldest short con in the book. So I'm down a grand in a scenario where Eugene, my bloodthirsty Russian friend, expects me to cash *two dimes* and bring the money back, not one. Well, at least if the Things are gone, I don't have to worry about meat cleavers. Wielded by them, anyway.

Wheel of fortune? That guy's wearing a hoody over there.

Nuh-uh.

Wait.

Do I seriously think a couple hoodie minions would dare steal counterfeit chips technically belonging to the Russian mob? I truly am losing it. This casino is vast. The Things are almost without a doubt moving my chips in here somewhere. I didn't check out the blackjack tables.

And there goes my stomach, down to the floor. The real problem crashes in on me like a ton of counterfeit chips in a sack with my name on it. *Iris.*

No, Mud.

Here's the issue. In this start-up chip-moving operation of mine, I'm the employer, the Things are my employees, and although I haven't offered benefits—perish *that* thought—they'll at least want a fair wage. A flat fee or percentage. Either way, I'm cooked. A girl made out of money wouldn't be passing counterfeit bones for the likes of Philippe and Eugene to begin with.

So I've come full circle, giving up an unpromising poker career for a life of crime, only to need some quick poker income to save life and limb. That little irony became a certainty yesterday, the minute Philippe said he wanted five grand. Or even earlier, when I made the decision to start my life of crime in the first place.

What was I thinking?

I'd heard the story on the street, that's what. A classy if somewhat shady guy has a boatload of chips to move. A full rack of blacks. Ten grand minimum, and that's before we look under his mattress. Later, this decidedly unclassy man suggests bigger scores in Vegas, making his threatening presence in my life almost tolerable. In fact, depending on the final chip count, grandfatherly even. That's enough motivation for *anyone* to stray from the straight and narrow.

Right?

There's Bob now, sitting at a mid-stakes game in the poker room, table two. He can run, but he can't hide.

I'm at the entrance in a heartbeat. Which is pretty quick, considering the state of my heart over the last ten minutes or so. Maybe I've calmed my nerves about possible theft by the Things—although I've heard inside pilfering is the single thing that takes a lot of retail establishments down, and judging by the way my mom used to operate when she worked at a Target during her heyday... yeah. But even setting that risk aside, this minimum-wage problem still weighs on me.

Not to mention the completely ridiculous pitter-patter that Bob, this almost total stranger, triggers just by sitting in my field of vision. He's cute, but still...

"Care for a seat, gorgeous?" A fawning floorman ogles my boobs.

"Um, yeah. Maybe at table two?" Anyone who can't figure out why I'd choose that particular table over the dozen others in this house needs to do a better job of keeping up.

"Need chips?"

"Uh-huh. All red." Out of my purse and into the floorman's hands go my remaining nine blacks plus the hundred in twenties from the test chip I cashed yesterday. This goes against the original plan. If those bones don't pass the wand-swipe test at the cage, where he's taking them, I'm done before getting started. But seriously, the buy-here-cash-there strategy, repeated again and again, beneath the probing gaze of the eyes in the sky, *that* plan never had a chance.

I grab the chair to Bob's immediate left, the position of supreme power in Hold 'em. Is there any better way for a girl to begin a relationship?

Speaking of power or lack thereof, Bob bought in for the minimum, just three measly stacks of red. That's normally a sign of weakness. Skittish players don't buy more chips than they can stomach losing. Some of them claim they're following a nifty new strategy, but in truth, they're running scared. The best players always buy in for the maximum so they can push the cowards around with mind-boggling bet sizes.

But I don't make him out to be yellow. He's taking a shot,

hoping for a quick score at higher stakes than he can afford. Of course, the downside of this strategy is that he could end up sleeping on his buddy's couch for a few days.

And I've got position on him, hee hee.

He folds a hand. Glances over at me. "Hey, Iris. We meet again."

"Long time no see, Bob."

With perfect timing, my two racks of reds arrive. "Here, let me assemble this massive collection of chips next to your little tiny one, and then we can chat." I start lining them up in a five-row triangle. Poker isn't all about math. Geometry plays a role. But mostly power.

Not to mention nerves. Where are the Things with at least a progress report?

A few chips tumble from the apex of my triangle, thanks to a twitch on my part.

"You okay?" Bob touches my wrist with a wildly electric hand, sending the most pleasant throb in the universe from his fingertip all the way to my elbow.

"Yeah, I, uh—"

"Hey, Carol!" Thing Two jumps in triumph at the entrance to the poker room, arms stretched up, hundred-dollar bills in one hand and a few remaining blacks in the other. Jesus Lord, could Eugene have hired a bigger imbecile? We need to be discreet here.

The Things didn't scam me. They're moving my chips… ever so sloppily… *and* they'll want to get paid.

"You're hyperventilating," Bob says. "You sure you're—"

"I'm fine, Bob. Really."

Slow it down, *Iris*. Deep breath in, then out. Go with the flow.

"On you," the dealer says.

I toss thirty dollars into the pot without looking at my cards, and everyone folds. My first win of the day.

Yay.

Bob's shaking his head in feigned wonder. "A little heavy for a bring-in raise."

I flash my widest smile and move in for the verbal kill. Hey, I might like this guy, but we're playing cards here. Any decent player leaves the affections at the door. "What's with the short buy-in? You didn't seem like the sort of guy who'd come into a game half-cocked."

Sly grin. "I'm taking a shot. What about you?"

"Me?"

Good question. I've moved all of the blacks in my purse already, and the Things have made great, albeit moronic, progress with the others. The time to skedaddle would have arrived, except I need to win at least a hundred to pay my hooded buddies a salary. Maybe more. "Truth is, I'm insane. Haven't you noticed?"

"Figured as much."

Can I bottle this man and take him home for a bender? They'll find me drunk in a gutter two nights from now, but he'll be so worth the hangover.

The game takes over, and I settle into a zone, folding hand after hand. My playing style has always been on the conservative side, if not downright somnambulant. Over the course of the next hour, only two favorable shuffles wake me from the dead. The first time, everybody fears the strong-card image I've created by not playing *anything*. They fold in terror the moment I raise with ace-queen. Small pot.

But later, some poor fool in a goofy hat draws pocket kings against my aces. Decent pot.

So now I'm up a couple hundred and eager to grasp at straws. We've unquestionably reached the defining moment when eleven consecutive bad months of poker have morphed into something resembling a hot streak. Sure, I can walk away with enough money to fully compensate the Things for their efforts, but who leaves the table in the middle of a rush?

Not Bob, that's for sure. He's been bullying *everyone* by using oversized bets to scoop pot after pot without having to show his cards a single time. Thanks to a tableful of folding wimps, his measly buy-in has doubled in size, making him far more formidable in this game, except against me, the little spider waiting to catch just the right two—

It's happening. The opening player limps for five, Bob raises to twenty-five, and I'm sitting in the catbird seat with pocket jacks.

"One hundred." I push a red stack forward across the felt.

Fold, fold, fold, fold, fold, and… "Three all day." Bob shoves a trinity of chip stacks into the pot.

Wow. That wasn't supposed to happen.

But I'm an imbecile who forgot to think two steps ahead, so it did.

No point in staring him down for tells. Our eyes can't meet. He's sitting right next to me and watching some goddamn sporting event on the wide-screen. Even worse, this devil of a former heart-throb has relaxed his body into a complete state of placid, unreadable immobility.

A hand on his leg might make him squirm enough to show a tell, but physical interaction between two players involved in a hand is frowned upon to the point where the lesser establishments in the wrong part of town would take me into the basement and hammer my thumbs. Or was that Paul Newman in the pool shark movie my mom used to love?

No matter. I can't afford unnecessary attention by the ever-lurking brass in this house, not as much as a simple warning, when in the middle of a chip-passing scam. A lesson I need to teach Thing Two after I finish throttling his thick neck.

Bob's bluffing. I know he is. He's been making this kind of move ever since I joined the table.

And yet… I might still cover payroll for the Things if I fold. Bought in for a thousand and there's eleven hundred right in front of me, my original red triangle plus one neat stack of reds right on top in the middle. Design is everything for us superstitious types.

Besides, go find *a single book* on poker strategy that says pocket jacks should do anything but fold when faced with a strong four-bet before the flop.

He'd expect that, though, wouldn't he? After watching me muck hand after hand, he's pegged me as a weak player following the standard fraidy-cat pre-flop strategy.

I'm calling.

Better yet, I'll shove all in and make *him* squirm.

Let the meat cleavers fall where they may.

Deep breath.

"Fold." I flip my cards too hard, sending them airborne. They fly almost far enough to strike the dealer—another possible ticket to the dungeon—before crash-landing at the base of her tray. The jack of clubs turns face up. Anyone at the table can guess that one of his three brothers lies hidden beside him, in this case staring down at the felt with a single eye.

Hand's over, so I can touch Bob now. Lightly, on his nice, warm, intoxicating wrist. "I showed you mine."

Long, deep sigh on his part. "This whole table will figure me out if I return the favor."

I bat my eyes.

"Still friends no matter what?" he asks.

"I doubt it."

He opens his cards on the table—ace-nine off-suit—then pushes from the table and starts racking his chips.

"You're a dick," I say.

"No, it's Bob. Let me buy you lunch."

"I've been working a new style," he says between forkfuls of salad. "I used to fold, fold, fold, just like you."

"Good luck with that! What if I had pocket aces?"

He levels a long, hard look on me. "Bet sizing tell. When the guy in the hat went after your rockets earlier, you only raised to fifty, because you wanted him to call. You bet a hundred against me, so I *knew* you had something vulnerable."

Swell. He used a simple deduction as the foundation for a reckless three-hundred-dollar bluff, and he got away with it.

Here I thought my main problem was the occasional chip-spraying tilt. Like after those gut-churning occasions when one of my monster hands falls prey to some snickering tourist's unimaginable luck, and I start playing hands like seven-six, because if he can parlay idiocy into a straight, why not me? Bob hasn't seen *that* little leak in my game yet.

"When did the world turn so dark?" I ask.

He chews on that for a beat or two. "When Dunkin Donuts crept ahead of Starbucks in the hit parade? I remember birds falling out of the sky. Dixieland Jazz started dying."

"Not where I live. That constant goddamn music seeps through the walls."

"Yeah?" He sets his fork down. "Where's that?"

"In the Quarter, with a friend."

"Sounds cozy, Iris."

"Not so much. See, she's out of town and I'm all by my lonesome."

Could I be any more forward without lowering the straps of my sundress right here at the buffet? But like I might have said before, the man has a baby face to die for. Not to mention the devil-on-the-shoulder gleam in his eye.

Deep breath. Gotta keep it together here. I'm supposed to be launching a business enterprise in this place, not chasing every hot customer who happens to chance by.

"Carol!" The Things wave from the cashier area up front.

Good God, I'd impossibly forgotten. This is what happens after playing bad poker and flirting with the most interesting man to come along since that bastard, Peter, two-timed me. Time to travel full circle *again,* returning to a life of counterfeit crime, where the men in my corner wear hoodies and fail to bathe very often.

Thing One arrives first, money in hand. Then comes his smiling partner.

"Thanks *so* much, guys." I'm tucking the money into my purse, holding back a hundred for them. Hopefully they're not thinking one apiece. "Most of this goes to Eugene, but I can—"

Thing Two waives me off. "We'll take our cut when you get out from under."

"But… that could take awhile."

"Not if you hurry." And with that, the two Things walk away.

Bob watches them in silence until they leave the buffet to disappear into an ocean of slot machines. "What was that all about?"

"Oh, nothing, really. Just me getting in deeper and deeper."

CHAPTER EIGHT

WHAT'S THE GIRLFRIEND EXPERIENCE like with Amy? Actually, she's calling herself Iris today, and I'm Bob. Whatever the names, though, I've seen the bad ending more than once. Her coldness when we played cards against each other at Snakes, a flashlight to the knee in the backseat of my car, the ugly scene at the gypsy casino.

But those encounters don't count. She hasn't acknowledged their existence today. We live in the present instead, starting with a single beignet shared at Café Du Monde. We'd have one each, but this perfectly fit woman, if not somewhat on the thin side, insists she's on a diet.

Then I buy another for myself, and she steals half of it. We kiss once to taste the sugar on each other's lips and again for the underlying flavor. Strawberry ChapStick in her case. The encore performance initiated by Iris leads to the warm elixir of her tongue against mine.

We browse through art galleries in the Quarter, Iris clutching my arm like a southern belle. She pauses before a striking painting of grand piano, outdoor deck, and the churning sea beyond. "Are you intimidated?"

By the talent? The accomplishment? What can a guy do but shrug? We'll never make *this* of ourselves, either for lack of talent or poor motivation. The thought lessens me and brings out the same mood in Iris, judging by her frown. But we play cards for a living, and what's wrong with that?

"Everything," she says, although I never raised the question aloud. She's speaking randomly or brooding over questionable career paths as much as I am now.

Outside, the sun warms us. We escape all hints of misdirected agendas by turning our backs on the arts and taking a long walk to the river. "I'm from Missouri," she confesses later, beside me on our bench.

Squa, squa, squa. The boldest seagulls peck pieces of a bread roll she stole from the Snake Eyes buffet.

"Kansas," I admit.

"Bad blood, Bobby boy, but I'll give you a mulligan."

"I lived in a hotel outside Winstar Casino in Oklahoma for a whole month."

"Seriously? One last chance, mister."

Squa, Squa. They fly off, but we linger. Iris tilts her head back, eyes closed. Seems relaxed enough to fall asleep, and that's a good thing. Last chances require serious deliberation.

A barge floats its way down the river. I drape an arm over Iris's shoulders, and she settles a hand on my leg.

After a lazy forever, a second barge happens by, and this one comes close enough to reveal its lettering.

"Alaska?" I offer.

"Let's head over to my place," she says.

A couple miles walking back, and we're almost at the galleries, but she skirts around that area until she locates and leads me up a musty stairway to a tiny flat above a shop. The blinds are partly shut. Filtered light provides only the dimmest illumination of a kitchenette, small living area, and bedroom through a side door. Then she closes the shades all the way and has to lead me by the hand until my eyes adjust to the darkness.

"The first time should be hidden," she whispers, "and quiet."

But we're up against the wall in no time flat, waking the dead with our moans and cries.

Later, she's opened the bedroom shade a tad. We're in our birthday suits, hands touching, a glow of either late-day sun or projected satisfaction casting us in gold. Smokers would be lighting up.

"Now that we're lovers, can I share my secrets?" Iris whispers. "The rule is *you* have to keep them to yourself, right?"

"Like attorney-client?"

A low rumble of laughter catches in her throat. "More like I'd have to kill you." She flips onto me in a move that would do any gymnast proud. "I've started passing bad chips."

Her mouth is on mine, and we sway in sync, her soft breasts against my chest, red hair tickling my nose. We're moaning back and forth. Grunting now, as our synchronized dance escalates from waltz to jitterbug.

Fourth of July comes and goes. My breath takes time to catch.

Finally, the recorder in my head clicks on, and the last five words she said echo through my brain. "Wait. What?"

"Counterfeit bones." Iris tells me this convoluted story about weird gangsters with eclectic names like Philippe, Eugene, Thing One—

"*And* Thing Two." She's got the sheet pulled over her head. Her words come out muffled.

"The hoodies? I figured they had some angle on you, but we're really just talking *Nerds* One and Two, aren't we?"

She lowers the sheet enough for an unobstructed peek at me. "This is serious, Bob. Don't make jokes about it. Geeks I could handle."

"Okay, fine. Why did you get sucked into this? We hit bad runs and play our way out of them all the time."

"*My* run is eleven months of dream-crushing bad." Deep sigh, accented by a vulnerable sheen in her eyes. "Let's start here. This flat I'm sharing? We're really talking squatter's rights, more or less. Ex-boyfriend's out of town for a few weeks and doesn't know I copied the key. Otherwise I'd be homeless."

That one sets me back a bit. I've had her on something of a

pedestal from day one. Not that being down-and-out is her fault necessarily, gambling addiction notwithstanding—

Her eyes flare. "Don't look so smug, buddy. I can read you like a book. What dive do *you* call home, your friend's couch?"

Iris gets me worse than she thinks with that line. My few remaining friends don't want to know me anymore, other than to hit me up for loan repayments. Does Runbad count as my only pal? That'd be one sorry state of affairs.

I start telling without thinking, disclosing more than I normally would in a case where revelations about poker losses, mental blackouts, a shady if not imagined character named Runbad, and a chronic sense of vague confusion might scare away a gal I'm really into, and not just in the physical sense. I do stop short of mentioning we've met before, back when she called herself Rebecca or Amy. Oh, such as yesterday for example, and the day before.

Iris should have the right to confess her own madness when she's comfortable enough to lower her shield more than she already has. So I finish with, "I've got the same Vegas dream as half the grinders in the country, but currently my mailing address is the backseat of my car."

"I *knew* it, Mister Three-hundred-dollar Bluff!" She's on top of me again, knees straddling my chest while she laughs her ass off. She calms enough to get off a question. "Did you go to college?"

"Four years at Alaska State."

"Oh, baloney, you've never been to Alaska in your life. I watched that barge float downriver, too, you know."

We start moving to a silent song with Cajun accent and Dixieland tone. Brief pause, and I open up a bit more. "Got my degree at Kansas State, actually, in journalism."

"Really? Then what the hell have you been doing?"

"Chasing the dream, just like anyone else. What's your story?"

"Don't laugh." She nibbles my earlobe. "A criminal justice major."

I almost lose it, but she asked me not to.

"My mom and I had no money, so I waitressed my way through," she says. "Maybe I should have stuck with that."

"Nah. You'll be going places once you kick it into gear."

"Like this?" Swaying a little harder now.

God, her skin is soft. Time to share one more secret. "Runbad says he'll stake me ten grand if I do him some favors."

That brings her up short. She hovers over me, gazing into my eyes for an extra beat. "You've sold your soul to the devil?" Then she's at my ear again. "I can top that," she whispers. "The Russian mob owns every inch of mine."

Several frenzied minutes after, we're catching our breath again, side by side, and gazing at the ceiling. "We should name these fixes we're in," Iris says. "Define, so we can defeat."

Doesn't take much thought for me to come up with a good label. "How about seven-deuce off-suit?"

"Nah, too hopeless. Show some ambition." She kicks the sheet off, and two wonderfully freckled breasts return to my almost wasted but still leering gaze. "How about pocket queens? The little ladies can get you into *so* much trouble."

"Nah. We're talking ace-nine off-suit."

That gets her laughing again, then fading into a smile with those cute dimples on full display. "I should throttle you."

"But first?"

We kiss long and hard, then go at it for the third or fourth event. Shuffle away, Iris. I'm not planning to fold anytime soon.

Much later, she's staring at me, all quiet and thoughtful.

I'm fine with the silent exchange. I'll bathe in the warmth of her body, her eyes, and the shadow of a smile.

She starts to speak, thinks it over, tries again. "Mike... can I call you your real name?"

"Not today. I put too much work into thinking of a new one."

"Bob, then. I know we just met, but... would you be willing to, um... be exclusive for a little while? Long enough to see how things play out?"

"You mean as in *mi casa es su casa*?"

"Yes, but try to win enough so I'm seeing more than the backseat of your car in my immediate future."

I'm loving the idea of a one-on-one with her, but my jaw surely drops somewhere in a duplicate world. My focus has been on building a bankroll and heading to Vegas for the longest time. All of a sudden, that whole deal feels hollow. Why the sudden ache for a relationship with a woman possibly crazier than I am? We're both spiraling in the wrong direction, and neither one has lifeline on their resume.

Her eyes well. "I shouldn't have asked such a thing. We're still strangers."

"No, we aren't. We shared our secrets. Now I'm your very own one-woman guy."

Long stare. Her deepest yet. "Just know I have a jealous heart."

An odd sensation sends a shiver down my back. Not quite déjà vu, more like a thousand-mile glimpse at my most recent past through an out-of-focus telescope.

The strangest dream awakens me. Runbad's at a turntable, setting a needle on the vinyl. The music clatters in a cadence like none I've ever heard.

Disorientation closes in, but Iris's soft breathing stills my panic. I haven't lost her to a blackout. Not yet, anyway.

Ace-nine off-suit. Funny how I got her with the same hand twice. First at Snakes a couple days ago and then—

Wow. Only the shadows of an unfamiliar room could have laid out an idea so threatening I'm having trouble breathing. It starts with an impossible supposition. What if my brief relationship with Amy just finished running its course *in reverse*? Like the record Runbad played in my dream. Or the hidden message in a Beatles song that could only be understood when played backward.

In my new, funhouse-mirror sequence of events, I didn't first meet Amy in a game where she fooled me into changing two stacks of reds for her counterfeit chips. No. We met at Snakes, all right, but on a completely different day—the one we just finished. She was dealing with the Things, playing poker with me, making love, and obtaining the promise I'd be a one-woman man. I started that day as Mike, then Ricky before settling on Bob, but we agreed to change names every day.

She next saw me when I had Cynthia all over me at the gypsy casino. She's Rebecca now, but I'm still Ricky—forgetting the new-name-each-day game, from her perspective—and she flies off the handle, throwing my promise of fidelity in my face. She would have tossed her chips in the same direction if the bouncers hadn't dragged me out. What else happened? Oh yeah, I passed two counterfeit chips to her.

Later... earlier? No, in this chronology, later, she found me with Cynthia in the backseat of my car. She said she didn't want to know me anymore.

Finally, we're back at what I'd thought was the first time we met, but in this scenario, the fourth. She acted like she didn't know me, as promised, and she introduced herself by her real name, Amy. I'd hurt her. Bad. Cheated on her.

"I'm so sorry," I whisper now.

She rolls over, facing me but still asleep. Her auburn hair is soft as silk in my fingers. Her expression that of an angel.

No, this is crazy. My insane thoughts will fade into the general chaos of fragmented dreams when the morning light wakes me.

One last stomach-churning idea keeps me from dozing. Amy didn't know me when we met at the casino today. Doesn't that mean, if I'm careening backward through time, we'll never cross paths again?

Otherwise, she would have recognized me, presuming *I'm the crazy one, not her.*

Or even worse, neither one of us is.

Her smartphone glows like a nightlight from the bed stand beside her. It'll show the date.

I'm afraid to look.

CHAPTER NINE

EVERY DAY A NEW name, so…

The breakfast I'm fixing is sure to pull *Stanley* out of bed by the nose. Scrambled eggs, toast, and especially bacon. A lovers' meal. A secret-sharers' banquet. He's up to speed on the Russians, and I've heard about his bargain with the devil—not in so many words, but reading between the lines. This imaginary friend calls himself Runbad, so who else could he be?

My new heartthrob might be one hell of a card player, but he's also several degrees shy of true north. Not that I hold it against him. I'm drawn to the nutsy type like a moth to a vacuum cleaner. They're thrilling.

Unpredictable.

But not always. There he is at the bedroom doorway scratching his side. The smell of bacon works every time. Now he's grabbing a seat at the table. My culinary skills are downright Pavlovian.

His hungry arrival is *my* clue to do the girlfriend thing. "Hey, sweetie." Quick peck on the cheek. Plate down in front of him. He'll dig in and love me all the more. I've fallen hard for the guy, and my mom taught me the handiest etiquette for cases like this.

"Hey, uh…"

"I'm Janet today, remember?"

"Oh. Yeah. Sorta."

What's with the pasty face? The flu's been going around. Time for girlfriend experience squared.

I'm all over him. Arms draped from behind, hands on his cool face, then down to an only slightly warmer chest. "What's wrong, baby? Did I wear you out? Your battery indicator's blinking orange like crazy."

"No, but don't let me look at your phone today, even if I beg. Okay?"

Stanley's talking crazy, so he must be fine. I *did* wear him out.

Now he's staring at the wall like blood's flowing down from the ceiling—a common plumbing problem here in the Quarter. I'll make a mental note to stop binge watching horror movies on Netflix.

"The calendar," he says, a crack in his voice. "It can't be right."

"Nope. Wrong month." We're well into May, but the March page is *so* much better. Mountains, trees, a lake... no Russians. "Listen, baby, I need to go handle something. Eat your breakfast and... I don't know. Crawl into bed again?"

"Yeah," he says. "Maybe."

My inner mom is rubbing her hands together with glee. And my inner whore? She's almost racing him to the bed. But we need to take care of this one little thing first. "You'll stay here and wait for me, Stanley, won't you?"

"Uh-huh. Got any more bacon in that pan?"

Perfect. But he's off, somehow. Haunted eyes.

Enter Eugene. We're back at his kitchen table, two thousand dollars in hundreds on my side, stack after stack of black chips on his. I'd be drooling, but his ferocious dog does the job for me, running a slobbery tongue up and down my leg. Where's a Taser when a gal needs one?

I should have worn jeans.

The balding Russian sweeps a hand across the fortune in bones. "Eight thousand left in collateral," he says.

The man's good at arithmetic. We started at ten, I laundered two, and that leaves eight. A little more arithmetic says I borrowed five thousand cash, and he added one as interest, putting us at six. But now I'm repaying two. I could keep moving chips two at a time until the debt is settled and the remaining collateral comes back to me. But I'm the impatient type, I guess. "About that, Eugene. How about I take four of these stacks and work my debt off in one fell swoop?"

Long stare at me.

Dark.

Ow. This damn dog is gonna get my shoe up his ass if he doesn't stop distracting the hell out of—

"You changing the deal we made, Lyla?"

The rage in Eugene's voice blows my hair back like a hurricane. My body shifts into quivering terror mode and I accidentally step on Bruno's paw.

Squee squee squee. The dog darts from beneath the table and heads for the nearest corner. Who can't feel bad for the poor thing? Or guilty. Later maybe. A reckless idea steals my complete focus. Maybe Bruno isn't the only creature whose bark is bigger than his bite.

I need to tighten up, stand my ground, beginning with a little test of strength before I go for the gold. I mean blacks.

"My name is *Janet* today. That's *my* decision, not yours."

"*Your* decision?" Eugene is on the balls of his feet, leaning over the table.

Hold steady, Janet. Stop that lip from trembling.

"Me and my boyfriend make the call on who we are each day." I manage to toss all of that on the table without stuttering one bit.

Eugene's eye-bulging face looks ready to explode. And it does. Into laughter. "Yosef!" he chokes out.

Thing Two's at the doorway in an instant.

"Take this tough little lady over to Philippe's. She needs a name lesson."

Uh-oh. Who thinks that sounds good? But my new, take-no-crap persona hasn't pushed the edge of the envelope quite hard enough yet. "Let's compromise. I'll take *three* of these stacks, Eugene. The Things have been helping me move them. You'll get your principal back quicker that way. Then I'll work off the thousand in interest."

"Things?" He's beside himself again, chortling almost to the floor. "I like you, girly. You've got moxie."

Yay.

♥ ♦ ♣ ♠

Enter Philippe. We're at *his* table now, a shoebox full of driver's licenses and passports spilled out between us. All showing a picture of *my* face.

"Go ahead," he says. "See if you can find a single Janet in that pile. We were supposed to consult with *you* before we had these made?"

"Wait. Where did you get my picture for these?" The larger question is why I'm looking at a couple dozen identities here. But the violation of my privacy trumps any irritation over mad Russian schemes.

"We have our ways."

Like I didn't expect *that* pat answer. Note to self: Stop leaving your window shades open when alone with the lights on at night. Telescoping cameras are a marvel these days, and you weren't just teasing the local peeping tom like you thought.

Besides, now that Mike's in my life, I don't need to find interesting ways for getting my nipples hard, and all the other stuff.

So I file that away into my ever-expanding personal stupidity cabinet, within the *no longer necessary* folder, and go for the better line of inquiry. "What the *hell* are you up to?"

I haven't forgotten the fact that Philippe is strong enough and mean enough to squeeze me into borscht, but a girl's gotta take a stand.

Worked with Eugene.

Philippe, too, apparently. Instead of pounding me into the floor or summoning Thing One to handle the job with a meat cleaver—which isn't likely, cuz if Eugene gave it back only one day after slaughtering a goat, he's far quicker than the typical neighbor borrowing a cup of sugar—where was I? Oh, yeah. Philippe is taken aback by my aggressive approach.

Wow. So call *me* the woman in charge now. Mmmm. Power is so—

"Hans! Bring the hatchet!"

Great. Quivering terror again, without a dog in sight for me to kick. "No, Philippe. *You're* the guy in charge here. Totally." This time I do stutter. But no tears. Or racking sobs. Chalk it up to personal growth. A scheming mind locked into overdrive. A secret mantra. *There's got to be a way out of this mess. There's got to be a way out of this mess.*

There's no place like home.

It worked! Dorothy was so on the ball. Not that I've traveled to Kansas or ever want to.

But Thing One isn't standing in the doorway with a bloodthirsty look in his normally vacant face, either. Maybe he isn't even in the damn building.

And Philippe? This balding Russian grandfather in the best of worlds, brutal enforcer in the worst, is laughing like crazy. He knocks his vodka bottle over, but it's empty, so no harm, no foul. The passports stay dry. He leaves the table and opens a cupboard.

Whoa. Rack upon rack of chips. Mostly black, but a few are white. Isn't that the color code used in California for a hundred? Or Spain? Could be, cuz from my vantage point here at the table, coupled with the twenty-twenty vision gifted to me either by a favorable gene pool or all the carrots I eat, we're looking at possibly a worldwide collection of counterfeit poker chips.

"Big factory," Philippe says.

"No shit, Sherlock." The reason for all the phony driver's licenses *and passports* has become exquisitely clear.

"We'll be partners, all over the world," he says.

The man's a frigging mind reader, and he's offering more wealth than I ever imagined. So why am I trembling like a leaf and begging the gods for a change in footwear to ruby-red slippers?

Philippe's in my face, worry lines wrinkling his. "Watch out for Eugene. He'll fuck us in the ass, first chance he gets."

So there's that.

Thing One shows up in the doorway, hatchet in hand.

And that.

"Put it away, you idiot," Philippe barks. "You'll frighten the girl."

But no, I'm not scared of these two anymore. My new grandfather needs me in one piece. Apparently, I've passed the test to become his favorite chip mover. Most likely his *only* one. Hiding out in run-down apartments on the bad side of town can't be conducive to making a wide circle of friends. And certainly not those greedy enough to risk prison time not only here in the friendly confines of America but also some country where the cells are damp and the meals are laced with maggots.

I watched *Papillion* with my mom, so I know.

Hey there, it's me. Amy.

I've got to remember that, cuz this new girl I'm becoming? She scares the hell out of me.

I'm away from the table, heading for the door on wobbly legs. "Chip run," I say. "I've got three grand to move for the guy I'm not supposed to trust."

"Go help her with that, Hans."

I wave that suggestion off with a sweep of my arm to the fortune-bearing cupboard.

"Don't you need him here to, I don't know, help protect the evil empire?"

Philippe's grin does little to brighten the sinister look in his eyes. "I've got guns for that."

Surely he does. Before he can open another cupboard—based on the movies I've seen, guys with murderous weaponry are always itching to show them off. *Meet my little friend*—I skirt past Thing One and make for the nearest exit. "Let's meet at the casino in a few hours, *Hans.*"

"Okay, Lyla."

I've got three options at the moment, all beginning with a brisk jog to my flat in the Quarter—hide under the bed, collapse into a fetal position, or whimper in Mike's arms. No, I mean Stanley today.

I'll bury my head in his chest, and not only because I want to tell him my swell new name.

CHAPTER TEN

I CAN'T STAY INSIDE. Not much to do in this little flat except watch TV, and that poses too large a threat. A flick or two of the remote, and I'll be gaping at the wrong date, off by days or even weeks, in some news channel's bottom-of-the-screen data scroll.

If I'm falling deeper into the past, I may have lost Amy/Janet before our relationship had a fair chance of getting started.

Don't want to verify.

Do I know already?

The logic is flawless. Timeline relentless. Our relationship has been running in reverse from ugly ending to one fine beginning.

Best head-in-the-sand approach? Leave the TV off and fix that damned calendar. Forget that mountain scene on the March page. The future always offers something better, such as the present, in my case. We're supposed to be deep into May at the moment. Quick peek at *that* calendar page—a barge loaded with trash on the way to the landfill. Hmmm. Yeah, that's the ticket.

Waste management in the proper perspective can be uplifting. Patriotic. Eco something. She probably won't mind all that much if I pull the tack out of the wall, flip the right page in position, and lock it in place.

There.

She can always switch it back when I'm feeling saner.

But these walls are closing in on me. I've gotta get outside.

Quick note in case she gets back before I do:

Amy,

What should I tell her, good-bye? If I'm careening downhill through the pages of time, I might never see her again. She didn't know me when we met yesterday, meaning we never crossed paths on whatever earlier day I'll fall into next.

These walls. The itch behind my eyes.

Just going out for some air.

Love you.

Come on. We just met. Scratch that out.

Thinking of you.

Uh-uh. Too Hallmark. One last stab at it or we just go with *back soon* and pray I'm not lying.

Wanting you.

Perfect.

I'm out the door and down the stairs, almost losing it at the sight of a folded newspaper in the bottom foyer. It'll show a date for sure.

Through the glass door at the bottom, and I'm out on the sidewalk.

Oh, yeah, baby. The combination of blazing sun and clammy air never did a guy a better solid. I slow to a shuffle, soaking in the wrought-iron balconies, the lazy tourists, maybe a gallery later, or a bar for a cool one. They call this place The Big Easy for a reason. Perfect tonic for my anxiety attack.

Oh, no, not a newsstand.

God damn.

Ambush at every corner.

Should I surrender to the inevitable and read what the papers show or keep my head buried deep, until I'm walking the earth with the dinosaurs?

Time to man up and see what the *Times-Picayune* has to say.

May thirteen.

Thirteen days earlier than the game at Snake Eyes.

So this is what a gravity-free environment feels like.

With no way to stay standing and not a bench in sight, I just sit on the curb like any other down-and-outer. Maybe somebody will toss me a dollar. Better yet, a DeLorean.

"Buy a weekly magazine," comes the voice from behind. "You won't be as far off."

Runbad settles down beside me, holding up a hand for a high five. Why not? We're quite a pair. Grayish T-shirts. Worn jeans. Uncombed hair. Mine, anyway. His is cropped too short to make much difference.

Hey, Suzie, look at the time-traveling *panhandlers* down in the gutter.

Yeah, I use plural for a reason. My run-ins with Amy have gone in reverse sequence, but the meetings with this grifter follow a consistent chronology. We're booked on the same flight, him and me.

"And both of us by choice," he says.

"Huh?" What's more inexplicable, that he can read my mind or misconstrue my motivation so badly?

Runbad lights up a smoke, breathes it in, and exhales with such a sigh of delight I'm wondering whether risking cancer might be worth it. Does disease matter at this point?

"You were dodging sidewalk cracks when we met," he says. "Thoughts all over the place and *so* hard to read. What did you truly want to sell your soul for—kiss the pretty girl or enter the World Series of Poker? The second possibility sounded so banal, you had to be leaning toward the first. But I couldn't be sure."

To ask a single question would undoubtedly lead to a dozen more. Still, I've gotta lob this one at him, or I won't be able to breathe. "Are you inside my head right now?"

"Not lately. Kills the mystery." He takes another drag. A master at slow motion. And reverse. A town like New Orleans, clinging to the past for comfort, serves as the perfect place for a guy like him, whoever he is. *Whatever* he might be.

A backflash to restraints on a bed brings a fresh bead of sweat to my forehead. At the age of eighteen, I spent two weeks in a mental hospital. Blackouts. Fugue episodes.

The pills they prescribed got me out of there, but they dulled me. Is quitting *then* catching up with me now? Billy's been back for a while. Now I'm dealing with imaginary time-travel tour guides? Only Amy feels real. *Janet.* Gotta get back to her flat.

So I drag myself up from the curb. "Always a pleasure, Runbad."

"Wait. Hear me out." He scrambles up next to me, matching my stride. "I offered ten large, *twice*, plus airfare and accommodations. Hell, I would have thrown in a Hertz rental, but you wouldn't have it. Mikey sold his soul to kiss the girl instead."

My legs stop working. I actually *have* met somebody a guy might sell his soul for. Not that I'll give *this fool* any ground. "Wait. I actually went for Vegas, somewhat, when I did you the favor at the gypsy casino."

"Halfhearted doesn't count," he says. "I had the ten grand in my hand, and you didn't take it. You've been all in from the start with the redhead."

A hooker in a doorway smiles at us. "Thirty bucks for a twofer," she offers.

"Maybe later," Runbad says, "I'll come back and cut a deal."

Gotta give this guy credit for a dry sense of humor.

Except he doesn't exist. Otherwise I'd be accepting the impossible. Reverse timelines? Devil's bargains? We're talking expired medical prescription, nothing more. I need to track down the doctor I used to have. "Okay, pal, you aren't really here. I get that. Help is only an electroshock away. But even if you *were* the devil, we never got anything in writing. In fact, I didn't even put in a request."

Runbad's laughter echoes on a street gone empty. "*If* I were the devil, am I not known as a trickster? Your deeds serve as the contract. You kept going after Amy. Four meetings with her so far and not a single lunge at my ten-grand Vegas stakes. Sure, I might have chosen for you, but I'll bet the judges in at least thirty states would back me up."

Well, what do you know? Let this guy go on talking and he'll say too much. Would Louisiana, the last state to grudgingly adopt the Uniform Commercial Code, ever go along with such a squirrely transaction?

Okay, now I *am* losing it. What do I think I'm gonna do here, sue the devil in court?"

Runbad motions to a diner. He's got the upper hand. As far as I can tell, the *only* hand.

I follow him in.

Ordinary things. The low murmur among regulars at the counter. Their meals are long gone, but these codgers have no reason to hurry.

The smiling hostess smells like cigarettes.

Hamburger sizzles on the grill.

A return to the world I trust.

Here at our booth by the window, the aroma of coffee sharpens my senses, undulls my wits, steels my resolve to cast all hallucinations out of my head.

Yet Runbad remains across the table, plain as day. "You're off the grid, Mike. Here's why."

Whatever this new spin might be, he keeps me waiting while he adds a cube of sugar to his cup, sips, grimaces, tries one more. And another. For the first time in our dysfunctional relationship, I'm hanging on this man's every word.

"Your girlfriend's been moving bad chips," he says. "Perfect counterfeits. But the day you met her at Snakes, the two blacks she shoved in your direction didn't pass the wand test at the cage."

Too big a coffee gulp burns my throat. I know where she got those bones.

"From you," he says. "A couple days earlier. But play the tape forward. She passes them back at Snakes, you trip across time, trade them for her reds, she moves forward, and so on. Round and round we go. An infinite loop powerful enough to knock you right off the grid."

Just one dagger into his ridiculous babble and I'll be out the door, back in the comfort of Amy's nest, instead of this galaxy far, far away. "Fine, Runbad. But you made the choice for me. You asked me for a favor. Lose a couple blacks at some dive of a casino. And I ran into Amy there. But the loop had already been triggered on *my* timeline, back at Snakes when she first passed them to me. I had no hand in that."

"Not hardly, Sonny Boy. If you'd taken the ten grand and headed to Vegas, somebody else might have blended into the past and given her the bad merchandise instead. In that case, no loop."

My head's swimming. He's bobbing and weaving me into the ropes.

"Think about it," he adds. "The initial day at Snake Eyes on *your* timeline? Either Amy *had never seen you before* and simply didn't size you up in a favorable way on first impression, or she'd been mad as a hen without breakfast because you cheated on her in the backseat of your car with some drunk blonde. Cynthia, I think her name was?"

Runbad goes for the sugar jar again. Not enough beets growing down there in hell? I'm not the only guy with issues. *Plop, plop, plop*, and he's talking again. "Door number one *or* door number two, depending on which choice you made earlier."

"You mean the choice you pushed me into?"

"Sorry you met her?"

He's got me there. I'm not even sorry I met *Runbad*. Without his time machine—surely he's the wizard behind the curtain—would I have spent any quality time with Amy? That's beside the point, though. The chronology still isn't right. "Runbad, I passed her the chips *after* I caught a flashlight in the knee. Your reverse-timeline wheels were already in motion before I knowingly did a goddamned thing to help you."

He's laughing again. A devil on top of his game. "Son, your first choice was to walk away from me on day one, when I pointed out the gypsy casino. You picked the pretty girl right then and there, and stuck with her every time I offered a Vegas stake."

"I didn't know her yet."

"You ached for her and didn't realize. Deep down, you've always hated playing cards for a living. That's where *I* came in." So he's my shrink now? Enough of this. I'm out of my seat and headed for Amy. Or Janet. Either one of her names is a lifeline.

CHAPTER ELEVEN

WHEW. THERE'S STANLEY NOW, sitting in the doorway.

How needy can a girl's heart get, compelling me to *run*, not walk, all the way from the bad side of town to my own little home sweet home? From the moment I left Philippe's, a worry's been gnawing away at me.

But he's here. I wasn't a one-night stand. My purse is bulging with thirty counterfeit chips—*three grand*—and I would have flushed every one of them to find him waiting.

Chalk this up as a freebie then. Still got my chips *and* my man.

Yay.

He isn't showing much life down there, though.

"I've been set up." He looks up with wide eyes, like someone who's been, I don't know, set up maybe.

"How so, sweetie?" I get down beside him, arm draped over his shoulder so I can lean in, steal a kiss on his cheek, a nibble of an earlobe. "Let's go upstairs, and I'll fix whatever's broken." My voice comes out throaty. Seductive. I'm making *myself* hot, let alone him.

"He guessed what I'd choose before I had a chance to step into the trap on my own. Never even told me the price. The man cut a bad deal."

If anything, Stanley's face has gotten paler than when I left him earlier. His conversation no more intelligible. But I'm here for this madman. I'll be his sounding board no matter what. "Who?"

"The devil."

Oh, of course! Who else could Stanley's nemesis have been? We're in straight-jacket crazy mode at the moment, and my best move is to play along until sanity comes knocking, but holding back at least a giggle is next to impossible. "Stanley, were you thinking the devil was gonna cut you a *good* deal? Come on up and tell me all about it. *In my bed.*"

Now we're trudging up the stairs without a stagger, so maybe he's snapping out of it. "Here's a choice," he says. "I'll pretend none of the impossible stuff ever happened, Janet."

"Works for me, but I'm Lyla."

He stops. Trains wild eyes on me. "Did the date change?"

Nope. He isn't quite in the mental state I'd been looking for yet. Such as fifty-one cards. I'm too realistic to think his deck will ever be full. "Just a couple more steps, baby. Good. Now through the door like this, see?"

Inside, I drop my purse on a chair and fish the driver's license out. "Lyla Banks. Not bad, I guess. Finishes with some promise."

Stanley snatches the license from my fingers and moves his lips reading my phony name. "Beats all the Lyla *Flounders* I've known."

"Ha ha. You would have loved the other IDs. Tomorrow I could be Penny Ballz. Or Cindy Eatz. These damn Russians and their corny humor."

He holds the license up for better lighting, studies the picture, stares at my face, then the picture again. "I don't get it."

"I'm jammed up real bad, sweetie. Or soon will be."

That's because of counterfeit chips good at casinos far and wide, including not only glamour spots like Cleveland but *Monaco*, too. Vast quantities of these bones aren't necessarily a good thing, either, even though I so want them to be. I'm at a crossroads between continuing on as a brilliant but damnably unlucky poker player or rising to jet-setting playgirl status with glittery earrings. Clearly the latter has its appeal, except for the inevitable on-the-lam episode, followed shortly by *rotting in a Turkish prison.*

My fantasies often come with broken edges, cuz my mom always said *don't step in the bullshit, buttercup. Trust me, it's there.* The more genteel types would call the problem Murphy's Law.

I want to explain this all to Stanley, I really do. The right words of wisdom, even from someone on tilt, could help me choose the good over the slippery slope. Except I've already cast my lot with hoodlums like Philippe and Eugene, plus two muscle-bound products of the Thing gene pool. So I'm stuck, unless Stanley helps me think of something clever.

"You think *you're* jammed up, Lyla? Listen to this."

Seriously? It's all about him and his *Needful Things* delusion? Two beers short of a six-pack but so like a man. We're dangerously close to our first fight here—a battle over whose situation is more fraught with peril. Or beginning with that but escalating to any number of pet peeves. Soon we'll be screaming so loud we won't remember the reason. He got potato chip crumbs on the sheets last night. Did I mention that?

But we're just getting started, Stanley and me. He's got those deep blue eyes. We're not talking cheating cad of an ex-boyfriend whose apartment I've temporarily stolen with the help of the spark-throwing key-copy machine at my local Ace Hardware. You snooze, you lose, Peter. Go ahead and fly to Haiti *for two whole weeks* with that blonde bimbo, Cynthia. Business trip, my ass. You never did anything nice like that for—

"Lyla! You're hyperventilating again, just like yesterday." Stanley's got me by the hand, leading me to the couch. Sits down beside me, arm over my shoulder.

Deep breath in, Lyla. Good. Now exhale ever so slowly. Mmmm.

He fetches a glass of water.

I try to smile.

"Anxiety attack?" he asks.

"Something like that. I have trouble letting go of things. Promise you won't ever break my heart?"

"No way would I think of such a thing."

But his eyes don't meet mine, like he's hiding some secret already.

Wait. I can't let insecurities get the best of me. My man's hurting inside. He had haunted eyes when I found him downstairs. Traces of worry still wrinkle his forehead, betraying the false show of bravado in his stab at a grin.

And I love him.

"Tell me what happened to *you*, Stanley."

He shrugs. Shakes his head. "Well, I guess the long and short of it is I sold my soul to kiss you, Lyla."

"Really?"

"Uh-huh."

This is special. So banana-cream nice a smile almost stretches my face apart. But mom's warning about BS cannot be ignored. "Would you do it again if the devil didn't trick you into it?"

"You bet." Not even the slightest hesitation or the tiniest bit of uncertainty flickers in his eyes.

I'm all in with this guy.

If I lose, I'll be felted worse than all of my bad poker beats and every failed relationship since I turned sixteen and eloped with mom's chiropractor. But my heart isn't the only thing fluttering. My head's in the mix. Wedding bells ring from ear to ear. I'd carry him to the bed if I had the upper-body strength.

Thankfully, he comes on his own.

Modesty precludes me from describing this next little bit. It's a drawn-shade, creaky-box-spring sort of a thing. Twice. And soon to be once more, but first, we need to catch our breath.

He's on his elbow, caressing my thigh with lazy strokes.

I'm trying to find the purr reflex cats utilize so well, but short of that, "Mmmm, don't stop," works just fine.

"So this problem of yours, Lyla..."

Yes! I've found me a good man. Notice how he set aside his story about the devil to talk about my Russian problem first? Thank heavens I didn't pick a fight when he seemed inclined to make this all about him, earlier on the couch. Here in my bed, he's sorted his priorities.

Not that I'm some mythical enchantress like Venus, Helen of Troy, or Angelina Jolie. I simply told Stanley before dimming the lights that if he desired something sounding a lot like hex, then words rhyming with bevel aren't allowed in my bedroom.

I wanted some hot and heavy action as much as he did, of course, but a calculated bluff can do a weak hand wonders.

Anyway, he'll get his turn soon enough. I'm not the type to clog the airwaves for any great length of time. Besides, since I didn't forbid words rhyming with *maiden*, and he can still slip Beelzebub beneath the sheets if he's sneaky, I haven't denied the man an opportunity to take charge.

So I better talk fast. "I'm falling in deep with a chip-moving scam that's sure to blow up in my face."

Long, hopefully thoughtful silence and, "These Russians. Are they holding a gun to your head?"

"Not in so many words, but where there's smoke, there's fire."

"Okay," he says, "let's break the problem into smaller pieces. What steps would you take to get out of this mess if you were so inclined?"

Wow. At least for now, my uninhibited loving touch has healed every crazy bone in this man's body. He's turned analytic, which is exactly what I need. "I'd have to get out from under. Opening step would be to move the three thousand in my purse. That handles the principal owed to Eugene."

"And then?"

"Well, at that point, he still has five thousand of my chips, but I only need two grand. One to pay off his interest, a few hundred for the Things, and the rest for the wardrobe upgrade I always wanted."

"And then?"

"Philippe can have the last thirty blacks as a get-out-of-my-life present."

Long pause. His fingertips doing wonders up and down my thigh again. Finally, "Go move some chips then. That's your best play whether you're in or you're out."

"Oh, Stanley, I love when you talk dirty to me."

We melt into passion again, which I won't bore you with, except to say slow is best and maybe the only way possible at this point, since we are only human, except sometimes Stanley seems like the Eveready Bunny.

And who wouldn't love one of those for Christmas?

So next I'm seeing lavender blue and dining on the finest chocolates while coasting to a soft landing in my mind's eye. Totally ready to hear out his plight. "This deal with the dev—I mean Prince of Darkness, what exactly did you mean when you said you sold your soul?"

No answer right away. He heads for the bathroom. Splashing sounds. Comes back with a fresher face and a few beads of water drooling down from his hair. "I guess I gave away the future, but not mine, exactly. These last few days have definitely been new to me."

"Stanley, that makes about as much sense as the old David Lynch movies my mom used to like. Ever see *Lost Highway?*"

"No, but the title sure fits." He edges onto the side of the bed, hands on his knees. I miss them all over me, so hopefully, the man's a quick storyteller.

"Lyla," he says, "if you found yourself tumbling backward through time, what would you do about it? Let's break *that* little problem into smaller pieces."

I'm sensing a degree of one-upmanship here, and I've already demonstrated my maddening flight to the darkest places during contests of will, so the best thing I can do is treat this as a rhetorical question for now. I'll hold my sometimes overly sharp tongue. Maybe a shrug. Nothing more.

Yet he's eyeing me expectantly, not at all in a challenging way.

Hey, I've been misreading signals for eleven consecutive months. Why stop now?

Soooo, what would I do in his hypothetical case, since he does want to know? "I guess I'd use my knowledge of the future to stop accidents waiting to happen."

"To you? This isn't playing out as a repeat of *my* life."

"No, I was thinking more like how Bill Murray helps all those people in *Groundhog Day.*"

That answer earns a fingertip caress through my hair. "You mean use my superpowers for good?"

"Sure. Dive right here under the sheets and we'll get started on that."

"Yeah, in a minute, but one more thing." He's staring into my eyes with such intensity I'm scared he did something bad, such as murder or worse, and the whole sell-your-soul idea is step one in a poorly concealed deceit. Like when somebody goes to the priest to confess but says it's a friend who committed the crime. "Lyla, the next time we fall asleep, if I'm not with you when you wake up, trust me that I'm doing everything possible to come back."

Oh, no. That's just what I meant. Prison time.

"You okay?" he says. "You're breathing too fast again."

"Sweetie, you didn't do something *really bad,* did you?"

He's under the blankets in a flash, wrapping me in his arms. "Of course not," he whispers. "I'm just wondering whether anyone ever tried selling their soul a second time to get what they really wanted."

"Which is?"

"Do you need to ask?" His lips on the back of my neck cast a rainbow of florescent shivers all the way down to my toes.

CHAPTER TWELVE

BED'S EMPTY. MUST HAVE slept too long.

"Lyla?"

Wait. New day, new name. She mentioned two possibilities yesterday. "Penny?" I've got a mind like a steel trap.

No answer.

"Cindy?"

Deafening silence.

Oh, no.

What made me think I'd wake up in the right place and time two mornings in a row? I could have skirted past her in this mad dash down the pages of history.

Hustling now. Bare feet smacking against the cold, hardwood floor. Into the kitchen and—

"Somebody's been eating my porridge." Runbad has his back to me, a box of Frosted Mini-Wheats in one hand, cornflakes in the other. He turns. Nods. "Hot coffee's on the burner."

Not interested. Except... smells like we're in a Starbucks. Give the guy credit for roasting a good brew. I pour a mugful, eyeing him, trying to keep my worries about Amy beneath the surface. "What are *you* doing here?"

"I come and go," he says.

That he does. If Runbad *is* the devil, I suppose walls aren't necessarily an issue.

But he's violating Amy's space, big-time. Mine, too.

Or not? "You're just an episode, pal. Let's call you a figment."

"Could be." He chooses cornflakes. Stashes the Mini-Wheats away. "You're good with odds. Should we say sixty percent chance you oughta run to Walgreens for a prescription refill?"

"I'm thinking more like seventy."

"Still leaves thirty that I'm real. A guy could go broke without a hedge against that kinda downside."

Got him there. "I'm already broke. Living out of my car. Remember Cynthia? She'll tell you all about it."

"All right then. Grab a seat at the table. Talk is cheap. Free, as a matter of fact."

So he wins round one. I settle into a chair, sip my coffee, glare at him. "Where's Amy?"

"Other side of town? We're talking *before* she copied a key to get in here." Runbad takes the spot across from me and starts shaking cereal into a bowl. "Maybe she's sleeping in somebody's car." He adds some milk. Goes for the sugar jar. "Not yours, though. Poor girl hasn't met you yet."

Deep breath. And then another. Neither one helps.

I'd kill the messenger, but who else might know how to rectify matters, re-steer my course *forward* in time, maybe accelerate it enough to get me back in sync with the rest of humanity?

Gotta keep him talking and see whether he might blab his way into showing his hand. The guy came after me for a reason. Only my soul? Nah, way more than that. He's been hounding me for favors from the beginning. Maybe I'm the only guy who can get them done.

But in case we are in fantasy land, I can crawl into bed when we're done talking and wait for Penny or Cindy or whoever-the-hell to show up with a warm compress for my forehead.

"I still want you to do a couple things for me," he says.

Bingo. "Forget Vegas," I say. "Ten grand sure would help
Amy. She's in over her head and needs some cash to work her
way out of it."

Runbad fishes in his shirt pocket, comes up with a cigarette.
"You mind?"

"Why ask? You've been blowing smoke up my butt from day
one."

"Good one." He flicks a lighter, gets the thing going. "I used
to drag a torch around, but cigarettes are so much more
satisfying."

"Yeah? I'll need to catch up on my Bible studies. Since when
does the devil carry a torch?"

Lazy shrug. "So maybe I'm somebody else. Anyway, suppose
I *can* move forward in time from one day to the next, unlike you.
Should I catch up with Amy and give her the dough?"

Here's where I need to find who truly has the upper hand. He
bet, and it's my turn to fold, call, or shove.

First, a nice, long sip of coffee. Man, this stuff is like heaven
in a cup. The savory steam caressing my nostrils, a burst of
flavor burning its way across my tongue. I'll take my time with
it.

Meanwhile, he's trying to freeze *me* out, puffing away on his
cigarette, pausing for a spoonful of cereal, then back to the
smoke.

Gotta believe he's accustomed to having people over a barrel.
If so, he might not be well experienced in the patience
department. But I can wait all day, folding hand after hand.
What's poker if not the world's longest pregnant pause?

"You looking for something more than that?" he asks.

"Could be." Man, was I ever right. He caved before I had a
chance to push my damn raise into the pot. Another sip of coffee.
Keeping him waiting. Then, "Let's talk about the favors you
want, first, though."

Runbad levels a long, thoughtful look on me. This guy does
not have devil's eyes. I wouldn't call them benevolent, though.
Probing. Deep. And a color that never seems to fit my memory

from the previous encounter. Brown today. Blue last time I saw him? Dark hair every time, cut almost as close as a razor job, but those crayon-box eyes... "You're at the cage in Snakes," he says, "and Sally calls me over to examine a couple bad chips in your possession. Let's call anything after that moment the future, and we're in the past."

"Okay," I say. "No, wait. Unless time froze at the cage, entire days must have gone by since then. That was Sunday. The future has to be up to Thursday or Friday by now."

"Not necessarily." He takes another go at the cereal bowl. Comes up chewing. "Let's say time froze, from your perspective."

Perfect. Got this man talking, and he's shedding clues all over the place. He just told me the exact point in time where I can sync back into the real world. Just need to reverse my direction and deadhead over there.

Somehow.

"You're a smart one," he says. "You and Amy both. But not the best match. If I wanted to kill two birds with one stone, maybe I'd convince you to pass those bad chips to her at the gypsy casino, knocking you off the grid where you can help me *and* triggering the events that broke you up. You know, like how she caught you naked with Cynthia in the backseat of your car."

I'm clenching my coffee mug with both hands now to keep from lunging over the table to take him out. "Where are you going with this?"

"Nowhere," he says. "Just throwing you another clue, since you're so big on them." He heads for the coffeepot on the stove, refills his cup, comes back to the table and raids the sugar jar again. "You know what everyone in the whole wide world has in common? We all spend our lives trying to manipulate the future for our own selfish needs. I'm no different."

"And you need my help."

"Like I said, Mike. You're quick." He shifts his focus to the wall calendar. Chuckles. "And you do know where the future lies." Turns to me again. "Back at Snakes. Ground zero. At the table you left. Seat five is a tourist. A woman. And seat eight is a middle-aged Asian man. Remember them?"

"Uh-huh." How could I forget anything from that first go-around with Amy? She bet eight, I raised to thirty, and when she took forever to fold, I studied the field. The entire lineup is an Instagram in my head. A couple hoodies, an Old Man Coffee, Amy, me, a couple empty chairs, the woman—he's right, a tourist—and the Asian with his Guns N' Roses shirt.

"Everybody at that table is important, Mike, but those two in particular must leave the building immediately. That's where *you* come in."

All of a sudden, maintaining a poker face is almost impossible. I've got my hands on my knees to hide the trembles. "Fine, Runbad. Put me back at the cage and I'll see they go home." The devil doesn't hold the monopoly on false promises. If he sends me to that point in time and pushes the forward arrow, I'm back to the future. The hell with those two other card players. I can track Amy down and mend fences with her. A happily ever after.

But the smirk on his face sure suggests otherwise. "Let's give it a go, cowboy."

The room dims a tad. Rays of sun pouring through the kitchen window dissolve into the ever-present man-made lighting of a modern casino. Cooler temps raise goose bumps on my flesh.

Sally's looking through the bars at me.

I'm back at the cashier's cage! I must have spit out the magic words.

There goes Amy with the Old Man Coffee. They're hurrying toward the exit, heads down, in a manner that can best be described as...

Sally's handheld chimes an off note.

I swivel back to her.

"Where'd you come up with these blacks, Mike?"

Yep. This is playing out just like before. I'd fallen for Amy's rigged chip swap.

I shrug, glance toward the exit where she's headed, then back at Sally.

How do I play this out? What's the next step? Gotta stop Amy and tell her the whole story. I know she thinks I'm nuts, and the truth will do nothing to dispel that notion, but what else can a guy—

"Pete!"

A uniformed security guy rises from a stool in a corner of the cage and…

Bright flash. I'm flying sideways, blinded.

Rays of sun.

Pouring in through the kitchen window.

No!

Runbad has the wrong look in his eyes. Compassion? *Pity?* The renewed urge to dive across the table and deck the guy makes the backs of my fists itch.

Long sip of his coffee. Eyeballing me. "For reasons I can't disclose at the moment, you'll never be able to chase after her that way. Can't even hurry over and ask the Asian or the tourist to leave." He plunges into his cereal again, leaving me to chew on frustration.

Not lost hope, though. This guy is full of—

"Mikey, did you look back at the table at all after you got to the cage? Maybe they already left. Game could be breaking up because of a couple things you'll do for me."

So there it is. We're back at the negotiating table, and I *still* might have the upper hand. Sure doesn't feel that way, but I've bulldozed tough players out of pots before. "Here's the deal, Runbad. *I* get to give Amy the ten grand, because you're gonna let me see her again."

And now what am I looking at, sheepishness?

"Actually, I'm a little short. Would five do the trick?"

This liar. "Whatever. *And* you'll let me out of this time warp."

"No can do," he says. "But how about I let you visit her more than once?"

"Fine." Two can play his game. I'll do the one favor if it's not too unreasonable, and then demand more before tackling the second. "One last thing. These solids you want. Nobody gets hurt by what I do for you, right?"

"That's up to you." Runbad sets his spoon down. Kicks away from the table. "I've shown you the line between before and after. Only one can be manipulated. If you trigger a butterfly effect by changing the past, people could die. Starting with Amy."

"What? Listen, asshole—"

"No, pal, *you* listen. Do not try to talk anyone out of showing up for the game." He heads for the door, slows, chuckles. "Nobody rewrites history, but sometimes blending into the past works just fine. You've done it a few times already."

And he's gone. End of negotiation.

Did I win?

CHAPTER THIRTEEN

I'M PENNY FOR THE day, but the new identity isn't necessarily a pointless ruse. I'm hitting a new casino. Different place, different name.

Not that anyone would follow such ridiculous reasoning. Changing names every day as a game with my boyfriend is one thing, but doing it as part of a counterfeiting scam?

I just don't follow the logic. Sometimes I think my new Russian buddies are toying with me and laughing their asses off. I'm pretty sure my failure to stay one step ahead of this dandy scheme's masterminds is because I don't think in Russian.

Anyway, Eugene told me about some place called a gypsy casino, where they accept Snake Eyes chips. Ever hear of such a thing? Me, neither, but I'm standing outside of it, under the awning to stay clear of the drizzle.

My immediate goal is to rid myself of any and all Things. One of them is standing in front of me with a hangdog expression on his face. I can't remember whether he's Thing One or Two, let alone his real name.

"This place is too small for both of us to be running around bouncing bad chips, Hans."

"It's Yosef."

"Yeah, like I said." So this Thing works for Eugene, the loan shark, not Philippe, the counterfeiter, although since the Things look almost the same and they've always got those hoodies on, they could be switching back and forth for all I know.

And why did somebody just take our picture from that black sedan over there? He speeds away, having added a nice pic of random chick standing next to hoodie for his *I visited New Orleans* Facebook album.

Meanwhile, Thing Two has been babbling away in a whiney tone.

"I'm sorry, what?"

"Hans and I need to make some money."

Good God, this is why I never intend to have any children. Unless they're Jonathan's—my man's name of the day, but he doesn't know that yet, cuz he wasn't in the bed *or anywhere in the apartment* when I woke up this morning. And that's another reason I can barely tolerate the company of a Thing at the moment, to the point of being rude and telling him to get lost, even though if this guy ever lost his temper, they'd be scraping me off the sidewalk. "Get lost, Hans."

"It's Yosef."

"Whatever." The comedy routine could go on all day, but I've got chips to move, then even more chips to move until I can fully pay off the Russians and be on my way. The three grand in my purse plus another two at Eugene's for good measure. I don't care how he and Philippe divide up whatever's left after that. In other words, I've made up my mind to walk the straight and narrow, no matter how many diamonds my Monaco earrings would have displayed.

And not because their bad cop/worse cop routine has gotten stale. Philippe actually updated his status to a man above the law when he showed me his boatload of chips, except upon deeper reflection, he became the worst cop ever.

Jonathan thinks *his* soul has been stolen? Imagine what too many counterfeit bones might do to mine. My mom always said—

Oh, hell, I should leave her out of this. Any halfway decent shrink would blame my unchecked greed and borderline gambling addiction on a poor upbringing, only I'm not buying it. Where I am and the direction I'm headed is on me.

Totally.

"Why do you need money, Yosef? It's not like you guys have a deficient wardrobe that keeps sucking away every last dime. Try having to buy shoes that match your hoodies sometime."

Weirdly, he turns shifty on me, signaling with lowered hands to keep my voice down. He leans in close, which I'm so not in the mood for. "We're into something big. Hans has a thousand, I have a thousand, but we need one more."

So the Things are boiler-room stock investors now? More than likely they're being duped by some con artist. And who better to help them than their two dastardly patrons? "Look, why don't you just hit up Eugene for a loan? Or borrow some chips from Philippe and start your own operation? Better yet, whatever this sting is you're getting yourselves into, go to them for advice. Crafty guys like those two can probably smell a scam a mile away."

"They don't trust us." The Thing has defeat in his voice. "Hans doesn't think they even like us. They remind him of, you know, profilers at the security checkpoint?"

Oh, poor widdle Thing, pulling out the race card like that. I've got problems of my own. Besides, who wouldn't be leery about allowing a couple muscle-bound Things who *never* lower their hoods to board an airplane? "Fine," I say. "Go *filch* some chips then. Philippe's got so goddamn many he'll never miss a few."

Wow, I've kneed him in the nuts with that one. His eyes have gone wide at the suggestion. "We're honorable men," he declares.

"Go home for your nine-times-a-day prayers then. I'm moving these chips on my own today." That's just downright nasty, and I know it.

The Thing shuffles away, all bent head and slumping shoulders.

What has he ever done to me? Nothing. So how would my mom handle this one? Tough-love time. She'd be chasing me with a ping-pong paddle.

"Sorry," I call. "We'll go back to Snakes tomorrow. Okay, sweetie?"

He waves me off.

"No, seriously, I kinda like you guys." As the words spill out of my mouth, something impossible dawns on me. I do like them. They're steadfast, loyal, and now that I think about it, they've acted protective of me from day one.

I'm running after him. "Tomorrow, Yosef?"

"Yeah, okay. I'll let Hans know."

Yosef doesn't turn to me, so I give him a quick hug from behind. "Wish me luck."

"You're too smart for that, Penny." His voice even keel now, and he's on his way home.

Did the stupid sedan driver slink around the block and snap another picture just now? This gypsy casino is far too small for that level of security. And where's Jonathan today, leaving not so much as another *wanting you* note on the kitchen counter? He definitely earned his eggs and bacon breakfast with that one, when I discovered his folded piece of paper from yesterday morning.

I hustle back under the canopy and through the entrance, brushing past a couple low-life scammers who won't have much luck at this kind of scummy place where *everybody* uses at least one hand to protect their wallets. Hey, guys, maybe try the parking lot of the local Churchill Downs for accidentally torn-up winning tickets. Is thoroughbred racing big around here? Being from a small town in Missouri, I never cared much for the ponies. Only the underground card games my mom used to run.

At first glance, this insufficiently lighted casino's interior comes across like the set for a *Caligula* remake, what with the nymphs on the ceiling and the red-papered walls. But the second impression pulls me forward. Row upon row of slot machines with their *clang, clang, clangs* and flashing lights. The frantic shouts of encouragement for the shooter at a craps table. And, above all, a sign for poker pointing up the stairs.

How many nice pairs of shoes can I buy if I stick with the Russians? How much fine jewelry might I own?

I am so torn.

CHAPTER FOURTEEN

I'M AN IDIOT. HOW could I let Runbad leave this apartment without telling me how to chase the Asian and the tourist from the game at Snakes? I can't simply sidle away from Sally at the cage, deadhead back to the table, and offer a hundred bucks apiece for them to go away. He already made that abundantly clear with his little time-travel demonstration at the cage. My needle gets stuck on empty the minute Sally calls for backup. That's my line between past and future. A barrier I can't cross.

Besides, I don't even know how to find the right coordinates for that particular time and place. We're still on a reverse flight to nowhere. And the favor Runbad wants is daunting at best. So the prospect of ever seeing Amy again... *that's* looking kinda grim.

I'll sure as hell try, though.

Now... what's the best strategy here?

I'll hang around and see whether Amy shows up. Runbad told me she doesn't have the key yet, but whatever definition I lay on him, trustworthy doesn't make the cut.

I pace the floor. Stare out the window down to the sidewalk below for a while. Switch the TV on. Switch the TV off.

Still waiting...

Still.

Oh, hell, no luck here, and the clock keeps ticking in the wrong direction. Away from her.

I leave and walk to the gypsy casino first. It's closer to Snakes, and I found her here once before. Except what, they pulled up stakes and moved away? No canopy to shelter me from the rain beginning to come down with a vengeance. No faded letters announcing *Casino* to passersby. Just the storefront of a wildly different operation.

As newly reconstituted—or before I last visited?—this place teaches some version of martial arts I can't even pronounce. Students in white pajamas tied closed with ropes keep brushing past me to hurry inside. They're getting just as wet as me, but judging by the eager smiles lighting their glistening faces, they are far more enthusiastic about the way the world has been turning lately.

No sign of Amy or whatever name du jour she's going by. Not a hint of Runbad, either, a demon normally well-versed at crashing into my life. Just a rumble of thunder.

I should hustle inside. A guy could drown out here. Except my current situation off the grid, out of the timeline, and flailing away in the past strongly suggests temporary immortality. Otherwise, what's the point? So go ahead, rain. Keep oozing down my forehead and into my eyes. I'm here for you.

I trudge away, pausing to check the newspaper stand.

And I swallow.

I've slipped a couple days back, away from her. We're now at T minus *fifteen*.

Is the version of Amy who hasn't met me yet really sleeping in somebody's car, like Runbad suggested? The idea of such a prospect calls for immediate surrender to the forces of nature. I lift my face to the soaking sky, but the pit in my stomach only opens wider... letting in a heavy dose of reality.

I can't look for her now. He said she might die if I change anything. Saying *hey there* to somebody a couple days before we ever officially saw each other probably qualifies as enough butterfly-style revision to stir up typhoons in China. Gotta think of that as a no-crossing sign. Little walking man in red with an x all over him. Certainly not green. Or even yellow.

Worst part is the way Runbad warned me. He didn't suggest Amy's peril in a threatening tone. More of a matter-of-fact statement with just enough emphasis to imply worry on his part, not malice. Making the risk real. But why the level of interest? *Somebody's been eating my porridge,* he said. Maybe she's been sleeping in the backseat of *his* car.

Great. At a time when positive thought might produce a favorable result somehow—hey, it works in a poker game, so why not in a supernatural con game?—I'm conjuring up even worse scenarios than the already awful here and now.

I need to chew on *this*, instead. Amy is alive at the moment in Snakes when the past melds into the future. This means she's breathing just fine every minute before then, unless I mess things up and somehow cause her *not* to be at ground zero. In that case, she's thrown onto a different path. Adding Russian mobsters to the mix sure makes the outcome scary. I can't be certain she'll survive. *That's* what Runbad was getting at when he warned me.

Okay, I'm still not entertaining positive thoughts, but they've definitely gotten more logical. I've gotta stay focused on one thing no matter how tough it is to say. *No Amy reunions* until I find my way to the point where she at least remembers meeting me. Like Runbad said in so many words, I'm allowed to blend into the past, as long as I don't do anything to change the stretch between T minus fifteen and T in such a way the takeoff gets aborted. We're talking predestined, albeit walking-in-the-blind, choreography as opposed to bull in the china shop.

So it's the Asian or the tourist I need to track down today. Find either one of them, do Runbad his favor, and flash forward to Amy, five thousand dollars in hand to bail her out of Russia. But with a strong encouragement thrown in for her to play cards at Snake Eyes the day before Memorial Day.

And if Runbad doesn't fork over the cash?

He will.

He better. Those mobsters are far more likely to sell Amy

into white slavery than ever think about letting her off the hook unless somebody pays them off fast. Damn it, Amy. You're way too smart to fall into their clutches but a little too reckless not to.

I won't call her greedy. Never being sure of the next day's meal creates ravenous hunger for the better things in life. Such as a roof and a real bed. I've snuggled up to her and looked into her eyes often enough to know. She's a scared little girl inside.

Okay, the question is how to find an Asian Guns N' Roses fan or a tourist with big hair and loopy earrings in a city of half a million or so? Go where they like to hunt. So I'm walking and walking, barely slowed by the random sightseeing souvenir shoppers I'm elbowing past. Up this street and across to the other, down the Riverwalk, then cutting off on an angle to the casino.

Like a one-man swat team, I storm in and clear the joint from corner to corner. Poker room, craps tables, roulette, the stools at the bar, the lounge area, wheel of fortune, the other bar, blackjack, Caribbean Stud—man, three-card monte offers better odds—out the front door and in again through the side, the men's room, surveillance from against the wall by the ladies' room, in and out of the gift shop... but no dice. Or I didn't recognize them. Where's a face on a milk carton when you need one?

Runbad hasn't done a thing to make this easy.

Night's closing in. I need somewhere to think. So I'm walking outside again, down this block and that in near darkness. Till I find the lot with three working light stands and go to my car beneath the one that isn't. Standing away from it for a minute.

We're in the past. What the hell happens if I find my old self sleeping inside? Talk about butterflies stirring up hurricanes.

Car's empty, thank God, and I'm crawling into the backseat of this little life raft for a few moments' solace from an unforgiving world. If I close my eyes, will they reopen during the Civil War? Doesn't matter. They're half-shut already, I'm breathing steady, and—

Swish, swish, swish. Huh! I peer through the wipers' crescent swipes and lurch the wheel just in time to avoid the railing. Easing to a stop now on a gravel shoulder.

Must have fallen asleep at the wheel.

No, wait, I wasn't driving, was I? And if so, why?

Better yet, where?

Gulfport, Mississippi.

Says so right on that sign.

And I'm here because...

It's hunting time? I don't have any other reason to be in Gulfport, unless they sell really good anti-fugue-episode medicine here. So I head into town, park outside the first riverboat, and head inside to case the joint the way I did in Snakes. Blackjack, craps, roulette... the whole nine yards. Downstairs and upstairs. But not a single Guns N' Roses fan or woman with big hair and loopy earrings do I find.

On to the next riverboat and up the entrance ramp.

Blackjack?

No.

Roulette?

Uh-uh.

Craps?

Whoa, Momma.

There's a middle-aged Asian in a Guns N' Roses T. Same thing he wore at Snakes.

Lucky shirt? For me, maybe. Enough to blast my pounding heart into overdrive.

I head on over, squeeze in beside him, and try to... blend in, I guess. But that means buying in and joining the fray, doesn't it?

I don't know the first thing about craps, or any other casino action not known as poker. I've never played. Why flush my money down the drain? Every form of gambling, from hungry slot machines to all the many different table games, has odds biased to the house. Sure, I'll buy lottery tickets at the truck stop where I shower when the jackpot's high enough, but that's just a matter of practicing the national religion. Anything within *these* four walls, though...

This game here has something to do with betting on a number called the point—like eight, for example—and praying said number gets rolled before a seven comes up. Yet the Guns N' Roses fan to my left keeps communicating to the housemen in code, shouting phrases like *the hard way, Buffalo, C&E* while spraying chips all over the board. I'm staring at him with *lost* surely written all over my face until he grins and motions to his array of chips scattered over various number combinations on the felt. "Side bets," he says.

"Right." Something almost clicks in my brain but fades too fast for me to latch on.

A houseman hands the dice to one of the players whose position is known as the shooter. I know this much but little more. Soon the dice are flying toward the back wall of the table, then hitting, bouncing back, spinning, and coming to rest as a six and a one. The dozen or so players gathered around the table join in a collective shoulder slump, with the odd grumble or two about their shitty luck and how all the money ends up in the house's hands sooner or later. It does seem to be flowing that way at the moment. Their bets are scooped away.

One of the board men gazes at me expectantly.

Now what? Oh. Crowded table. Casual observers aren't wanted. "Change?" I fish a hundred bucks out of my wallet and toss it onto the felt, silently cursing Runbad for putting me in a position where I have to spend money on a house game that, by definition, has odds tough enough to crush the savviest players if they stay long. And I'm a rank amateur without the slightest knowledge of the rules, understanding of the action, or—of utmost importance—grasp of a plan for convincing a guy to leave a poker game eighty miles away that won't even start until fifteen days in the future.

Befriend him? For whatever reason, the action pauses for a shift change or something. Two suits leave, and a couple new ones start setting up. This is my chance.

Rules of engagement for breaking the ice are to talk up the weather, babble about sports, or state the obvious. "You're running good," I say.

Should work. The rows of blacks and greens in his tray add up to three thousand or more. This guy is *solidly* ahead unless he bought in deep.

He grins. "Good luck's the test of the man where I come from."

Seems to me bad luck would be the larger trial, but arguments and small talk do not go hand in hand. So, "Where's that?"

"Hong Kong, but I get around."

"Me, too. I'm from New Orleans at the moment."

"Oh, yeah?" he says. "I'll be out that way for Memorial Day weekend." He motions down at his Guns N' Roses T-shirt. "Concert."

A safecracker would say he just heard one of the tumblers click. Part of me wants to gape open-mouthed at the way this guy just played into my hand, but a wizened voice in the back of my head asks whether *I'm* the one playing into Runbad's. Mental note: *Next time you see him, ask why he needs you as his bitch. He could have sidled next to this guy and handled whatever needs to be done here on his own.*

But regardless, the beginnings of a script just surfaced, and I better recite what few lines I know. "I'm Mike."

"Tak. Good to know you."

"Yeah."

I've got chips now. Twenty reds. Still don't know what to do.

"Bet the pass line," Tak says. "Pays even odds."

"Oh, like red and black in roulette?"

He nods. "Good for beginners."

"Yep, that's me." Hopefully I'm not this easy to read in poker, or if so, no wonder my luck's been down.

I toss a chip down. "Pass line?"

One of the housemen scoops it to an oval labeled *pass.*

Okay, good. How hard can this be?

The next shooter sends the dice flying. They bang the end of the table, bounce around, and come up fours.

"Hard eight!" Tak yells.

Chips get shoved in his direction by the house. God only knows why.

"Another side bet, Tak?"

"I'll bet on anything," he says. "See the woman in the hat coming toward us down that aisle? Wanna go five bucks she stops at a slot machine before getting this far?"

Wow. Tumbler number two. This is like flopping a monster hand in Hold' em. Absolutely no skill involved, but I've still earned a payoff. *Or* it's the classic scene where the mark gets to win a small bet only to lose his whole bankroll when the sting kicks in.

Still, if Runbad's playing me, how can he be sure I'll find such a great angle in what Tak just said?

"When it comes to proposition bets," I say," I prefer the long game."

The dice roll again, bounce around, come up a three and a five. Must be a good thing. Not only does nobody lose their bet, a few players toss more chips into the pit. But not Tak. "*Long* game?" he asks.

"Yeah. Hear me out. I'll be in New Orleans the day before Memorial Day."

"Okay."

"Suppose I wager that you and I meet in a poker game at Snake Eyes, I'll out-bet a redhead who just sat down. She'll fold and switch seats. Then, maybe ten minutes later, I'll head for the cage, and the cashier will shout *Pete* so loud the whole table will hear it."

He laughs. Shakes his head. "No way I'm falling for that scam. You could rig the whole thing."

"Oh, but that's not the bet," I say. "I'm going a hundred bucks you'll get so caught up in the action you won't be able to leave the table and walk straight out of the casino when you hear her shout."

Tak's face reddens. I've called him a compulsive gambler. "Make it a thousand, smartass. What time of day should we meet?"

Hook, line, and sinker.

CHAPTER FIFTEEN

SO HERE I AM, Penny again.

Missing my man.

Pushing him out of my mind so I can focus on moving chips at the gypsy casino without getting caught.

Folding hand after hand in a worn-out poker room, after a little bad luck at blackjack and even worse at roulette. The immediate field offers only moderate challenge but more than a smattering of annoyance. We're looking at two elderly men, one with a funny hat and both easily predictable, two tourists, three regular players with headphones and steely gazes—this trio is to be avoided except when holding the strongest hand—and one really annoying jerk of a wannabe pro who just showed the table his hole cards after chasing a stronger hand out of the pot with a bluff.

Hubris.

For the most part, a guy thing. Or kid. The smarty pants in question looks to be all of nineteen.

Trust me. I know a thing or two about fake IDs. I've got *that* going for me but not much else, such as possessing sufficient planning skill to consider all likely outcomes when trading an honest life for a heavy dose of crime. Oh, sure, I did focus on the two ends of the spectrum. Here we have point A, where I jet-set from Monaco to Macau, dangling rubies on my fingers. And there's point B, where my head is shaved and a tin plate of gruel is shoved through the bars as my meal.

But how about a monkey wrench known as leakage? That's where I walk into a casino with three thousand in bad chips, hoping to swap it all for the same amount in cash. Yet blackjack, roulette, craps, and all the games I play in order to change these bones will inevitably take a bite out of the mothership. The odds favor the house, after all. So I'm two hundred short at the moment, with a thousand counterfeit chips still to move as I sit here and watch Mister Gloater make an ass of himself.

Okay, enough musing. Things can change in a heartbeat.

Except another round of cards is dealt, and mine come up a seven and a three. Next hand, ten-six. Another deal brings queen-deuce. Then six-three, jack-four, nine-six. The action is ignoring me. Chips thumbing their noses as they fly around the table and refuse to help put a dent in my losses. I jinxed myself into a run of dead cards by folding something good.

Yep. It was *my* strong hand that kid bluffed out of the pot, putting me two-fifty behind now that I've scurried to the one game where the odds should be in my favor, eleven bad months in a row be damned.

King-seven, eight-four, ten-deuce. When will this end? And why do they only show sporting events on those stupid TVs hanging down from the ceilings everywhere I look? They can't downstream a closed-captioned HGTV show? Or the Food Channel? Teach me how to make a rhubarb pie for Stewart. Please.

Stewart. My missing boyfriend who started as Mike and now might be *Mr. Dumped Me?* If he doesn't show up soon, I'll forget how to name him.

Then I'll be forced to face my problems all by my lonesome.

Such as this quick review of the math. I received ten thousand in chips from Philippe, for which I paid five. This was money borrowed from Eugene, and I've already repaid two, but he's a fierce usury loyalist, meaning I now owe him four, not three.

Still, he's holding chips as collateral I might get to use. Five thousand in value, after deducting the two I already moved and the three I toted here in my purse a couple hours ago. Therefore, not a problem, right?

Five grand is more than enough to make me whole, especially since I swore off my continued involvement in this counterfeiting scam earlier today with every intention of passing only enough bones to pay off the Russians and maybe buy a few extra skirts and some fancier shoes. My jewelry needs an upgrade, too, but we're talking places like Claire's as opposed to Diamonds Plus.

I refer to the Russians in the plural case, cuz the seemingly independent loan shark and equally aloof counterfeiter are no doubt in cahoots, with the shared goal of keeping me under their collective thumbs forever. That's a big reason for deciding to flee this scam before it devours me. Plus, about a half dozen *Mom always saids,* all with *honesty is the best policy* as their common theme.

Except she did agree the ability to lie convincingly can be so strong a success indicator as to trump whatever misguided morality would otherwise give me pause. Or maybe that's my take on her wisdom. Am I to remember with unfailing accuracy every damn bit of advice she threw at me? Mom played poker. Actions speak louder than words. If bluffing is okay, misrepresenting phony chips can't be far behind.

Where was I? Oh. Suppose I'm having the slightest change of heart over walking the straight and narrow, cuz for a woman with no job or prospects, other than a useless college degree, I might end up walking the streets. There's *no way,* so don't even think we're heading in that direction—but a job as a waitress, cashier, assistant librarian, administrative assistant, receptionist, corporate team member in any capacity, or schoolmarm doesn't offer the kind of excitement and glamour I've always hoped would be mine. Whereas successfully moving a cupboard full of counterfeit chips all over the world might be just the ticket.

So I'm wavering a teeny tiny bit, which brings me back to the math, and the problem of leakage. I didn't lose two-fifty today because of some freak stroll down the wrong end of the normal distribution where the wide and wonderful hump of success dives into oblivion for the unlucky few.

The business model for every casino keeps profitability at the very top of the priority list. Even higher than down-sliding singer/celebrities and yummy buffets. That means the house makes a small profit on every game I'll play, except poker, where the ordinary fields I've been up against tax me quite nicely on their own of late. If I walk into a casino with a thousand to trade, I'll typically limp out with something like nine hundred in cash. Maybe less.

Queen-four.

Fold.

Seven-six.

Fold.

Queen-ten.

Take a shot with it?

Fold.

And still nothing but baseball games to watch while I freeze to death in this cold seat.

A waitress stops at our table. "Drinks?"

Nuh-uh. I wouldn't be able to stop.

Here's the new formula for a rack of counterfeit chips. Five thousand for Philippe, a thousand for Eugene, a thousand in leakage, maybe five hundred for the Things in providing whatever level of protection their muscle has to offer—not to mention sometimes helping me move the bones—and just twenty-five hundred for little old me.

Of course *eventually* I'll squirrel away enough twenty-five-hundred-dollar scores to avoid borrowing from Eugene and maybe negotiate a better deal with Philippe, using the old *I'll quit otherwise* strategy. That's not the immediate problem, though. The pressing issue is I took three thousand in chips from a loan shark, and he'll want that much in cash dividends before he's willing to part with any more collateral. At least that's the attitude I sensed back in his apartment when he and his dog were snarling at me.

Do Russian mobsters justify beating women by relying on the *whiney, thankless, and highly unreliable bitch* excuse? If so, none of the possible outcomes bode well for me, whether I throw myself before the mercy of Eugene's court now or eventually cut him out of the action and put the squeeze on Philippe for a bigger taste.

Woe is me comes to mind, a phrase specifically coined for jams of this magnitude.

But wait. What's this? I'm peering at my hole cards in the very next hand, and my eyes water at the sight of the ace of spades partnered with the beautiful ace of diamonds. Winning is a God-given right with pocket aces in Hold'em. They do just that over eighty percent of the time.

My tummy tingles from what happens next. The gloater bets twenty dollars, and the action folds to me. My first inclination is to nurse this kid along and not scare him out of the pot. My new worst friend bought in for less than the max, but he does have two-fifty in front of him, which I'm happy to win.

Strategy time. I should do no more than raise the minimum allowed by the rules, just twenty dollars, to build the pot a little while keeping him in the hand. Almost nobody folds against a min raise. But on the day Stewart was Bob, a face-to-face part of my life and not a nagging worry, he told me to raise the same amount no matter what hand I held. That way, the competition won't read me so easily.

I raise the bet to sixty.

The kid tanks. That's poker lingo for sitting befuddled for an excruciatingly long period of time. His slumping shoulders say he'll fold and I'll be cursing the dead, who Stewart will soon be when I get my hands on him.

But lo and behold, the kid calls, and here comes the flop. The deuce of clubs, queen of clubs, and... ace of hearts. I almost swallow my tongue. The nice starting hand of mine has grown into a monster. A set of aces. That's poker terminology for *hot damn!*

He'll check to me for sure, since I raised him before the flop.

Hands almost always play out that way, unless this guy is a complete—

"All in," he says.

Christmas came early. The mean side of me wants to slow roll the goof, pretending to puzzle over whether to call or to fold for as long as *he* tanked, before shoving my chips across the felt and showing him what he's up against. But my mom taught me better. "Call," I say almost immediately, and I flip over my hand.

He glances at my monster, shrugs, and turns over the six and seven of clubs.

Oh.

I'm still something like a three-to-one favorite, but he could beat me with a flush if a club hits, unless I'm lucky enough to outdraw him—like if I upgrade *my own hand* by picking up a pair for a full house. But keep in mind, I've been distinctly unlucky for about eleven months running. So I don't want to see another club hit the felt. Not. Ever.

Stop twitching, knee. I've got to stay optimistic. The deck is *loaded* with suits not known as clubs.

I wait without breathing.

The dealer turns over the king of diamonds.

Good. Just one more card to go.

Long, pregnant pause. Poker rooms the world over wait a few beats before showing the final card, much to the annoyance of almost every player. The house enjoys building up the suspense, without regard to possible heart attacks by those involved in the hand or stifling boredom by those who aren't.

Finally, the last card hits the felt.

The four of clubs.

I might as well go to Eugene's place five hundred short and let him kill me now. This friendly card game is way worse than that.

So I'm wringing my hands at Eugene's now, sitting on the front stoop of his duplex.

"He went to the store for some milk," Thing One says.

Ah, those ulcers. A pity the poor guy has so much stress in his life. "Wait. Don't you work for Philippe?"

"We switch back and forth. Anyway, I noticed you sitting alone out here, and... you know."

So the Thing is nice enough to sit with me, minimizing the danger some random thug on this bad side of town might think it hot to shove me against a brick wall in the alley over there. My temporary protector would be far less useful against the unbridled fury of the Russian mob, such as when Eugene learns I'm short a few dollars, but I shouldn't hold that against him.

We sit in silence for a while. Then, "Just so you know, we only pray five times a day, not nine," he says.

Great. Now not only is my stomach churning, my cheeks burn. "I shouldn't have demeaned Yosef like that, Hans. I've got problems at home, and they make me..."

"Flighty?"

Wow. That isn't the word I was groping for, but give him credit for nailing it. I've gone from teetering on the ledge before Stewart disappeared to a hot mess after. "It doesn't matter," I say. "This disrespectful chip mule will be dead soon, anyway. When Eugene gets here, he's gonna learn I'm five hundred dollars short."

The Thing gazes at me for the longest time, as if he's weighing whether to help me, which he can't. Then he reaches into the pocket of his hoodie, retrieves a small wad of hundreds, counts out five, and presses them into my palm.

The Good-Samaritan gesture doesn't register, except for one possibility. "No, I can't take a loan from you. I'm in deep enough already."

"It's not like that," he says. "Just pay it back when you can. I won't even ask."

"B-but Yosef said you and he are saving up for something you really need."

"You know what he calls you, Penny?"

"Nothing good, I'm sure."

His eyes burn into mine. "Little sister."

I cry so easily, and there's no tissue in sight. Takes a while for me to compose myself. His arm over my shoulder helps.

I need to adjust my Thing-detecting meter. From the start, I've thought of these two as part of the unwashed thug masses, but on closer inspection, Hans does have clean nails. My mom always told me to judge a man by his hands. And what's wrong with something of a masculine scent?

Little sister.

Hans and Yosef aren't Things anymore.

He's fishing in his pocket again. Pulls out a creased photo of a dark-haired beauty with a smile on her face that could turn the whole world green. "Yosef says you look like her."

"I'm not that pretty. Who is she?"

As he puts the photo back, I'm reading the tremble in his hand as the predictor of a great weight of sadness soon to blot out the sun. Too late to take back the question, though.

"Elsa was my sister and Yosef's wife."

"Oh, no. Is she…"

"They call it collateral damage. You know, when the Americans aim their missile at the number four on their list, but they hit your house instead."

"I'm so sorry, Hans."

He shrugs. "These are… problems at home."

He's made me small, but not in a mean way. More like a lecture from my mom.

We sit forever on the stoop. The sun brightens just a tad, and he punches my arm in a friendly way. Moods change. Even throat-clenching ones.

I put his five hundred into my purse. "I won't use this unless I absolutely need it. Maybe Eugene will understand the shortage when I explain the concept of leakage to him."

"Leakage?"

"It's the long story of my life."

More silence. More waiting. "Why do you and Yosef wear hoodies all the time?"

"We're being watched," he says.

"Got it."

Making themselves more conspicuous is nonsensical at best, suggesting their paranoia comes flavored with more than a pinch of craziness at worst, but I do go for that type.

CHAPTER SIXTEEN

I'VE GOTTA GET AWAY from my Guns N' Roses pal, Tak, before our prop bet unravels. The longer we keep talking, the more likely we'll bond. Then he won't stay angry enough to try winning a grand off me in New Orleans two weeks from now. For the moment, his pursed lips and furrowed brow convey the intense desire to prove he *can* leave a poker game in the middle of the action. Hopefully he'll follow through and bolt from the game at Snakes, like Runbad wants. That's supposedly my ticket to Amy.

A shooter throws the dice, all eyes follow, and I skedaddle.

Where's the door? These casinos set up their meandering walkways like gauntlets, hoping to bludgeon us suckers into overstaying our budgets. They've tossed slot machines in my way, roulette tables, three- and four-card poker, black—

Holy crap. The sight of a slump-shouldered devil playing twenty-one alone at a high-stake table stops me in my tracks.

Other than the body language, Runbad may be the most dapper guy in the house. Dinner jacket. Pressed shirt open at the collar. Gray slacks. Sloshing drink. Bloodshot eyes. Okay, on closer inspection, maybe not so dapper.

I grab the seat beside him. "Hey."

He barely acknowledges me. Takes a gulp of whiskey or whatever. Signals the dealer for a hit.

The house is more than happy to oblige. A flick of the wrist later, the jack of clubs busts the seventeen Runbad should have stood pat with. House had a six.

The dealer scoops up the bet, shifts his attention to me, and flashes a winner of a smile, as in *we want your money so much we'll pretend to like you.* Another fine disciple in the Church of Fleecing Rubes. "Chips?"

Not at these stakes. A placard on a corner of the table sets the minimum bet at a hundred bucks. I'll damn well give all I have to Amy when I find her. Not one penny to this place.

"No, I'm heading out in a minute." And then, to Runbad, "How did *you* get here?" This question is near the bottom of the priority list, borderline irrelevant, and pretty much a nonstarter in any context. Demons get around. Yeah, and if I were good at icebreakers, I'd be in sales. Got lucky earlier with Tak, but good fortune only goes so far.

Nevertheless, he does stop drinking long enough to glance my way. "Maybe I hitched a ride." He's got a telltale slur to his speech, something I could cash in on at a poker table, but not so much when I'm relying on the guy to steer my roller coaster uphill.

Runbad busts another hand, then motions to the dealer. "Phil and I go way back. Met on an archery range years ago."

"Damn straight," the dealer says. He does have the look of someone my buddy here might pal around with. Close-cropped hair. Tattoos peeking out beneath both sleeves. But in their vastly different lines of work, what kind of dynamic would play? Maybe my sinking-fast friend with diminishing chips beats the daylights out of Phil during target practice, only to repay all that and more, playing blackjack with—

The money meant for Amy! "Are you kidding me, Runbad?"

The game stops. A pit boss ambles over.

The dealer waves him off. "We're good here. You know how loud these northerners get."

The suit closes in on us, anyway, clearly itching to get the last word in. "Ain't a spectator sport, kid. Buy some chips or go home."

A kid reference gets my blood up *every* time, but in this case, his slight has some validity. The man's at least sixty, and that might be ten years too generous. I'd respond with something snarky about ex-Snakes employees retiring on riverboats, except getting what's left of Amy's bankroll out of the casino is the main priority at the moment. "Let's go home, Runbad. I'll drive."

"Suits me," he slurs. "This table's getting old."

Kudos to a guy half-sauced for getting in the dig I wanted to go for. But as sharp as his wits might still be, he has a lot of trouble wobbling off his chair.

"No way you're the devil."

"Never said I was. Let's go grab a drink."

Later, after the second cup of coffee at a diner next to the pawn shop, he's beginning to look sober.

I dig deep for the chart topper from my long list of questions. "Who are you, really?"

He winks. "My mom came from Venus. She married a guy from Mars."

"Have another coffee."

One steaming cup and a pit stop later, "Why do you want Tak to leave the poker game at Snakes?"

Big smile. Warm, if such a thing is possible. "A woman's walking by outside. They'll cross paths, stare into each other's eyes, and before you know it, we'll be hearing wedding bells."

"Uh-huh. So you're a matchmaker now?"

"Not a good one," he says. "Things go badly. Turns out they aren't the be-all and end-all they've been looking for. Lots of good sex at first, though." Another wink.

"No, really, Runbad. What's the story here?"

"Let's just say for now I have my reasons."

We're getting nowhere, as usual.

Stubborn to the point of idiocy, I try a different line of interrogation. "Why didn't you introduce your little dating service to Tak on your own?"

"Apprentice training." His greenish eyes no longer show the

slightest sign of sway. Give the man an Academy Award for his earlier performance at the casino. Which means… he lost on purpose and feigned drunkenness to come across as a born loser? Easy task for a master at blending into his surroundings. And from what I've observed of the grifter, he took to this particular role like a duck to water. But to what end?

I'm almost afraid to ask the next question. "How much of the five grand do you have left for Amy?"

He sets his coffee down. Bores holes in my eyes. "Mike, I'm going to give you a word of advice. Let Amy play her way out of the jam on her own. She'll respect herself more for it, and that's important."

"So I'm guessing every dime is gone?"

He shrugs. "I've still got a thousand. That's enough to let her know how much you care. Plus whatever you've got in your own wallet, I guess."

I don't throw my coffee at him and beat him senseless with the cup. I do slam it down hard enough to get my hand with the spray. "We're done." I'm up from the table, shaking burnt fingers and making a beeline to the door.

"You'll never see her again."

Yeah, like this guy can make a difference. He's probably careening down the sands of time even more out of control than I am, without any idea how to set either one of us on the right course.

No, that's not it. I mean, even if he's flailing in the same whirlpool, he proved he can get me to Amy when he flashed me forward to the cage at Snakes. He *can* help, but he never will, out of spite if for no better reason.

I'll have to figure out how to reach her on my—

"Want a furlough from your time ship?" he calls.

I should keep walking. But even the strongest players grasp at straws when their luck runs bad. "A what?"

"You handled Tak for me, so you've earned that much." He hurries up to me. "Don't forget to take this with you," and he presses a thin money roll into my hand.

I slip it into my pocket. "Look, we had a deal. Don't expect any more—"

The room dims and relights, like somebody plugged one too many toasters in the socket.

Another fade.

One more.

Total blackness, and I'm reaching for a pillar to steady myself.

Hold on. This doesn't feel right. If the generators would just kick in so I could see what I'm—

Oh, do they ever. Bright light. Warm. Exactly like…

I'm basking in the sun. The pillar I'm leaning on?

An ornamental tree.

And out the door of Snakes marches Amy, flanked by a hoodie on either side of her.

Hologram? Hallucination? My mouth's too dry to ask.

She catches my eye. Stops. Long pause without the hint of her smile.

The hoodies pull closer to her until she says something low and fast. One peels off and walks away. The other takes his time. He gives me the once-over with a smoldering glare, and gets my shoulder almost hard enough to knock me over on his way out of Dodge, brushing past me and then stopping. Looks like he's ready to mix it up, but I can hardly stand straight at this point, let alone trade blows with this muscle-bound monk.

"No, Yosef," she says. "Leave Stewart alone."

Those few words take the fight out of him. He nods to her, turns on his heel, and walks away without giving me so much as a second glance.

Is this real, or did I just witness a queenly figment of my imagination, protected by her royal guards? My heart wants to believe I'm gaping at Amy. It's pounding away like nuts. But my brain is caught mid-gear, between coma and spin cycle. Neither one helps me articulate anything of importance other than, "So I'm Stewart? What should I call you today?"

"Pissed."

CHAPTER SEVENTEEN

THE DAY MY MISSING man meanders back into my life begins with the smack in my head known as leakage, and now here I am, still Penny, sitting with Hans on a porch in a bad part of town. We're watching a balding man approach from down the sidewalk. He's in a state of perfect balance, toting two shopping bags, one in each hand. This is a Russian named Eugene if ever I saw one. Closing in on the stoop, he steps carefully, avoiding a sidewalk crack, thereby demonstrating allegiance to irrational superstition. Small world. That's the guiding principal I use when everything else fails, which is to say, quite frequently.

Could be worse. I could be a gambler turned criminal.

Oh, wait.

He nods to Hans, smiles at me—a good sign, seeing as I'm five hundred bucks short unless I dip into Hans's *save it for a rainy day or murderous Russians* donation fund—and heads on up the stairs.

The dog starts barking, I make a mental note to buy some pepper spray, and we're all three inside Eugene's place a turn of the doorknob later.

Next stop is his kitchen table. Me and the loan shark, anyway. Hans takes a position across from us by the sink, arms folded, and totally in protective soldiering mode. Also known as muscle.

Barring a sudden invasion by some warring tribe from down the street, Eugene and Philippe should seriously consider double locks, mace, and Tasers, all of which can be found online or maybe at the neighborhood hardware store, in lieu of the headaches associated with payroll, employee benefits, and arguments about whether flag day should be an observable holiday.

I do like Hans and Yosef a lot now, but if they qualify for unemployment, wouldn't they be happier with—

"Well?"

Wow. A simple word delivered with maximum force in a Russian accent is literally capable of knocking me out of my chair. Good thing I arrested my fall by grabbing the edge of the table, or I'd be sitting on the snarling dog right now.

"Girly, why is your mind always a thousand miles away?"

I'd point out that my name of the day is Penny, not a belittling term such as *girly*. Except if I provoke him into shouting a half dozen words or so, rather than just the one, I might get blown right out a window. Instead, I open my purse, extract a wad of twenty-five one-hundred-dollar bills, leaving Hans's incredibly self-sacrificing loan hidden beneath, and I start counting them out on the table.

"That looks short," he says, about halfway through, but not from his seat at the table. No, about a quarter of the way into my demonstration of basic arithmetic, he leaves his chair to walk around behind me, where he can simultaneously peer at the largess I'm bestowing and breathe down the back of my neck.

"Oh, yeah... see..."

Good God, did my voice just crack from fear? I've gotta come across as a gal in control. Where's the water? I stare directly into Hans's eyes with a silent plea for either a bottle of Aquafina or whatever might pour into a glass from the sink, as long as it doesn't come out rusty. Sadly, we haven't established a system of signals, let alone rehearsed them yet. This conversation will not be well hydrated.

"Um... Eugene, there's a little problem I hadn't quite anticipated. Let's call it leakage."

"Leakage?" He grabs me by the hair with ease, cuz my poorly timed laziness led me to skip the shampoo while showering this morning. I tied my unwashed mess into a ponytail, instead.

Everything kicks into a faster gear. On the counter, next to the sink, sits a barrel-shaped holder loaded with various handy kitchen implements such as spatulas, oversized spoons, a meat thermometer, and a couple serving forks, plus the few odd paperclips, erasers, and coins forgotten on the bottom if it's anything like mine. Hans forgoes those miscellaneous office supplies and goes directly for a fork with tines wide and nasty enough to do a considerable amount of damage to any and all mean Russians.

Meanwhile, at the same split second, *yanked* might be a better term than *grabbed* when it comes to what Eugene has done with my hair. I'm sitting with head bent back, eyes wide, and legs splayed out in front of me. I almost don't see Hans grab the fork, except for my twenty-twenty bottom peripheral vision, if there is such a thing.

Eugene would easily see the deadly fork in the grip of my wonderful pal if he weren't focusing his entire attention down on my tilted face. Let this be a lesson on the values of multitasking for anyone who later finds themselves in a similar situation and thinks they have the upper hand.

I'm barely able to do this next thing. Catch Hans's furious gaze, purse my lips, furrow my brow, and sweep a shaky hand from left to right as an improvised and, yes, unrehearsed sign for *back down*. Two, maybe three stunned seconds have passed from yank to signal. Two, maybe three more uncomprehending moments pass before I give up on the subtle-hint approach and go with a raspy shout. "Back down!"

The pull on my hair immediately slackens.

Hans lets go of the fork, dropping it into the barrel with a clunk.

Eugene doesn't do anything after loosening his grip on my hair, which is a vast improvement over what he'd been up to.

As for me, I've just learned something so spectacularly valuable I'm wondering how I'd never heard of it before. Clearly, my mom had some Yoda-like teacher in her early years, cuz she couldn't have come up with all of her homespun motherly advice on her own. But did she sneak out of the classroom early the day he taught *this* little lesson? *Unexpected demonstrations of authority can stun even the nastiest people.*

Now, despite a state of fear nearing petrification, I must gather myself, take control, and sound like I mean it. Deep breath in. Let it out easy. And, "Eugene, I'm your mule. Yours and Philippe's. If either or both of you don't start showing the *respect* I deserve, you will not have a flunky who can magically convert phony chips into cash. Cuz honestly, your bench looks kinda thin. People who pass counterfeit bones without getting caught don't grow on trees. And—"

I've run out of clichés, but no matter. The point has been made. Eugene releases my hair entirely and laughs in what might come across to many as a scoffing manner but sure sounds face-saving to me.

"Leakage," I start to say, but eye to eye is best for this conversation, so, "Eugene, can we sit across from each other like we were before? Otherwise, I'll need to swivel my neck completely around to see you."

He laughs even louder, clearly catching the *Exorcist* reference, another of my mom's favorite movies. Regrettably, she insisted we watch the bad sequels, too.

Presto. Eugene returns to his chair. "You were saying, Penny?"

"I can't possibly move chips without losing some."

He sneers. "Because you're a lowlife gambling junkie of a whore?"

Great. The concept of respect only goes so far with this guy. Now we've got Hans inching back to the slaughter barrel and me smarting at least a little bit—honestly somewhat more than a small fraction—cuz lately I've wondered. Not about the whore part. My mom raised me right, and anybody who thinks otherwise can step forward to read my lips while I practice my back-and-forth slapping technique. And watch out for where I aim my kick.

But the gambling junkie part? He pushed a button there.

I'm probably at the point of diminishing returns with my show of verbal muscle. And hand signals have been a complete failure with Hans today. Best strategy now is to stabilize the situation by neutralizing my overly hot-blooded ally while tossing some logic at my foe in a way he'll understand. "Hans, would you pour me a glass of water, please?"

He does.

"Thank you."

The water isn't rusty. It goes down just fine. I take my time with the drink, cuz low-life gambling junkies willing and able to move chips without getting caught really won't grow on trees in the Russian's mind, unless I act scared and easily replaceable.

"Eugene, you loaned me money and wanted a taste in return. Vig. You put up five thousand and asked for six back. I've been fine with that. It's how the system works all over the world." I pause, take a sip, let that much sink in.

"Now picture this. I walk into a casino to do what I do, and the house wants *their* piece of the action. Who are we to deny them? If I don't lose a little, maybe they'll watch me more closely, or kick me out altogether."

Long silence. Then a grandfatherly smile. A spread of his hands. "Yeah. Like the vig I charge you. The patronage I get from Philippe. But don't *ever* push it if you want to stay pretty."

Uh-oh.

The threat is hollow. I know it and so does he. But *patronage?* This means the Philippe/Eugene relationship has nothing to do with being in cahoots and everything to do with chain of command. I'll never get rid of the money-grubbing Eugene to partner exclusively with Philippe at perhaps a better price, cuz *Eugene is the boss, lieutenant, captain, godfather or whatever they call it in the frozen motherland lurking across the narrow sea from Alaska.*

If I remain involved in this scheme, I won't net more than about twenty-five percent. Might as well get used to this fact or walk, once I settle whatever debt remains with this loan shark and earn a decent enough profit to make the entire annoying episode of Amy the criminal almost worthwhile. "Eugene, we started at five thousand in cash and a thousand in vig. Now I've returned forty-five hundred."

He's sitting there nodding, so I press on. "Let me have another three thousand in chips, and I'll be back in a few days with your fifteen hundred in cash."

"You come back with two thousand," he says.

"No, here, let me go through the math with—"

"*Two fucking thousand.*" He pounds the table with his fist, sending the dog scurrying into the next room. Hans reaches for the fork again.

As for me, I'll do just fine if I don't act scared. "Can you explain what you mean?" My voice comes out completely calm. I'm so proud of me, and my mom would be, too. Eugene can't see my twitchy knee, so all is still somewhat good. Luckily Hans is behind him, and Russian mobsters lack the ability to swivel *their* heads completely around, or Eugene would know that his soldier is more loyal to me than to him.

I have my very own muscle now. Yay.

"You're five hundred short today sweetheart, and I charge a penalty for that."

"Okay, fair enough." I could dig into my purse and use Hans's loan to rectify this little shortfall, but I'm a self-help kinda gal. Hans will get his money back the minute we walk out of here.

And we do, five minutes later, after handshakes all around.

Handshakes. What better sign of respect could I hope for? I've maintained a seat at the table, as opposed to one beneath it, like the dog. Also, if I don't decide to exit this counterfeiting enterprise altogether, twenty-five percent of everything in Philippe's cupboard would be okay, I guess. More than okay.

Once outside, the sidewalk beneath my feet has a cloud-nine

feel to it. Hans and I walk together in silence for a block or so. Then I stop, get the five hundred out of my purse, and hand it over. "I won't be needing this, but please know how much your loan meant to me."

"You were awesome back there," he says.

"Nah." But my cloud elevates to at least a ten.

A hooded figure approaches from down the street. Yosef.

Hand pumps go from one hoodie to the next. A shy hello to me. And we're soon all walking together.

"It's been a long day," I say, "but I'm wired. Let's hit Snake Eyes for an hour or two before we call it."

They nod.

But first, "Guys? I'm itching to know something, if you don't mind telling me."

"Shoot," Yosef says.

"The three grand you're looking to save. What's it for?"

I catch a quick glance between the two. Then they speak simultaneously.

"Better hoodies with lining."

"A poker stake."

This comes out *better poker hoodies stake with lining*, but I can't make any sense of their hurried words even after sorting them into the proper sequence. Still, what really does make sense in a world where a five-hundred-dollar shortage costs me half a yard more, my new best friends go through life with poorly insulated hoods on their heads, my boyfriend thinks he's being scammed by the devil, and I'm veering so far across the line between good girl and bad my mom must be rolling in her grave? "I can give you some pointers how to play, if you want."

"No need," Hans says. "We're ready to kill."

Uh-huh. I noticed that.

CHAPTER EIGHTEEN

MY MOTHER WAS NO saint. Just ask the pitchfork- and torch-wielding soccer moms who claimed she embezzled from their uniform fund. Boy, did we have to leave *that* town in a hurry. But she did take me to churches of the chip, dice, and card variety, where she'd indulge her passion for reads and deceptions while I played outside, waiting for the day I'd be old enough to practice her faith.

Now I'm a big girl with my own soul to save.

Hans, Yosef, and I behold the very place to get started—a temple drawing worshippers from every denomination. Forget the lack of stone pillars. Snakes' towering brick structure offers all the false hope the multitudes have been looking for. Another twenty paces and we'll cross the holy boundary between lazy southern heat and the frenetic clamor of a gambling house.

My hooded pal, Yosef, spreads his arms like a pilgrim at the Promised Land. "Fill our pockets, for we are deserving," he says.

Or maybe I'm paraphrasing something more concise, such as *yeah, baby*. Either way, oh ye of too much faith. We need to *work* for any results worth talking about. Snakes' doors will not spill open to spit hundred-dollar bills at us, like an oversized ATM gone wild. Not a single penny, let alone the three grand or so needed if I truly want to get out of this Russian mess and forget about my high-wire pursuit of staggering riches without a net.

Churches pass the plate. Why should a casino be any different? Money only travels in one direction here without at least a token effort to reverse the flow. That means going through the effort to exchange good chips for bad. I dole out a couple blacks each to Hans and Yosef, palm two for myself, and leave the rest in my purse. We'll only stay long enough for me to get the edge off. A quick genuflection and bow of the head. Nothing more.

Eugene is so wrong about my urges.

"Meet out here in an hour?" I say.

They nod and we all head inside.

Oh, the depravity in this church of the damned. Noisy slot machines scream for money, drawing on gaming themes based on every TV show since the dawn of creation. *Friends. Seinfeld. Walking Dead.* That last one casts a pall of doom over the entire array.

The craps tables are out, because I just don't get it. Roulette maybe? Wheel of fortune? The flip-of-a-coin choices in my uncertain and perilous future get thrown in my face at every turn.

Poker? People always say if you fall off a horse, then get right back on it, but my mom never came up with such nonsense. Not in all her infinite wisdom. I'm pretty sure she would have agreed a set of aces losing to some idiot's lucky flush requires a period of seething anger almost as long as Lent before the losing party will be ready for another hand.

So blackjack it is.

Maybe the questionable outcomes of my decisions in life have been caused by these kinds of emotional thought processes, but I'm changing my bad chips for good ones at the first ten-dollar-limit table I see, anyway.

Here's an empty one. The dealer looks lonesome. *Carrie,* according to the name tag with its smiley picture that doesn't do the high cheekbones of her underfed face enough justice. I grab a seat before her and satisfy her hunger by offering a couple scrumptious blacks for two stacks of reds.

Mission accomplished. I've laundered my chips. But I can't run off with these ill-gotten gains. We want the eyes in the sky to perceive me as a *round* peg in a round hole, not a square one. That means playing a while. The customers here, they come to gamble. Eugene had it right to a certain extent. When within these four walls, I am a low-life gambling junkie. Gotta be.

Away we go. I place a small bet, the cards get dealt, and a seventeen lands on my doorstep. I should hold right there against the dealer's six. "Stay." They have signals for every move in blackjack, with forward swipes of the cards for a hit, a left-to-right wave for stay, and a few other little wrinkles, but just ask Hans how successful my attempts at sign language have been lately.

The dealer doesn't seem to mind a bit of conversation here and there. She nods, flips over a king, busts out with a queen, and I'm ten bucks richer.

On and on the hands go.

"Hit."

"Stay."

"Stay."

"Hit."

I check my watch. Time is *crawling*. See this, Eugene? The junkie thing? It's a *role* I'm playing. Nothing more.

"Hit... stay... stay... stay... hit... stay... stay." God. Maybe twenty-one isn't the game for me. I need the mortal combat of no-limit poker to get the blood flowing. "Carrie, can you just place my bets and play my hands for me while I close my eyes for a bit? Let me know if I win."

This slip of a girl dealing the cards—who, incidentally, makes me want to increase my roadwork to achieve a similar size-two frame—she's been all smiles since I sat down, but now her laugh at my suggestion carries more than a hint of nervousness. Like she just heard a comment out of left field and maybe the moment has come to signal the camera people upstairs so they'll elevate my scrutiny code from yellow to orange.

I need to keep my mouth shut and do my job. "Stay."

Perhaps if I increase my bet sizing a tad. Just to keep the old eyes open. I'll go twenty-five bucks just this one time. For snickers. There. Five reds instead of two carries far more weight. The game's still boring as hell, but... "Hit."

Damn.

One more time. I won't bust out twice in a row. Even if I do, I can double up to fifty and get it all back. "Hit."

Oh, come on. Seriously? Okay, people, I warned you about the fifty. Give me a second to make a nice, lucky stack of—

A gentle nudge against my shoulder. "Hold out your hand, Penny."

"Not now, Yosef, I'm busy."

"Hold it out."

Wait. This guy—formally known as Thing Two and tilting my terminology back in that direction—this guy is supposed to be shy around me. That's the dynamic.

The dealer is waiting. These people make their money on tips. A buck here, a couple bucks there for winning hands. Or maybe instead, a ten or a twenty at the end of a session, win or lose. But tokes can't happen with any high degree of frequency when the cards aren't being dealt. Carrie stands there with impressive patience, but I can see the pain deep within those stoic eyes.

Or maybe I want to perceive her as an ally in this cold, cruel world. Otherwise, it's all about me, and not in a good way. We need to kick the action back into gear. At least long enough to win my fifty bucks back. "Sorry, Carrie. This'll just take a second." And to Yosef, "If I hold out my hand, will you go away?"

Carrie smiles. But who can't see the tears behind her mask?

Yosef doesn't say a word.

"Fine." I hold out my hand.

He drops a sterling-silver bracelet in my palm. It holds just a single charm. A little tree.

"What… what is this?"

"Where Hans and I come from, it's the symbol for strength," he says.

These guys. With all their kindness. Wisdom. Timing. How the hell did they fall into the hire-a-thug racket? "Have we been an hour yet, Yosef?"

"No, not yet."

"Let's get out of here." My throat's almost too lumpy to choke the words out.

I gather my nice, cleanly washed but somewhat short chips.

"Color up?" Carrie asks. Dealers everywhere hide their anguish over a player's departure by offering a simple courtesy. They'll happily trade blacks for any hundred-dollar increments of reds I might have, so I won't have to carry so many chips to the cashier window. A cynic would say they're simply taking steps to avoid the possibility of running short of reds and having to slow the game down while they replenish them. But I prefer the humanitarian angle.

I decline her offer with a shake of my head. The objective here is to move faulty bones, not get them back. I do tip her a dime, though.

Yosef and I head for the cage, his token of affection still warming the palm of my hand. Something must be said, or he'll get the wrong idea. "Yosef, I have a man, more or less." And damn you, Stewart, for disappearing so long—almost *two days*— that the footnote is required.

My personal hoodie stops, I stop, and we look at each other.

"Yes, but do you have a brother, Penny?"

Thank heavens the gaming tables all around us carry boxes of tissue for moments like this.

There. All better. He hardly noticed. Who wouldn't catch a cold the way they crank up the air conditioning in these casinos? My best friends wear their hoodies for a reason today.

Hans hooks up with us in the lobby, he and Yosef fork over their cash, and we're somehow thirty dollars ahead, despite my brief detour into the desperate world of low-life gamblers. Which means they won, and they're turning their winnings over to me, the boss lady. We're in the patronage business now. I've become their Eugene. But these two can rest secure in the knowledge I'll never yank *their* hair the way my boss did with me. They wear hoodies for more than one reason, soon to be lined and with a poker stake to boot if their dreams come true.

And why shouldn't they? We boss ladies are all about dreams. "Guys, you're on my list. When I finish moving this three grand, a thousand goes to you. For all you've done already, it isn't enough."

"You're quitting then?" Yosef's pursed lips and probing eyes turn the question into a plea.

I can't answer. His bracelet fits beautifully on my wrist, but I may need more trees.

CHAPTER NINETEEN

ON OUR WAY OUT of Snake Eyes, this swell gambling house, my Stewart's still missing. Where is he, the louse? When what to my wondering eyes should appear? A bug-eyed missing boyfriend and eight solid reasons why I should kick his sorry butt from here to next Christmas.

All starting with *you* and ending with *had me worried.*

Big-time.

About Stewart? Yeah, but I'd be lying if I didn't add *about me too.* Honestly, how well is this awesome gal doing on her own? If not for the two warmhearted hoodies flanking me, my support group without Stewart would be about the same size now as when my downward spiral finally lands me in a Turkish prison.

That's pretty small.

Zilch.

Nada.

So yeah, I should be mad he scared me into thinking I was a one-night stand. But the longer I run through the list of best ways to strangle him, the more his body language says *Hey, I'm a guy who just got rescued from being shipwrecked on a deserted island somewhere.* He's taking me in with wonder, delight, even joy. The upward curves at the sides of his mouth, forming something known as a goofy smile, give it away.

Still, before I let my heart completely melt to a simmering puddle of pureed sugar plums, shouldn't I hold on to this anger long enough to thrash him a little? True, we haven't known each other even one tenth the time needed to qualify as short, but *I took this man inside of me,* more than once. I let my guard down with him. Told him all about myself. All about my Russians. He said he's a one-woman man.

Also, I tend to get hurt a lot. Latest ex-boyfriend dumped me for a vacation in Haiti with a blonde floozy who might happen to be well-endowed but couldn't possibly possess my winning personality.

Come on. My thieving nature has its appeal, no? For guys who like the bad girls?

Right. Except they keep using and losing me. Maybe I should take up smoking to push my badness over the top. Who doesn't love a gravelly voice?

Regardless, the moment has come to get rid of my escorts. "This is my man, guys. He and I need to have a little talk. Did either of you happen to bring, I don't know, maybe a whiffle bat?"

"That's love talking," Hans says. "Time to split." He touches my wrist with enough reassurance to add another tree to my charm bracelet. "Later." And he peels away.

One sweetie of a hoodie gone and one to go. But Yosef doesn't get the message. He heads straight for Stewart, gives him the old shoulder roll, and stops for more action. This muscle-bound big brother of mine has enough raw power to turn any man into a splat on the sidewalk.

"No, Yosef. Leave Stewart alone." I don't want my man getting pummeled. No way. My heart's boiling over with early spring Christmas joy at the mere sight of him, two-day unexplained absence or not.

But I won't show it. Gotta maintain at least *some* dignity here.

Except... where'd the ground go? My feet barely touch the sidewalk in what hopefully comes across as a purposeful march to my recalcitrant boyfriend, for a tongue lashing at the very least, if not a well-placed knee.

"So I'm Stewart?" he says. "What should I call *you* today?"

"Pissed." But that's as far as my angry-bird act can go. I wrap my arms around his neck. Stare into those beautiful blues. "Baby, I missed you so bad."

Good God, could I say anything cornier?

No matter. Our lips are melting into each other now, my breasts pushing against his chest where they belong. If my vocal chords are launching anything more at this man, the sound must be the mmm ringing in my ears.

After what can only be described as a blackout—I'll need to check with Stewart later for verification. Always go to the experts—we're walking hand in swinging hand toward who cares where. "I'm Penny this evening," I say.

"So we're talking what, a couple of days gone by?"

I stop moving and he does, too. Good. Time to search this man's eyes for unwavering honesty. "If you're *faking* a return from a state of wandering, drooling fugue, just know I have friends who own riding crops."

"Nerds One and Two?"

"They have names. And don't try changing the subject."

He takes a deep breath. Blows it out. "I was falling backward into the past, and you got away. Now I'm selling my soul to spend time with you."

Wow. Who wouldn't cave at the delivery of a line with universal application from a tryst in a flowery meadow to the opening conversation in a dimly lit bar? My arms itch to wrap themselves around his neck again, but a teeny bit of additional assurance sure would be nice.

"He isn't the devil, Penny. I've figured that much out."

Uh-huh. So much for reassurance. But I'm crazy about this lovable man. I love this crazy man. Man, this is crazy love. And so on. Just ask my pounding heart, my gaspy breath, and the tingle from head to toes. "Let's go to your place, handsome."

"The backseat of my car?"

"Sounds cozy."

I'm a kept woman this morning, waking up in my boyfriend's car.

Big step up from the cardboard box my mom and I once called home, especially since I'm a sloppy sleeper. Henry's snoring on the floor now where I accidentally rolled him at some point, leaving the whole backseat in its entirety to little old me, Jasmine.

Now, what to do with the sixteen hundred bucks he pressed into my hand before we went at it?

Foot-nudge time. "Henry?"

"Ung."

"Henry, honey, I'm up now, so you should be, too." Yeah, I can be bossy that way. We members of the gentler sex had better be, or Russian mobsters and sleepy boyfriends will walk all over us.

"Ung."

This is not going well. I flutter a hundred-dollar bill onto his head.

No response.

The next one, folded into a paper airplane, crash-lands into his ear.

"Wh-what?"

"I can't accept this money. You're changing the whole dynamic of our relationship, and *not* for the better."

Eyes open now. Looking up at me from down on the floor. "I drove all the way to Mississippi to play craps on a riverboat just so you could have it."

"You what?"

"It should have been five thousand, Penny. No, ten, but—"

"That'd be worse. And my name's Jasmine today."

I open the door and get out, grabbing my bra, my panties, my sundress and hurrying into them before whoever minds this lot has a chance to get a pretty good eyeful. "Nice digs you've dragged me to, Henry. Where's the stream for us to bathe in?"

"There's a truck stop with showers down the road." He's dragging himself out of the car, his own clothing in tow. The two bills I dropped to wake him threaten to blow off the floor and into the breeze, but he shuts the door fast.

"Stream, my ass," he says. "We're living much larger than that." Yet he's twisting his neck this way and that way and bending from side to side like somebody all stiff from sleeping on the floor of a car.

CHAPTER TWENTY

JASMINE AND I FOLLOW my old sidewalk past the graveyard of imaginary friends. No mocking jokes spill over the stone wall today. I need no reminders of my latest failure. Billy isn't the guy under my skin this morning.

Damn you, Runbad, you chain-smoking con man. Where's the Vegas-sized bankroll? That'd be plenty of money to get Jasmine out from under. But a mere thousand bucks? The combination of that and the few hundred I had in my wallet brought little more than a note of irritation to her expression last night. She took the money without a word and didn't exactly tell me to stick it in my ear, but that's where one of the C-notes landed this morning when she airmailed it all back to me.

This is a woman who mixes it up with Russian mobsters. A gutsy, self-reliant type if ever I've seen one. Sixteen hundred bucks is way less than she'd swallow her pride to accept. Different story with the right offer, though. Yeah, she might *say* your broken promises of five grand or ten would have been even more debasing, but faced with that kind of money—a one-time shot at evening her life score if not putting her ahead—Jasmine's expression and tone wouldn't have had *don't demean me* written all over them.

You're laughing somewhere, but I don't give up that easily.

So only for now—I have pride, too, and I never back off without putting it all on the line—*only* for now, the money's back in my pocket. I'll find the proper moment to bring the matter up again.

Meanwhile, Jasmine swings my arm with hers, hand in hand, and she hums, *hums* after choosing a night in my backseat rather than risk getting caught squatting in her ex-boyfriend's place. And what can I do but live in awe of this homeless jewel?

Towel rentals at the truck stop are a couple of bucks. Maybe I can spring for *that* and get away with it.

We slow at the sight of a raggedy man sitting on his hoard of newspapers and cardboard. "Gonna be a hot one, dearie," he says.

"I can snatch an umbrella for shade if you want one, Charlie."

That's my Jasmine. She's on a first-name basis with the downtrodden. Panhandlers on the street. Unlucky poker players falling backward through time except when granted the rare furlough. Thanks for that, Runbad, but you're still a chiseler at best. Five grand would have solved this angel's problems and given her a small bankroll to boot.

"Toothbrush would help," Charlie says. "And some salt. We're low on the essentials down here."

"I'll shop around."

He blows her a kiss.

Jasmine returns the favor, then squeezes my hand all the warmer and hums all the happier. An Irish ditty to greet a morning sun that hasn't turned brutal yet. Birds sing from their perches in blossoming trees. The aroma of freshly brewed coffee wafts out of a nearby hole-in-the-wall café.

How can I stay angry? But should I risk spoiling the lighter mood by telling what needs to be told? The time will never be good for pointing out how my presence at her side might be occasional at best until I find a way to seize the upper hand from Runbad. Can't stray too far into the explanation, either. I'm supposed to blend in here, not change the past.

Otherwise, suppose I cover every detail of my predicament,

and she suggests something out of the box such as skipping town and never again setting foot in the off-the-grid shadows where Runbad holds court. Away from lurking Russians, too. Would that work? Maybe yes, maybe no. But if she doesn't show up at Snakes the day before Memorial Day, and she isn't all bent out of shape that morning from catching me and Cynthia in the backseat of my car, the past has clearly been changed.

What then? Maybe a timeline-fixated universe cleaves us in two, and our doubles wander into Snakes, anyway. That's the best case. And the worst? Let's not go there. Undeniable worry shadowed Runbad's face when he sprang Amy's possible death on me. His expression made the risk real.

So now what? Outside the poker room, I'm a reliable guy, but a dose of deception wrapped in a coating of truth might work best here. I squeeze her hand harder and slow our carefree walk until we stop and turn to face each other. Eye to eye. Her smile faltering a tad, because I've pressed my lips into heavy-news mode. "Jasmine, I want to be here with you *all the time.*"

"Me, too," she says in a voice quiet enough to signal she knows something's up.

A cloud shades the sun. We're tuned into an unhappy frequency now. Those kids down the sidewalk playing catch? They've scattered.

"See the cemetery back there?" I say. "Somebody flings jokes over the wall at me."

"A ghost?" She follows my gaze toward Billy's uneasy resting place. The old wall. The few odd statues tall enough to poke their heads up over it. A couple crows circling. Spooky New Orleans at its finest. My instability at its worst.

"No, a skeleton." I try a different tack. "I've always been missing a card or two from my deck. You get that, right?"

She's eying me now. Warm hand on my cheek. "Who has a full six-pack that I'd give two cents to know? There's nothing I don't like about you."

"Same here, but listen." To what? Where am I going with this? One loving touch, two liquid eyes, and I'm on the verge of babbling in circles. But that's the thing, right? Billy's voice has been shouting the message for years. "Jasmine, my crazy side needs space. Demands it sometimes. So I forget where I am now and then. I hide in the shade of a blackout."

She looks down at her shoes. Takes it personally. This isn't going well.

A monarch butterfly dances spasmodically from the thick trunk of a big old tree to flutter beside us before moving on. That's the frequency we need to latch on to here. I use a finger under her chin to coax her gaze back into mine. Those pretty gray-greens do their magic, pulling better words out of me. "We haven't been a thing for long, Jasmine, but I'm hooked. When I'm not with you, nothing much matters."

"Don't make me shackle you to the bed." There's the smile, the dimples, the twinkle in her eye. She's got me by the hand again, dragging me forward. "Charlie needs salt. Where's this truck stop you've been talking about?"

So we've processed this, more or less. Maybe she won't feel low next time I disappear into Runbad's reverse spiral. The fear that she may is even worse than the heartache I'll feel when I can't find her.

The place we're headed comes into view. A time-tested answer to eclectic needs. The vast lot offers quiet corners for parking and sleeping. Gas pumps for the thirsty. A convenience store that sells *everything,* including lockers and showers down the hall. The diner, where we can chow down on bacon, eggs, oatmeal, and those melt-in-your-mouth biscuits they're famous for.

Satisfaction is laid out before us, complete with a welcome sign, but she stops us short. "You could call," she says.

Uh-oh. The *no smartphone* excuse won't fly here. Where there's a will, there's a way. And I wonder... if I scratch Runbad's back with another favor, who says the laws of physics, microwave signals, and time can't be bent? "I'll try, but—"

"You could call."

From her mouth to God's ears.

Fifty paces later, after dodging sidewalk cracks, oil spills, and discarded gum, I pull the screen door by the handle and motion her inside like a knight and his maiden fair. A Maid Marian for sure, because she's grabbing a shaker of salt off a shelf and slipping it into her purse for a five-finger discount before the door finishes creaking behind us.

Guilty instinct has me casing the joint for security cameras in a visual sweep so jerky I wrench my own neck.

"Be cool, big guy," she says.

"Sorry. I'm not cut out for the Robin Hood thing."

That stops her. She's looking me over with mouth open, eyes squinting, like a lightbulb goes off in her head. "Where'd you come up with the sixteen hundred, Henry?"

"Six was mine. The other grand came from my partner in crime."

She arches her brows.

"You know, Runbad."

"Okay, and this buddy who might be real, but maybe not... what'd *he* do to earn it?"

"Nothing good, I'm sure."

She holds out a hand. "Fork it over, Robin. Just the thousand. You keep the change."

Later, when we're out on the sidewalk again, a higher sun baking the last glistens of shower from her hair, I'm thinking the raggedy man has a big payday coming. We're nowhere near the original plan, but I'd rather see her use the money for charity than make me give it back to Runbad.

Yet when we reach the makeshift home Charlie claims in the shade of a willow tree, she offers only a toothbrush she swiped. And the salt.

He closes a leathery hand around her gifts. "Always a dearie," he says, "but where's the pepper?"

Yeah. I'm kinda wondering the same thing. Maybe she's following the best-case scenario. My thousand plus the black Snake Eyes chips and hundred-dollar bills I spotted earlier in her purse could be enough to get her out from under the Russians if

I'm overly optimistic. But the gleam in her eye when I handed her the money said different. Her fierce pride comes into play. And the Robin Hood context doesn't fit into any self-help scenario I can think of.

I won't ask. We all have our secrets. She's happy at the moment. That's my new mission in life.

On and on we walk. Into one side of the Quarter and out the other, passing a zillion shops, bars, galleries, and tourists along the way. A small street parade complete with trombone and jugglers captivates us for a little while. We're able to elbow ourselves right up to the curb and take in a rendition of "The Saints" that almost does justice to the great Louis Armstrong. We buy ice-cream cones after that. I hope this epic salted caramel flavor stays on as a fad in the future, if I can ever find my way back to the present.

Snakes lurks only three blocks away, but I don't see the point in playing poker in the past. And Jasmine hasn't said a thing about her need to move bad chips today. That's a good thing. This counterfeit scheme lurches my stomach down a roller-coaster hill every time I think on it. I don't want to worry about her more than she'd want me to... which is not at all. So I steer her by the elbow around a corner and down a different street.

"Pascal's Manale?" she says.

"They don't open till five."

"The barbeque shrimp is to die for."

"It's a helluva hike from here."

"To *die* for, Henry."

Sure, why not? We've already reached midafternoon, thanks to a late rise and slow pace. So what better way to cover the rest of our idle hours than walk another four or five miles? Sure, we could street-car a good part of the distance, but she isn't complaining, and I enjoy matching strides with her wherever she wants to go.

Halfway there, as we follow a sidewalk shaded by big enough oaks to keep the sun from boiling our brains, she comes up with this: "Deep down, you know, don't you?"

"Know what?"

Jasmine doesn't answer. Maybe she's forgotten the question already. Hot southern days like this one tend to fog even those minds less shaky than mine.

But an hour and a half later, when we're wearing our paper bibs and completely high on the barbeque juices staining our chins and fingers, she comes at me with this: "Suppose Runbad isn't real. You've considered that, right?"

No, not lately, but, "Yeah, early on. Way more goes on with this guy than I could ever imagine on my own."

"See, that's the thing," she says. "I meet somebody and never need to ask myself the question."

I get where she's going with this. Given a past full of imaginary friends, how can I be sure which ones aren't? But that's a quandary nobody should think about too hard, especially me. Trusting my better ability to distinguish reality from fantasy in recent times keeps me fully upright and confident of a future without bed restraints. "He's real, Jasmine."

"Say no more."

Much later, when we're snuggled together in the backseat of my car again, and I mistake her purr for a half-asleep snore, she throws the old gentle elbow into my ribs. "Call me?" she says.

Yeah, she's got the same worry keeping her awake that I do. How long is Runbad gonna let my vacation last?

CHAPTER TWENTY-ONE

ANOTHER DAY SPENT WITH my tattered-wing angel. The goddess of ambiguous realities. Spewer of false chips. Love of my life.

I'm filing the memories by name now.

Jasmine.

We robbed from the rich, gave to the poor, and painted the town with our feet, living large before finishing the day in the shadows.

Then we fell asleep.

But now, tomorrow, I'm alone on a bench by the river with nothing to wrap my arms around but a sliver of early dawn sun.

I don't even know her next name.

Or mine.

Runbad comes around from behind the bench to sit beside me. No surprise there. He lives for finding me when my soul is on empty. "Early riser today, Mike?"

Wrong name. Unless... "Are we back at ground zero?"

"You mean *day* zero? Forget about it. You carry a couple bad bones to the cashier and boom."

Good way to put it. A few minutes at the cage and my unstable present explodes into an even shakier past. Not that I'm complaining. I've seen the light. This is all about saving Amy from *her* problems, not worrying over mine. I wouldn't even know her, let alone have a chance to help, if I hadn't fallen off the grid.

A wind gust from the north brings goose bumps to my flesh. A front must have plowed through overnight. Runbad's wearing a fleece to protect against the early-morning chill, but I'm happy to sit here in shirtsleeves. The bracing air sweeps the cobwebs away quite nicely.

So I can deal with this guy.

Wheel and deal.

Squa, squa, squa. The seagulls start another day, triggering a déjà vu... from when, exactly? A barge I might have seen before floats toward the dawn sun. Someone else is watching it, a little way down the walk, alone on another bench.

I wonder.

"Careful not to bump into yourself," Runbad says, ever the mind reader.

"When are we, Runbad?"

"A day after the last one you spent with her."

That's a relief. I've moved forward instead of backward these past twenty-four hours. The dinosaurs can wait. Awkward confrontations, too. We're still in a stretch of time when, during my previous *on-the-grid* existence, I happened to be out of town, visiting my sister. I won't be running into myself today. Just dealing with Runbad. "And you want another favor."

"Last one." He lights up a cigarette.

This man's lungs should be black from all the smoke he's inhaled just during the time spent with *me*. But he's something other than flesh and blood. A different form of being entirely.

Maybe another Billy tossing jokes over the cemetery wall? No. I can't stray down that path and still function... or help Amy out of a jam she won't admit she can't handle.

Okay. Say he's real then. Chain-smoking, time-traveling instigators don't just pop up out of nowhere. If I haven't conjured him out of some overly creative corner of my addled mind, *and I haven't*, then he's likely been around awhile. Maybe

145

a long while. And in that case, others must have seen him, written about him, described him. As a devil's lackey, a demon, some fallen god—a sinister footnote in the pages of mythological lore.

An Internet search would find something, and my lack of a smartphone is no excuse. Libraries spill over with computers.

Meanwhile, what clues do I have until the nearest one opens? Runbad matches Asian gamblers with their soulmates for relationships that fail once all the sex gets old. Cuts one-sided deals with suckers like me for the fun of it. He's mischievous, bordering on malicious.

What else do I know? I need to start taking notes. "What's your real name?"

He blows a smoke ring, watches it die in the breeze. "At the casino, they call me Pete. What's yours?"

"I'll let you know when Amy tells me. A phone would be nice. She'll start worrying the minute she wakes up in an empty car."

"You think you're so special she'd care that much?"

"Yeah, but that isn't the problem. She doesn't think highly enough about herself. I disappear without a word, and she'll look inward."

He reaches into his jacket pocket and comes up with one of those black antiques that flips open for a call. Would he pull it out if it couldn't do the time-jumping thing I'm hoping for? He's holding my new goal in life. And no doubt part of the next deal.

"Do you remember the tourist at your final table, Mikey?"

Yep. Here we go. "Ground zero?"

"Uh-huh."

"Sure I do." Big hair, loopy earrings. She seemed to know me, which suggests whatever favor Runbad wants could work. The connection she felt wasn't necessarily the result of some randomly crossed path in an earlier card game. Recent events have me redefining randomness as something decided upon by shifty puppet masters. Tak knew me at the table, too, because I'd blended into his past to track him down in Gulfport weeks earlier. "Let me guess. You want her to leave the table."

He goes for his pocket again and comes up with a small glass pyramid. "This might help." He hands it over.

A paperweight. Heavy in my hand. "I'd rather have that phone, Pete."

"So we're on a first-name basis now, Ethan? That'll be your name when you call Amy. No, I think she's going by Connie now. Or Sue? Depends on which number you dial."

The phone rests in his hand, inches from mine. Knowing this guy, if I try to snatch it away, we'll be talking Charlie Brown, Lucy, and the football. "I can pick different days?"

Runbad snubs his spent cigarette out on the bench. "If you punch zero zero, that'll catch Amy at the table that day—ground zero, like you said. Maybe you can tip her off on what's coming."

"Which is?"

"New boyfriend at the very least."

"No way."

Okay, so she was bent out of shape at Snakes. Who wouldn't be, after catching me red-handed with Cynthia in the backseat of my car?... The one-night stand I can barely remember except for Amy's flashlight banging against my naked-as-a-jailbird knee.

I'll win her back.

But something larger hangs in the air. Runbad's timeline is off. The flashlight scene happens *before* the Snakes scene, in a real world where the clocks all turn in the right direction. So why would I need to warn—

"Dial zero one and you get the day before Snakes. Go with oh eight and you're a week and a day out. That's the one you just spent with her." He hands me the phone. "One brief call a day. The battery's old. It'll tire out if you overuse it."

Something resembling gratitude washes over me, except Runbad's most likely the culprit behind my entire backflip through time in the first place. "Okay."

But what if he isn't? "Thanks, man."

"The tourist," he says. "She needs to leave the table."

"I get to visit Amy again if she does."

"Deal… if she does."

"Right. So let me guess. This tourist's soul mate happens to be walking by outside. Just like Tak's."

Runbad gets off the bench and stretches. "Not right away. A few weeks from then."

This guy and his riddles. "Then why does she need to leave the game?"

"Handle the tourist, and I might show you."

He's gone down the sidewalk.

CHAPTER TWENTY-TWO

BEEP-BEEP... KAPOW.

Ung.

Beep-beep... kapow

Go away. Jasmine is sleeping.

No, not Jasmine. That was yesterday. Today I'm—

Beep-beep... kapow.

All right already. Where's my damn phone?

Beep-beep... kapow. "H-Hello?"

"Hey, it's Ethan. Did I wake you?"

"No. I had to get up and answer the phone."

"Hah."

"So... you're Ethan?"

"Uh-huh. And you are..."

"Connie." Cuz this is a new day... I think. Yeah. Getting light outside. And I'm waking up alone after spending the night in my boyfriend's car. I've been sleeping around in Fords lately. "What does this say about me, Ethan?"

"Huh?"

"Come on. We need to click better than that. Can't you read my mind today?"

"Never could. Does it say you wish I were there? That's what mine's saying."

"Then why aren't you?" Wait. Stop it. What the hell is wrong with me? Being cotton-mouthed sleepy is no excuse for coming across as needy. I mean, yes, of course I'm needy. Who isn't? But *sounding* like I am? Whininess leads to solitude sooner or later. My mom used to say she owned the playbook for failed relationships. No thank you for *that* hand-me-down, Mother.

"I'm in a bad place, right now, Connie."

He's in a bad place? Try waking up in the backseat of somebody's car with a crick in the neck. I need to get out and stretch.

There.

Oh my God. This lot has people milling about. There oughta be better signage. *No parking! Connie's naked in here.*

I'm back in the car again, cowering.

Why is the phone on the floor? "Hello?"

"Connie? I thought we got disconnected."

"No, but listen… can we find a frillier place to call home?"

"Yeah, Connie, when I get back."

"You okay, baby?"

"Uh-huh. I just wanted to call and say… I love you."

Phone's back on the floor again. Fell right out of my hand because of my man. My crazy, lovable, poker-playing, hallucinating, dream of a man. *He loves me.*

"Ethan? Can you hear me down there? I love you, too." But my phone hides out of sight, somewhere under the front seat. It bounced and then ricocheted into the worst possible spot. I can't get at the stupid thing without opening the door, getting out, and… where are my goddamn panties? "Ethan, hang on a sec."

We lose the connection by the time I fish the phone out from beneath the seat while bending down from outside the car in such a manner as to surely let anyone and everyone in the lot get a good look at my bare butt. Especially since I grab their attention by shouting *I love you* again in the general direction of where the phone must be, in a voice screechy enough to wake the dead. I'm pretty sure his tinny response is something like *call you tomorrow* when I close in on the elusive device, but we've lost contact before I can get directions to where his bad place might be or why he felt the need to go there *today*.

Not that I gave him much opportunity to explain. I'm a morning person but not a crack-of-dawn one, and now he knows that about me. Tomorrow I'll tell him my favorite soft drink. Lovers should learn something new about each other *every* day, especially those lucky ones who've transcended from the physical act to the spoken endearment. Big word there, *transcended*. This is what Ethan's done to my vocabulary, raising me to a higher plane, where words like *epiphany* and *redemption* are next in line for the grabbing.

What can I say? He's made an honest woman out of me. I mean, if a day on the town, a roll in the backseat, and three little words can drop this much happiness onto my head, what the hell do I need any ill-gotten gains for? My mom missed the boat here, never laying anything even remotely Hallmark on me, such as *love can calm a thieving heart*. I suppose she was too busy hustling us from town to town, one step ahead of the law.

Not that I'm gonna toss in the gutter whatever money's left over after I've moved the last bones and paid Eugene off. A girl needs to buy a new robe from time to time. Hasn't my immediate situation in this less-than-vacant lot proven the point? And maybe several pairs of nicer shoes, if only as a souvenir reminder of how far off course my life can spin in the absence of adoration by a wonderful man.

I can't peg my future happiness on him, though. That's on *me*. I will not falter, even if he realizes the obvious at some point—that he can do better—and he dumps me before I have a decent chance to coax him to the altar and—

Oh... my mind just went to the place where the imaginings of brokenheartedness trigger the barf reflex. Thankfully I didn't, cuz this car's our bed and I'd certainly kill *him* if he did something like that. I'm scooting out the other door, just in case another wave takes me down, but mostly cuz on this side, the entire automobile acts as the perfect shield against lascivious gazers. Fancy words are dropping straight out of the sky in my new, star-struck existence.

Okay then. A quick scurry into bra, panties, and sundress, and I'm ready to face another day, beginning with a stroll to the truck stop. The showers and laundromat beckon not only me but yesterday's outfit as well. Thankfully I always keep crammed in my purse the emergency replacement ensemble I'm now wearing, hidden from any prying eyes beneath certain items that probably should be covered as well. Namely almost twenty counterfeit poker chips, give or take. Plenty of room for a handkerchief or scarf on top to cover it all next time.

Any ladies out there? Shop at Coach, go for their bulkier purse line, and, for emergency replacement ensemble space, lose the two extra pairs of sunglasses, thirteen pens, the little flashlight, the package of tissue—befriend Russian mobsters and that last item won't be a problem—the dozen ChapSticks you can never find…

Am I babbling worse than ever? This must be true love.

And not the sisterly kind, although now that my hair shines and my face glows with cleanliness and a newly laundered replacement set of clothing is stuffed into the purse, my two bestest hoody pals become the next destination. No, we didn't miss a chapter just now. Love leads to long moments of light-headed bliss, absorbing entire two-hour stretches of skipping down the sidewalk, smiling at the early-morning butterflies that fluttered at me from across the cemetery wall, and saying hi to Charlie, not to mention the time spent inside with washing machine, showers, and a shaker of pepper to go with yesterday's salt. I paid for it too. I'm a good girl now.

The sudden fit of honesty threw me off. I had to double back two blocks after I remembered buying the pepper for my favorite homeless friend. But I'm fully awake now, ready for action, and no longer as absent-minded.

Except wait. Since Hans, Yosef, and I didn't become fast

friends on day one, and I later had weightier issues on my mind, I never asked them where they live, let alone got a phone number or two.

No worries. I should stop at Philippe's first, anyway, and hit him with the news of my transformation into a girl who might still do a lot of things, but few of them dishonest... before I get stupid again and change my mind. He and Eugene need a new mule. Also, Hans or Yosef might be hanging around as part of their thug-for-hire gig, so maybe I can kill two birds with one stone. I've got a small donation in my purse for them.

Another hour walking and I'm back in a neighborhood even my happy mood doesn't allow me to see in a favorable light. Maybe a little fresh paint on the worn buildings would help. Tuck-pointing here and there. A release of white-winged birds to chase the pigeons and crows away. And weed killer by the bucketful. My Russian partners in crime need me and my neighborhood improvement ideas far more than I ever needed them. I know this now. Love has elevated me from an insecure, underachieving, low-self-esteem wallow to a million-dollar grin.

Up the stairs of Philippe's stoop I go, careful not to trip over the broken slats, and I'm ringing the bell. Waiting. Ringing again. Neglect rears its ugly hair everywhere, even in the wiring.

So I knock.

And again a little harder.

Hopefully he doesn't respond to unexpected visitors in shotgun-wielding, freedom-fighter mode. I read about unfortunate shootings all the time, and they aren't always on purpose.

Wait, there he is, peering out the window blinds off to the side. Wave, Connie. Flash an innocent smile.

Finally, after ample time passes for him to stow away any heavy artillery he'd been readying, Philippe creaks the door open, pokes his balding head out, and grimaces at me. This is what vodka benders can do to a man the next morning. He isn't even all the way dressed, only in jeans, showing his white-haired chest and ample gut to all passersby. But hey, who am I to criticize after my earlier display in Ethan's parking lot?

I widen my smile.

He doesn't. "That's an untrustworthy grin," he says. "I used to know a woman like you. The friendlier she got, the harder the news."

"Yeah? Well, invite me in then, so we can talk."

Chapter Twenty-Three

I **DIDN'T WALK THROUGH** a door between worlds.

No thunderclap transformed my surroundings into all kinds of wrong.

I called Connie. Nothing more.

But I'm standing behind the bench now, the river at my back, with no hope of processing an impossible apparition filling the space where an ordinary park used to be, not five minutes ago. The red-brick building with its enormously tall, arched windows and ornate green roof has no business in my field of vision.

Maybe my connection with Connie created its own magic. I'd love to run with the idea, but let's face it. This ridiculous moment has Runbad written all over it. A total departure from reality.

I reach for the back of the bench to regain balance... and I'm flat on my ass. The bench is gone. The river's missing.

And exactly what is this monstrosity across a busy street where grass grew minutes earlier? The Harold Washington Library Center according to that light-pole banner high above me.

Harold who?

Worker bees scurry up and down the sidewalk without giving me a second glance. I'm just another homeless dude rendered invisible for lack of proper context. They wear jackets and coats. I'm shivering in shirtsleeves. My careening mind has dropped the temperature to what's gotta be a northern climate, and definitely not the month of May anymore.

The passersby walk purposefully and without trepidation. Who wouldn't envy the lack of terror? Look at me down here, sitting on a sidewalk crack, between a bad omen and a hard place. No doubt a practical joke by Runbad. He's gone from verbal sparring to massive choreography. I asked for a library, and there it is.

A gust of wind sends discarded newspaper pages flying in my direction. A section catches a passing woman's leg. She trips, arrests her fall, and regains her balance by kicking a screaming sports headline right in my face.

Blackhawks Win.

So I'm in… Chicago? And oh, by the way, it's late February. Where's the reset button? The fractured timeline between points A and B has fallen into a wormhole, and string theory wraps around my throat till I'm gasping for breath. Sure, my earlier time-travel misadventures had me questioning my lucidity, but adding warped space to the mix could seal the deal.

I drove to Gulfport. Can't remember a thing about the trip, yet the story line was logical. I *could* have done it.

I walked into Snakes a few times and into a gypsy casino in a bad part of town. Easy enough for anyone to do.

But have I now sprouted wings complete with a jet pack?

This question keeps me occupied for many desperate moments before I grasp at the better of two possible conclusions like a drowning swimmer lunging for a lifeline. Runbad has awesome abilities.

Because no, I have not regressed into total lunacy. To prove the point, I must stand up now, dust myself off, and blend into the hordes of vertical, mentally stable pedestrians. My road to salvation forks in a couple logical directions, toward either the stoplight on the corner to the left or the one on my right. Fifty to a hundred paces either way. The congested street separating me from the library has too many lanes for me to try crossing without signals, if, in fact, the traffic is real.

Of course it is. Listen to the horns! Smell the exhaust fumes belching out the back of that truck! The nearest car speeding by just tossed its wind in my face.

So I march left. And I stop at the corner with everyone else. Actual people I can reach out and touch.

As if that proves anything.

Sure it does.

Don't walk.

The crossing sign is genuine enough. Otherwise, why would everyone wait here with me?

Don't walk.

Don't walk.

Walk. I'm on my way across, elbow to elbow with my fellow sane Chicagoans.

On the other side, most of them continue down the sidewalk, but I peel toward a library where a simple Internet search might reveal some answers about Runbad. Angel or demon? Captain Kirk helping me explore new worlds, or the devil dragging me down the road to perdition?

Somebody's footfalls sound behind me. The unmistakable click of high-heeled shoes. Good. I don't want to be alone with my thoughts or I'll risk figuring out that this world I've strayed into is one massive hallucination. Distractions, please! I'll play the gallant knight for someone. So I open the door, hold it, and turn to await passage and maybe a thank you by…

Her.

Forty something.

Big hair.

Loopy earrings.

A canvas purse slung over her shoulder.

The tourist.

Yeah. Why not?

So what am I dealing with in Runbad? A guy with access to an extra dimension or two, thus rendering the broad gulfs of space and time irrelevant? A chain-smoking navigator leading me from the wrong coordinates to the right ones... me a time-traveling infant with no muscle memory... him the wise parent using a shake of the metaphysical rattle?

Gotta think Captain Kirk here. I have not lost my marbles. Not when a newborn belief in science fiction can bail out my sanity.

But I've almost lost *her* in my frantic attempts to rescue my mind. The door closes in my face, and by the time I reopen it to hurry inside, she's out of sight.

This is a library? Where are the books? I'm standing in a vast, museum-like lobby with marble-tiled floors, a circular railed area in the center, upper floor balconies looking down from above, art on most walls, a massive American flag on another, wooden benches here and there, a monitor-lined reception station and... there she is, heading for an escalator.

What's my play here? No idea except to chase her onto the moving stairs, just behind some chattering kids who've crowded in between us. Up to the second floor... then off at the third, toward a bank of elevators. Thankfully, when the doors open, a few other people get on with us. I need time to come up with an introduction, let alone think of some way of convincing this woman to exit a card game that won't even happen until months from now, a thousand miles south of here.

Ding. Doors open. People pour out, and... wow. Forget museum. Think greenhouse instead. An incredible open atrium beneath green-tinted glass. She heads for one of the small tables gathered about, glances right and then left as if guarding a secret, then grabs a chair and sets up court, rummaging through her purse, and coming up with... crystals?

I sit nearby but not too close. We time-traveling madmen have to be discreet or we'll scare off the people only borderline crazy. Believers in fortune-tellers, horoscopes, and healing stones aren't necessarily all skittish, but this one seems insecure over her eccentricity.

I'll need an icebreaker if she glances my way. What would

Runbad do? He's the crafty one. Somehow I don't think another prop bet will do the trick here. The tourist is no compulsive gambler. She's more the starry-eyed type, like the chick in *Independence Day* who looks up to the heavens and—

Yeah, there's my angle. She's into the occult but insecure about it. People like her want to bond with someone like-minded, don't they? For validation of their sanity? I sure can relate to *that* concept.

I need to be into the same things she is. A believer in séances, magic, dark angels... *pyramids?* Runbad gave me one. Said it might do the trick. So I go for my pocket, latch on to the paperweight trinket, and set it on the table in front of me.

No dice. She hasn't noticed. Too focused on her crystals and whatever needs healing. I'd go grab the stones and press them into my head if I thought they'd do *me* any good. Except let's face it. Too many rocks in there already.

So now I'm looking to the heavens for the wonders they might offer *me*, up through the glass ceiling, at a broken overcast of dark clouds, patches of blue, a slivery ray of sun fighting its way out, taking aim, and—

Bzzzzz.

My pyramid vibrates like the signal for a sandwich order waiting at the counter. Except instead of a pulsing light, we're looking at a steady green glow, a thin ray reaching upward toward the sky.

I feel the weight of curious eyes from every occupied table within fifty feet. Hers, too, and that's a good thing, but am I supposed to run a play for all of these others, as well? I still don't even know what the game is.

Bzzzzz.

Gotta cover it with my hand. End the show-and-tell for the masses and direct a sheepish shrug at *her,* as if nobody else in this place matters. We're skittish about our beliefs, the tourist and I. Two frightened souls in a sea of mocking doubters. What better way to bond?

But she isn't watching anymore. She gathers her crystals,

slips them back into her purse, and pushes from her table. *Click, click, click* go her heels toward the elevator bank behind me. She reaches my side. Continues on…

Come on, Runbad. What do I do now—

…and stops. "What *is* that?" Her voice comes out hushed. She glances away for a quick, head-swivel scan of the room and then back at me.

"Oh, you know."

"No, really," she whispers.

The pyramid isn't humming anymore, but its green glow impossibly penetrates my palm to shoot out the top of my hand undiminished. Good one, Runbad.

The tourist grabs a seat beside me. Big dark hair, wide greenish eyes. A little mist in there. She isn't here for a come-on. More of a pilgrimage. "Where'd you get it?"

"Tibet." The ridiculous lie gets me started on a roll. I follow by matching her whispers with the lowest voice I can come up with and still hear myself speaking. Spinning some total BS about a barefoot journey through the desert, a Sherpa-guided mountain climb, the ancient palace I approached on my knees. And the monks, of course. These sacred places of enlightenment always overflow with fanatics. Just ask Christian Bale.

And she's hanging on my every word. Hands clasped on the table. Her deer-in-the-headlights stare begging for enlightenment. This is an unforgiving world for nutcases. Believe me, I know.

"Can I tell you something?" I say.

The tourist nods, unable to speak. She's leaning ever closer, almost on my lap. But not at all in a flirty way. She's the disciple. I'm Yoda.

"What's your name?" I ask.

"Carly."

"I'm Michael." *Mike* would never stoop to this nonsense, no matter the goal. Besides, the situation calls for an angelic name. "Carly, it's really a shame you won't be in New Orleans for Memorial Day weekend." Of course, I already know she will be.

And she knows, too. Her jaw drops at what can't be a crazy coincidence in her mind. She'll see it more as a hand-of-God sort of moment. So much so that she takes long moments to gather herself. "Oh, but I will be!" She isn't whispering anymore. Her voice is almost loud enough to echo off the walls.

Eyes from all around are on me again. And her. I slip the pyramid back in my pocket with a show of furtiveness. "You can't repeat to *anyone* what I'm gonna tell you."

"No. Never."

"I mean it, Carly. I've searched the Internet. Ransacked libraries. There isn't a word written down about what the monks told me."

"You can trust me, Michael."

A pang of guilt slows me. Yeah, I can bluff with the best of 'em in a poker game, but I've never been comfortable with everyday lying, not to mention a tale *this* tall. But it's all for the greater good. Me getting to see Connie again, or whatever her name might be tomorrow. Plus, according to Runbad, Carly will leave the game to meet her true love one day.

That last part gives me greater pause. Why does he want her to leave if there's no real urgency? In Tak's case, his future soul mate happens to be wandering just outside the casino at the time. *Am* I doing good here or falling for some trick of Runbad's? No question I'm driven at least a little by selfishness, salivating for his end of the bargain—the opportunity to spend time with Amy again.

Doesn't matter.

Amy needs me either way. She's made the wrong friends. She's in too deep and doesn't get it. Did I seriously think for a second that she took my thousand bucks to buy her way out of the jam? She had the same double-down expression I've seen in hundreds of card games. I've given her the stake to *play* her way out of the Russian mess, not pay her way out. But because of the unforgiving waves of bad luck even the best players deal with, we're talking a forty percent chance or higher she'll lose the extra grand before the Russians ever see a dime of it.

Maybe Runbad will come up with some kind of pyramid to

help me help Amy. I'd do another of his pointless favors for that.

Meanwhile… "You'll see me there that Sunday, Carly. In the card room at Snakes. But you've gotta act like you don't know me. We can't draw attention to ourselves."

Silent, reverent nod.

"Two invisible stars will align with the sun in the early afternoon that day. New Orleans is the ground zero location for the effect. At first, that'll rain bad karma down on the planet. So we have to be inside."

She's eating this up. I should do seminars.

"Okay, now here's the trick. When my pyramid clicks on, like it did just now, *I'll know* the sunlight has evolved into healing mode. That's when I'll leave the poker room and head on out. You should follow."

"What will the sun heal?" she asks.

"Everything, but especially our souls."

You can beam me up now, Runbad. She's hooked.

But he doesn't. I'm still here with my starry-eyed new friend. Just like with Tak, the longer this conversation continues, the greater the chance I'll stray into the stupid, to the point even the most faithful see through the fraud.

So I'm out of here. A warm squeeze of her shoulder before heading to the elevators with the magical pyramid secured in my pocket. Quick stop on the third floor, though. The directory by the elevator says they've got computers down there.

Googling Runbad doesn't get me far at first. *Matchmaker* gives me pages of dating service hits. *Cigarette* pulls up cancer. *Poker syake* begets poker stake and the need for a better spell checker. Nothing useful from *poker stake,* either. I need to dig deeper.

How about… *trickster?*

Bingo. A mythological figure appearing in the legend of many cultures. Really? I'd always regarded the term as a figure of speech. A label. But Wikipedia goes on and on for entire pages. References in African American oral history. American Indian. Chinese. Chilean. Sure sounds like a guy who gets around. Like Runbad, for example. The trickster is known as a boundary crosser. One who violates principals of social and natural order, playfully disrupting normal life and then reestablishing it on a new basis.

I tool around some more, typing *one-sided deal* into the search box, and get something that immediately kicks my broken mind into gear. *How to deal with one-sided love.*

Well, I suppose I'd look around for Cupid, wouldn't I?

Cupid. A lot of print in the Wikipedia article. Hallmark kind of stuff. More of it. Still more. I'm wasting my time with—

Wait. Here's something. Medieval mythographers viewed Cupid as a demon of fornication. One writer of the time regarded him as a seductive but malicious figure who exploits desire to draw people into an allegorical underworld of vice.

And who wrote this opinion? Theodulf of *Orleans.*

Yeah. A trickster might regard *New Orleans* as an ironically satisfying place to plant his modern-day roots. My heart's pounding in my ears. I've figured Runbad out. He's a trickster, all right, and the name he said I'd figure out sooner or later is right here in my face. *Cupid.* The son of Venus and Mars. *He told me that!*

The long article doesn't give a hint how to best this chain-smoking devil, but I know his name now, and knowledge is power, isn't it?

Not out here in the cold. I floated down two floors to the ground level, my body on automatic while my mind chewed on a letter of complaint to all greeting card companies far and wide. Then I wandered out the door to the hockey-loving city Runbad unceremoniously dropped me into. I know that's a snowflake fluttering in the breeze. I know a short-sleeve shirt isn't the ticket for this kind of weather. And I know the lazy Mississippi still isn't flowing behind me.

This is what tricksters do.

"Taxi!".

CHAPTER TWENTY-FOUR

LOOK AT ME AND Philippe all domesticated at his kitchen table. Isn't this nice? Only he's hitting the vodka bottle *hard*, he hasn't bothered to throw a shirt on, and he's got an especially bad look in his eyes. This from a guy who never has good ones.

So yeah, my knee wants to twitch, but I'm holding it steady.

The conversation is going okay, all things considered. He hasn't punched his fist through the wall yet, *or through me,* at the news of my retirement plans. A lucky happenstance, given the fact Hans isn't here to have my back.

"You *can't* quit on me," Philippe growls. "You were born into this life."

What? Maybe *I* should be the one punching walls. "Who are you to say—"

Philippe pushes from the table to pace the floor. "Your mother had a sheet wider than the motherland. Apple doesn't fall far from the tree, no?"

Oh my God. He checked me out. Don't they believe in employee authorizations where he came from? Privacy rights?

He stops to glare at me. "How long ago did she kill herself? Eleven months? Tell me you haven't been reeling ever since."

"That's enough, Philippe!" Is nothing sacred? He's fighting dirty. Nobody needs reminders of a crippling grief almost passed.

And guilt. I left her for college. Then deserted her again a year after graduation to drift from cardroom to cardroom until the broad Mississippi and ever wider Gulf said I had nowhere farther south to fall. I'd gone looking to find myself, leaving my better half behind to overdose on whatever medication she'd been taking for her migraines. "Her death was an accident. So you can just go fuck your—"

"Rose and I were an item once, when she was your age. Looked just like you. Crafty and beautiful."

He steals my breath away with *that* little news item. All I can do is stare with eyes gone so misty I can barely see. "You're lying. I found you randomly. A friend of a friend. You never knew my mother."

He grabs the half-empty vodka bottle from the table. Chugs. Smirks. Strips me naked with bloodshot eyes. "You don't think *my* friends can't find yours and bring you home?"

God. He's driven me into a corner so dark any random roaches scurrying by are blinded from a lifetime of deprived sunlight. But don't worry. Anyone looking for the reckless, wryly funny, devil-may-care Amy persona I've fit into as a cocoon for so long—without wasting a dime on navel-contemplating therapy, I might add—anyone looking for more shits and giggles needs only skip ahead a tad. I'll be back. I promise not to let this vodka-swilling monster wreck the lovely flowered trellis between my happiness and all the ugly stuff. The wall I've spent a lifetime constructing. But for now, I've clenched my fists so hard the nails bite into my flesh. I can only speak in measured tones or I'll start shrieking and never stop. "What... are... you... telling... me?"

Philippe's pacing the floor again. "What am I telling you? That I wasn't cut out for pony rides. Or Disneyland. But now that you're grown, I'm here for you. *If* you're here for me."

Enough of this. I'm out of my chair and heading for the door. Only no. He is *not* getting the last word. I whirl to face him. "Here for me? What about *her?* Do you know we spent a whole summer living on the street when I was sixteen? Just like Charlie."

"Charlie?" He stares at me, wrinkling his forehead in confusion like the idiot he is.

"To you he'd be a random homeless guy, cuz you aren't worthy enough to know him."

The bottle flies past me, smashing into the wall and exploding into wet shards of glass. They do nothing to dampen a fury in the air I could cut with a carving knife just before burying it in his head.

"I offered to help a dozen times," he shouts. "But she was too proud. And hateful. She kept me from meeting you... *my own flesh and blood*. Foolish pride. Spiteful hate. No, the apple *doesn't* fall far."

My knees buckle. He's calling her hateful. And me... hateful. This bastard who also happens to be *my dad.*

Deep breath in. Then out.

And another.

Happy thoughts. Ethan loves me. *Mike* loves me.

"Fine," he growls. "Don't be my daughter. Get the hell out of here!"

I don't need a second invitation. A shaky twist of the knob, and I'm out the door, sobbing.

The lock latches behind me.

Now what? Do I stir up the neighbors by shouting every curse I know? Throw my shoe at the window in case he's peeking out at me?

No. He doesn't deserve anything I have to offer, not even spite. I'll just focus on reconstruction after yet another cluster in my life. Rebuild what this lousy, drunken Russian gangster just did his best to break into a thousand pieces.

A new wall isn't easy to make when I'm grinding my teeth, but I'm well practiced, so I sit and get started. Brick one—I just quit a life of crime. Ethan counts for three more. Mike another five. And Charlie by the truck stop? Good old Charlie's always there for me as a touchstone. Eleven bricks more.

My eyes are drying. Sure, my face is probably all puffy, but I'll work up a smile eventually, and that should help.

Except my mind won't let go of the buried emotions Philippe dredged up. Or the reflections on what I might have done differently. A steadier presence in my mom's life might have saved both of us.

I'm so terribly sorry, Mother.

And I'm crying again.

Hans crosses from the street to the sidewalk to the stoop, sits beside me, and drapes an arm across my shoulders. "Hey there, pumpkin, what's the matter?"

"N-nothing."

But he holds on tight, anyway. Comforts me forever. Till the next day at least or the one after that. He holds me till I'm funny again and no longer Amy. I'm back to being Connie.

He turns to the door behind us. "I should end that guy."

"No."

"World would be a better place."

I stare Hans down with all the ferocity I can muster. "Never ever. Get it?" I was an orphan once already and it's no fun, believe me. What would Annie be without the elusive Daddy Warbucks? Just a poor little redhead with too many curls. See? I'm funny again.

Not that Hans notices. He's shaking his head. "You're a tough little bitch."

"I'll bet you say that to all the girls."

"Truth."

Yosef lopes toward us from down the sidewalk. That's the bond between these two, dating back to when I knew them as Things. If I see one, the other can't be far behind. Like me and Ethan these days, except for when he's in bad places, dealing with the devil or whatever. It better be the devil, cuz if this particular Satan is wearing high-heel shoes, I'll strangle Ethan like the tough little bitch I've now been christened. But I refuse to let my mind go there. Jealousy is a weakness. A form of self-doubt. Not the right state of mind, or heart, for somebody who just emancipated herself from the fatherland... literally.

"'Sup?" Yosef looks up at me, then Hans, then me again.

J. M. FRASER

"C'mere. I've got something for both of you." I fish beneath the bad chips in my purse and come up with the thousand bucks Henry gave me.

They're flanking me now, a hoodie sitting on either side. Studying the money in crinkle-eyed confusion.

"It's payday, guys. But I don't have an accounting department, so don't expect 1099s in the mail next January."

More confusion. Even a hint of embarrassment in Hans's flushing cheeks.

"You moved chips. You handled security. And so this is the money you earned."

"No," Yosef says. "No, no, no. It's way too much."

Hans doesn't say anything, but he's shaking his head.

Wow. Shouldn't gifting money be easy? Apparently not.

So what's the protocol for getting these guys the extra grand they've been looking for while simultaneously keeping them from losing face? "Listen. You told me you needed a thousand more dollars for lined hoodies and a poker stake. And you worked for me, giving me what I needed. So now *in return* I'm paying what *you* need. That's an even bargain where I come from."

"Ah, you didn't come from where we do," Hans says. "If I cheat you on the price of a rug, you'll still offer to pay for the shipping?"

The joke sounds mildly insulting, but they're both chortling, and each now seems comfortable with the fistfuls of money I've forked over. So I'll take one for the greater good and grin with them.

Hans ruffles my hair. "Okay," he says. And to Yosef, "It's pure?"

"Yeah, I think so. Uh-huh."

Good. I've passed through the gauntlet of unwanted charity and come out the other side still their friend.

"Nine days, then." Hans says.

"Till you play? Why not right away? Snakes has a high-hand hourly payoff today. A hundred bucks. Maybe you'll—"

"Spiritual cleansing," Yosef says.

"Prayer," Hans adds. "And then we'll do it."

Wow. I should try a little of that. Anything to reverse the last eleven consecutive months of pain. And not only at the card tables.

Hans gets his smartphone out and tools through the calendar. "The day before your Memorial Day. It's fitting."

"Yeah." I'm all caught up in this now. Anything to get my mind off other things... *Anything.* "Sundays are great. Lots of tourists. If we play at the same table, I can keep an eye on you and let you know if I spot any weaknesses."

But they're frowning. I've accidentally thrown their masculinity under the bus again. "It's just a little-sister thing," I add.

"Uh-uh. Stay away," Yosef says. "We'll be..."

"Nervous," Hans says.

The hell I won't show. These two need a supporter on their first day at the felt. They could've practiced online till the cows came home, but live play is totally different.

I've challenged them enough for one day, though. And anyway, who doesn't like surprises? If I happen to wander into the casino at the same time they're playing, they'll be fine with it. "Okay, I guess. Good luck then. You'll get your start here and end up in Vegas for sure."

"Place to be," Yosef says.

"Paradise," Hans adds.

We stand. Hugs all around, and I'm off, leaving the two former Things alone for their nine-day sabbatical and my loser of a deadbeat Russian dad hopefully gone from my life forever. Maybe I'll pass some chips to while away the rest of my day. And take a long walk. All the way to Ethan's car.

When he shows up, I want to be there for him. That's what lovers do, especially after a mostly bad day.

CHAPTER TWENTY-FIVE

TWENTY-SIX HOURS ON a bus? I'm bored out of my mind after only four. Alone in a rear seat with nothing to do but nail yet another Sudoku puzzle or stare out the window and see firsthand why people in Indiana are referred to as flatlanders. Thanks again, Runbad. At just a hundred twenty bucks, this bargain-basement milk-run is the only affordable way home for a guy denied any more wormhole privileges.

I grab the phone out of my pocket, but my attempts to reach Amy on any of the two-digit options Runbad provided yield nothing but a low hum. *One call a day,* he said. That means I've gotta wait several more hours until midnight ushers tomorrow into my life—or whatever day that turns out to be.

Shouldn't call her so late, though, in case she's sleeping. Although our dates may be out of sync, the hands on the clock seem to match. After all, I did wake her up when I called at the crack of dawn this morning from my bench on the Riverwalk, just before my thousand-mile trek through time and space got started.

But with four hours down and twenty-two to go, I'll go crazy if I don't make that midnight call.

The flat plains of Indiana racing by my window have darkened now to the point I'm getting sleepy. I nod off, awaken to more nothingness outside, and doze again until the bus jolts to a stop. We've reached some backwater town for a ten-minute break.

Down the aisle and out the door I go in search of fresh air.

Nope. Exhaust fumes.

So I go for a vending machine by the curb, but one of my half-dozen fellow passengers stands in the way between me and a junk-food splurge. He's one of those plump, bookish types with glasses way thicker than stylish and curly hair woven too tight for a comb to matter. My age, more or less. Thirty at the oldest. He's lost his change in the machine despite a remarkably dogged persistence at working the pull-knob. Now he slips the leather satchel off his shoulder and goes at it with both hands.

That doesn't work, either.

"I can help." I pound the glass at just the right spot with a well-practiced thrust. Amy isn't the only one with a history of going for the five-finger discount when times get tough. Sadly, I don't have charity for homeless guys like Charlie as an excuse for developing the expertise. Just a couple poker runs so bad I wouldn't have eaten much otherwise.

A packet of M&M's almost shakes loose from the twist of metal holding it captive. I try the old machine-shake to finish the job.

Presto.

"Hey, thanks." My traveling buddy fishes his candy out of the slot at the bottom, then looks up at me. "So you're the new guy, I guess. I'm Freddie."

"Mike," I say out of reflex. Then, "What do you mean, new guy?"

He stares for a couple beats and shakes his head. "My bad. You wouldn't know yet, unless Peter told you. I take it he didn't say anything?"

Peter? Hmm. Didn't Runbad say the people at the casino call him Pete? But my mind's also racing to something I need to consider whenever confronted with comments out of left field. This Peter character could be a friend I've yet to meet during some future journey into the past. Twisty timelines can be awfully confusing. Hopefully the end result of the Peter episode I've yet to enjoy won't be a flashlight getting thrown at my knee by the brokenhearted girlfriend I've unknowingly cheated on.

My stomach lurches at the reminder Amy hasn't been burned in *her* timeline yet by my little Cynthia tryst. And I don't know how to stop it from happening. Talk about a relationship threatened by a wall of churning clouds.

"Hey, are you still with me?" Freddie says.

"Sorry, I get lost in space sometimes. Don't take it personally."

He grabs his book bag from the ground and hefts it over his shoulder again. "Yeah, I remember reading that about you."

"About *me*? Where?"

"In the journal. Come on. I'll fill you in." And he heads away from the bus toward a nearby grassy area.

I'm torn. My transportation to Amy in New Orleans is a couple minutes from leaving the station without me, and all signs indicate I'm safe to chase her down without changing the past. My just-completed Chicago visit may have been in February—months before the first encounter on either of our timelines—but the weather has turned sultry here in Indiana, and the swarm of insects at the nearest light pole shouts the same message. I somehow snoozed my way back to the right page of the calendar—the one I left this morning. No point wondering *how* these things happen anymore. I'll go with the flow.

"You coming?" Freddie closes in on a picnic table, but the bus has been revving its engines so I've got to—

Huh? No, that can't be right. The rumbling has gone quiet. I turn back to look… blink… and blink again. The plume of exhaust out the back of the bus hangs still in the air, *frozen*, as if somebody switched the remote from play to pause.

I start turning away toward Freddie but stop halfway. It's time to get a grip. My lack of more double take than those two little blinks worries me more than the visible halt in time. If sudden flips from real to impossible go down this smooth, I've either lost it for sure or acclimated so deeply into my new existence I'll never find a way out.

"Over here," Freddie calls.

"Hold on." Part of me wants to just walk away from this mess. Freddie, the frozen bus, this out-of-the-way town. Why would we have stopped here in the first place?

So... how about an exit strategy? If I've been off the grid lately, maybe a sprint to that stand of trees over there would transition me to an *off the off the grid* existence in a new dimension that doesn't involve me constantly getting denied the basic human necessities anyone would need. Water—the Riverwalk I enjoy in the mornings. Food—a muffaletta now and again in a *New Orleans* restaurant. Shelter—my car. Love—I've gotta get back to her.

But the Big Easy is too far a walk from here, the bus isn't going anywhere, and there's Freddie, who read about me in some journal.

My chubby new peep grabs a seat at the table and starts pulling things out of his satchel. Way more stuff comes out than could possibly fit inside, but I'm not even blinking anymore. Books, pamphlets, legal pads, scrolls, *more* books—time-weathered but dog-eared the modern way, with Post-it notes—and a couple clipboards holding wads of documents together.

I sit across from him, racking my brain for the best possible of a million questions, the unreliable flow of time and space always threatening to cut a conversation short before anything meaningful gets exchanged.

"Let's start with Peter," Freddie says, beating me to the punch, "whom you know as..."

I wasn't expecting a pop quiz, but this one's easy. "You mean Runbad?"

Freddie grins. "Yeah. Give your friend kudos for coming up with some clever names. This latest one is way better than Pan. Anyway, he's a... how to put this?" He opens a book. Pages through it. Glances at a legal pad.

"Trickster?"

"Sorta. Good translation. We know them more as jinns. Born of fire and smoke rather than clay. They fall into the vast category of overly ambitious, ancient civilizations idiotic enough to incur the wrath of the Big Guy. All the whining and finger-pointing in the world didn't save them from getting scattered to the four winds. Nomadic morons these days, although most of them do have jobs."

I'm lapping this up. Pretty good odds my curly-haired friend here is setting me up for some one-sided deal, ala Runbad, but any basher of my chain-smoking puppet master is worth a listen, at least for a little while.

"These guys have been working stiffs for ages," he continues. "They're trying to get in good with the Big Guy again, for a seat at the table or at least not on the wrong side of the door. In Peter's case, he's been on the Cupid detail for hundreds of years."

"I knew it!"

"Yeah, well, know this. Cupids are a royal pain in the ass, because they're unionized. Just try to bust one of them for sleeping on the job, or even worse, dicking around with the customers. The grievance-filing process takes forever. Even if we win, the inevitable appeal ties us into knots for ages. We still haven't sentenced Peter for his role in the Henry the Eighth clusterfuck."

"Uh-huh." The background story has taken such a ridiculous turn, a jog to the trees for whatever dimension lies beyond is looking pretty good right now. Maybe I'll lob one more question to keep Freddie going, but know this. I'm bolting soon. "So... what do you mean *we* win? Are you part of some club I don't know about?"

"The ruling class. No, that doesn't quite nail it." Freddie makes a show out of cleaning his glasses on his sleeve. He clears his throat. "Look, we've got some really good people for explaining the big picture, but they're all—"

"Sorry I asked. Look, it's been nice meeting you, but I think I'll—"

Freddie raises a meaty hand. "Hold on a sec. You'll wanna hear this story. Peter's doing his typical half-assed Cupid job until, one day, he falls for a redhead he was supposed to match with somebody else. And she goes for him, too, until she catches him cheating with a hot blonde. See, at Peter's core he's always a jinn, and that's the kind of idiotic behavior they're famous for. So she slaps the crap out of him and gets in a few kicks, too. She's a regular hellcat when you rile her up."

"Wait. Back up. Did you say redhead?"

"See? Now I've got your attention." Freddie adjusts his glasses. Opens a book to a sketch of palm trees and a hut. The facing page shows a doll with pins sticking out of it. He shows me several more pages written by hand, then closes the book. "We keep track of our Cupids best we can. In Peter's case, he runs off to Haiti with his tail between his legs, along with the blonde, who happens to be another jinn, by the way. That island's a great place for plotting, which is never a good thing for jinns to be doing. But he comes up empty. No idea what to do, until…"

Freddie pauses with a self-satisfied smirk, like he's hooked me now, which he obviously has. I'll grab all of those books, scrolls, and journals to pore through them myself if he doesn't get to the point pretty quick.

"Stop," I say. "Just to clarify, the redhead who dumped Runbad wouldn't happen to be named Amy, would she?"

He shrugs. "Depends on which day it is."

"Right." My heart's sinking to the floor.

"Anyway, when Peter gets back, a bratty little girl with *way* more power than any of us gets hold of him and suggests the genie-in-the-bottle scam. Peter jumps in with both feet, but he needs approval. So he gets all dolled up one day, white suit and everything, and shows up at our headquarters. We have a meeting… him, me, my boss, my boss's boss, and another guy a couple levels higher up the pay grade."

Geez. Can he drag this out any slower? "Yeah, okay, and then?"

"He lays out the scam. In fact, it's already under way, which is *so* typical for a jinn. Go ahead and get started without asking permission first. Anyway, since he'd be messing with timelines in the process—*and already did to a certain extent*—he needs proper sign-off by all the right people. We don't take even the smallest tweaks of the past lightly, especially by untrustworthy jinns."

Freddie unrolls a scroll with *Genie request* written on the top of the first page in flowery script, a few paragraphs of handwritten gobbledygook in the middle, and a bunch of signatures at the bottom. "So he gets the sign-offs, but they come with a couple catches. First, he's not allowed to alter past events in a significant way, because the future's shaky enough without yanking support beams out of the framework."

I cringe at how this story is matching up with recent events in my own messed-up life. A redhead, an instigator of a hot blonde, and a warning. Runbad *insisted* that I don't change the past, just blend in with it. Now I see why.

If I'm not hallucinating here.

So which door do I open now?

(1) Everything's been a figment of my imagination from day one, and it's time to run for the trees.

(2) I'm fine, but I'm being buffeted by layer upon layer of tall tale, first by Runbad and now this guy, so it's time to run for the trees.

(3) This is all happening and everything's true, so it's time to run for the trees.

I'm leaning toward lunacy.

And running.

But door number three keeps me at the table. If Amy is Runbad's target in some scam, I need to learn enough to help her.

"Second," Freddie says, "and boy, we had a huge argument over *these* terms." He flips to the next page of the scroll, showing more script, marred in several places by cross-outs and alterations in red. "When he's done running the scam, whether it works or not, he's gotta sit down with Amy, or whatever name she's going by. He has to tell her what he started out as—a jinn—what he wanted to become—a human—and what he attempted as his ticket over—the scam. Big row over those terms, cuz this is a woman who slapped him around once already. *Hold on,* he says, *I wanna win her over, but I have to let her know what a lying, cheating bastard I am first?... Even if the scam doesn't work and I've got nothing to show for it?*"

Crap. If we're talking door number three and this is all real, Runbad's gonna march back into Amy's life—presuming he hasn't already—while I languish somewhere in the past. If he goes after her at the point in time I think he will, just after I leave the final table at Snakes and while Amy's still seething over the Cynthia incident, there's no telling what might happen. Yeah, he might spell out every bad thing he's ever done, but she'll be on the rebound after dumping me, and she might be susceptible to his chain-smoking, snake-oil charms.

Amy deserves so much better. I'm not pitching myself here, either. Pull me out of the equation, and she's still supposed to get way more than a loser like Runbad. Not even the Brothers Grimm could paint a simple fairy tale with so much red—pre-Disney, I mean.

"So that's the story." Freddie starts cramming all the books and paperwork back into his bag.

"Wait. Hold on. You didn't tell me what the scam is."

"It's older than the hills." He fishes around in the satchel, comes out with a fresh book, even thicker and moldier than the ones he put away. He opens it to the middle, adjusts his glasses higher on his nose, and starts to read. "Wherefore, heretofore, and with every regard to…"

"Come on. Seriously, Freddie? Just tell me the highlights."

"Fine." He shoves the book back into the bag. "Here's the deal in a nutshell. The scammer grants three wishes, and, in return, the sucker gullibly performs three favors using at least as much connivance and deception as a jinn might try."

"Uh-huh. And when does this happen?"

"It already did." Freddie holds up a finger. "One, he let you visit Amy."

He lifts another. "Two, you got to visit her again. Overnighters each time, complete with mornings after. He was overly generous with the favors."

And a third. "Three, he gave you a phone to call her with."

"Fine. He granted three wishes, which I wouldn't have needed if he didn't throw me off the grid. But I never connived or—"

He's rolling his eyes, and I say no more. Passing counterfeit chips to Amy, tricking the Asian, totally leading the tourist astray... Guilty as charged.

"Okay. Wonderful. He scammed me. So he isn't a jinn anymore?"

"That's the size of it." Freddie gets up and grabs his satchel. "He's human now, and you're the new rookie on our Cupid team. We'll fill you in on the details after you've had a chance to, I don't know, absorb your revised circumstances?"

"What? No way! You and Runbad can't just randomly pull a guy off the street and—"

"Sure we can. Anyone's fair game if you catch them in between the first life and the one that comes after."

He's walking away, opposite the bus, heading for the stand of trees I wanted to go for.

I try to speak. Fail. Swallow.

"Don't worry," he calls, "you'll be fine." He points to the bus, now idling again. "Hurry or you'll miss your ride. We haven't taught you how to click your ruby slippers yet.".

CHAPTER TWENTY-SIX

BEEP-BEEP… KAPOW.

Hah! I wasn't asleep yet, you noisy roadrunner. Try to pounce on *me*, will you? Just living for the chance to blast me awake, huh? Well, pounce this. I'll cram you so deep in my purse no one will ever hear you again. Bwa-ha-ha!

Pesky bird.

Thinking he can wake me…

Damn.

He actually did.

Twenty questions now to fall back asleep.

What was I doing?

Sleeping. Yeah.

And what just happened?

A couple annoying beeps and a kapow. I almost rolled off the seat, I answered the phone, and I had it out with my little bird. But that's all better now.

Good. So what did you say?

To the bird? Nothing kind. But shush now. I'm almost there again.

No, when you answered the phone.

When I… oh, crap. I buried the phone in my purse. Where'd it go? Not on the seat. The floor? It's too dark in here. Maybe if I open the door and... okay, good. Light's on.

Quick inventory.

Purse?

Check.

Crumpled lottery ticket on the floor?

Oh, Jason. Haven't you ever heard of the second-chance drawing?

If this thing isn't totally expired yet, it could be worth... huh? That date doesn't make any sense at all.

Beep-beep... kapow.

Got you this time! In my purse, where I shoved you. Right here under the chips. No. Caught in my emergency bra maybe?

Beep-beep... kapow.

Beneath the emergency panties. You can run, but you can't hide, little phone.

"H-hello?"

"Hey!"

"Jason baby?"

"Yeah, it's me. And I'm calling this chick named..."

"Claudiopolis."

"Claudia for short?"

"Jason, listen, are you in the counterfeiting racket, too? Cuz I'm looking at this lottery ticket here, and the purchase date hasn't happened yet."

Noticeable pause. Something's up. If he's gotten himself involved with Russians, I'll die. They creep into your head and plant a news flash in there you *never* wanted to hear, reminding you of unhappiness you'd almost...

"Claudia, are you crying?"

"N-no. It's just this... this everything. Why am I sleeping alone in your car?"

"I'm on my way back, I promise. On the bus right now."

"No, it's not that. I've been reeling. Somebody was kind enough to point that out."

"Who? Not—"

"Doesn't matter who. I'm not gonna keep acting needy and

pushing myself on you this way anymore. I'm going back to my apartment, *his* apartment and—"

"No! You can't go there. What if he comes back?"

Wow. Panic? I've never seen this side of him. "Jason, are you jealous?"

Another pause. He is. And I'm so insecure to want him to be. The neediness purge is harder than I thought. Might be a twelve-step kinda thing like the alcoholics deal with. The gamblers.

Sign me up.

"Uh-uh," he says. "I'm just worried for you."

"Not even a little bit... jealous?"

"Okay, yeah. A little."

And I'm smiling now. Just like that. It's a sickness.

Twelve steps. Starting tomorrow morning. "What's with this lottery ticket, Jason?"

Here we go again with the pause. This is why I hate phone conversations. I can't stare in his eyes and connect.

"I'm time-traveling, Claudia."

"You're..."

"I can't tell you much or I might change things. Supposedly that's bad, although I don't know what to believe anymore."

That's my man. If I could just cuddle up with him and fix him breakfast in the morning, he'd be fine. We'd both be fine. "Why are you on a bus, baby?"

"Cheapest way home from Chicago. That's part of the long story I shouldn't tell you."

"Hurry back, Jason. I miss you."

Crackle... "Love"... crackle.

"I love you, too. You're my everything."

Crackle.

"Jason?"

No answer.

I should sleep.

I can't sleep.

I close my eyes, count sheep, count counterfeit sheep, count all the Jasons in my life... count... count... cry a little...

And now, hours later, I guess, it's morning. My phone didn't need to wake me. The sunlight does a good job.

No hurry to sit up, though. I'll just lie here and listen to the sound of his voice. Stuck in my head like a song. His midnight song.

Or I could hit redial for the real deal.

Nothing. No ring. No automatic jump to voice mail. Jason, you beautiful thing. I love you, but you really need to buy better stuff. Your house... the car, I mean. Whatever crappy phone you're using. This is America, Jason. Why are we living in its bargain basement?

More hours. My walk to the truck stop. My shower. Scrambled eggs. Packaged Pop-Tarts for Charlie, cuz that's what he wanted. Those are the highlights. Who needs to hear every footfall? I'm at the entrance to Snake Eyes now, alone without Jason. Without Hans. Or Yosef. My hoodies are getting spiritually cleansed for their big day at the felt. Remember?

And I've got the rest of these chips to move. Three-grand cash payment to Eugene, and I'll be done. I'll become a teacher. Or a waitress like my mom used to be, in between poker games and busted scams.

Not Hooters. Never that, or even worse, dancing on a pole. I'm worth so much more than that.

Jason loves me.

Through the doors from peaceful southern order to chaos. Slot noise, bright lights, signs pointing this way and that, from one form of gambling to another, and I need twelve steps so badly now, cuz my heart's pounding a mile a minute.

Oh no.

Him.

Philippe.

Playing alone against a dealer at the first blackjack table in my path.

He needs to be subtler. I'm not that stupid.

I take a seat beside him, but he hardly acknowledges my presence. Just a hint of a smirk to mock what I'm thinking. That he never dressed up like this for me? Suit jacket, pressed slacks. He looks almost human, except the lights make his hair-challenged head shine too much.

No, not that. Well, maybe a little, but I'm mostly thinking the other thing. "Why are you stalking me, Philippe?"

He's chuckling now, making me the fool.

The dealer motions to my purse and arches her brows cuz I haven't bought in.

I shoot her a look that surely will kill if I have my way. "I asked you a question, *Dad.*"

"I'm sitting here," he says without meeting my eyes, while signaling for a hit and then busting out with a jack on his fifteen cuz there truly is a righteous God. "You followed *me* here, not the other way around. Didn't you notice?"

"Notice *this.* It's all about placement. You're right by the entrance. Do you think my mom didn't teach me how to run a good scam? You know*, the woman you dumped in the prime of life?*"

He's got my eye now while the dealer reshuffles, and he better be careful. No more smirks. No sarcastic remarks. Or I'll be scratching *his* eyes out.

Philippe motions to his chips. Some reds. A few greens. Mostly the blacks. A tidy stack of fifteen or so. "I used to have a daughter working for me. I'm on my own today."

Pffft. My anger deflates like a stale balloon. Replaced by... pity? Sadness? This man is more alone than I am. "Don't I have any brothers or sisters?" The question might sound dismissive, but I don't mean it that way.

He stands with eighteen and wins a bet. "No."

"It's just *us* then?"

Philippe raises a hand to slow the dealer. He turns to me. Now *his* look could kill. He hasn't caught on that I'm begging here.

Where's the tissue? Every table's supposed to have a box. Unwritten rule.

My rule.

"I want Paris for you." He's looking down at the blacks again but doesn't see how they'll poison me.

"Yes. But I want... I want... I want you to take better care of yourself." I push from the table so he can get back to his game. This player. The only blood relative I have.

"Yeah, sister. I'll floss three times a day."

My chip-laden, emergency-clothes-laden purse catches him flush against the cheek. I swear, officer, the crazy thing took on a life of its own.

I'm heading for the door. Hurrying before security can tackle me and kick my ass. Or worse—ban me. I still have some chips to move. A debt to repay Eugene. And then I'll be free.

To his credit, Philippe isn't laughing. Or smirking. The man I now know as Dad just sits there with a hand on his face when I take one quick glance behind. I almost go back.

CHAPTER TWENTY-SEVEN

MY BUS HOPSCOTCHES FROM town to town, picking up a passenger here, spitting a few out over there. The streetlamps cast pools of light in the darkness, but they can't stretch far enough to keep the disembarking souls from disappearing into the gloom of night. A path I could soon follow.

Freddie suggested as much, but I won't think about it.

I latch my mind on to Claudia for sanctuary from darker notions. She and I didn't talk long, or well enough. Static overwhelmed our voices, ending my midnight call. Just as well. We need face-to-face time so I can look in her eyes while I explain all that's happened. Not just to me but to *us*. She needs to hear and believe the whole nine yards. Forward and back. Inside and out.

And she'll never buy a word of my story without the body language. The sincerity in my unwavering gaze.

Otherwise, I can't protect her from Runbad.

My only halfway decent angle is to tell her *every single thing that happened*. The entire convoluted tale. Beginning with the first time I met her at Snakes, or the first time *she met me* two weeks earlier, or my first encounter with Runbad.

Or the second.

When stuck in a loop, where's the beginning?

I need to find it and keep her out of the circle, changing the shaky future by yanking a few support beams out of the past. They say not to do that? Their rules, not mine. Runbad started this mess with his timeline tweaks. Enabled by a bunch of tricksters—Cynthia, Freddie, and every otherworldly suit who signed off on the genie scam. Whatever happens next is on them.

As soon as I hook up with Amy, I can warn her to never set foot in Snakes on Memorial Day weekend, or the gypsy casino where I passed those bad chips to her a couple days before. If we avoid the scam, maybe Runbad won't find anyone else to play. And if denied the way to transform from a jinn to a man, could be he'll give up on Amy and move on.

Slim chance? When given nothing but straws, all I can do is grasp.

But she and I might never meet if I pull the needle out of the groove. Will I lose all memory of the best that life ever offered me?

This bus is hitting every pothole known to man. I'm getting carsick.

Freddie's words crash through my wall. *In between the first life and the one that comes after.*

Why didn't I push back at him? He was lying. Adding more bullshit to the huge pile Runbad's been building.

Had to be.

But his suggestion has the ring of truth now, in this darkened bus. Perfect explanation for why Runbad could pluck me off the street to serve as the foil for his tricks. And why this gang of schemers can force me to handle whatever ridiculous Cupid assignments they have in mind going forward.

Here I am. Come and get me. I can fly. I can leap back and forth through the shadows of my life.

Except I'm missing a compass for holding a true course. So they move me around with theirs, I guess.

After all, I'm lost in limbo, aren't I? Caught in between the first life and the one that comes after. Rudderless. Clueless. Easy prey.

More Guns N' Roses fans in need of redirection? I'm their man.

More tourists?

I'm their zombie.

In so many words, he told me I died.

What else could he mean? Why else have I had the memory lapses, the dazed time jumps, the world with no future beyond a line at the Snake Eyes cage, separating me from those who went on living?

I'm blowing now, not breathing.

Deep one in.

Pushing it out.

Something doesn't make sense, though. I fish a pen from my pocket and slam it into the edge of my seat, *hard*. Forceful enough to pierce the fake leather, leaving a hole where the point entered.

This part I don't get.

Could a ghost damage the seat?

Could a wandering spirit make physical love to Amy?

Whatever I've become isn't so easily defined.

"Careful where you aim that pen."

Someone's sitting next to me. Blonde hair. Ponytail. The little girl must have climbed aboard at the last stop. I was too obsessed to notice her. Or she suddenly appeared out of nowhere. Fifty-fifty odds either way, based on how things have been going.

"Do you mind if I turn the light on and sketch?" she asks.

"Sure."

But she doesn't. She's looking up at the seat lights above us, no doubt wishing she had longer arms. How old is this kid, six? Seven? And her parents let her travel alone?

No, they're probably sitting somewhere else on the bus, and she wandered away when they fell asleep. Kids do that.

I get the light for her.

"Thanks." She's got a pad on her lap. A pencil in her hand. She starts sketching away.

I shift my focus out the window to brood in the darkness. There's gotta be a way out of all this.

A farmhouse drifts by. The porchlight is on, and I can make out a tree on the lawn until we round a bend in the highway. The landscape becomes featureless until the next farm. Is it tomorrow yet? I fish the phone out of my pocket and punch a number.

Nothing. Not a tone or beep or anything.

"Wow. That thing's old-looking." The girl snatches it out of my hand.

I grab it back and cram it into my pocket again, away from little girls who need to worry about whatever stick figures they're drawing and *not* my one avenue to Amy lately.

"You're *rude*."

She's right. I'm so obsessed I can't even humor a little kid. That isn't me. Normally I go out of my way.

Well, I *did* get the light for her, at least.

I check on her drawing. Best way to make up is to say something nice about whatever she's— The shape of a face has been born. Mid-length hair showering bangs across the forehead. A familiar nose. Recognizable mouth. She sketches the first eye. Then the other.

She's sketching Amy.

The back of my neck tingles.

What is this girl? Another jinn? Or whatever Freddie is?

"Not hardly." She gazes at me with eyes so deep I lose my way in them. This is no little kid.

"I'm Gabriella, you're Michael, she's Amy, and the others are a very bad crowd. Do you get all that? Especially the last part?"

Deep breath in. Blow out.

"I'll take that as a yes. And look, I'm no angel, either. Should have been. Deserved to be. But I'm not. I made a mistake or two along the line that got blown way out of proportion. So now, for atonement, I return favors sometimes. Lucky you."

"Favors?"

"Long story."

Yep. She's a jinn all right. I'll be getting off this bus at the next stop.

"Don't be silly." She flips to a blank page on the pad and speed-sketches an arrow pointing up. Then a second beside it, going the opposite way. "These are your boundaries. Up. Down. Not very high or low. Just like in real life. You can climb stairs or fly in an airplane, I guess, but don't expect to sprout wings."

"Real life as opposed to wherever I am at the moment?"

"Exactly." She's drawing two horizontal arrows now, and they're *long*. Stretching to each end of the page before seemingly wrapping around the back. They return again to the front and race to each end once more, forming a parallel, then three lines, and four.

I'm getting dizzy. I find refuge out the window and the steady blackness beyond.

"You have no boundaries sideways," she says. "That's how you got from New Orleans to Chicago in the blink of an eye. When a person strays beyond the first life but doesn't quite find the second, a couple more dimensions become available. But you're no ghost, so keep the damn pen in your pocket unless you have letters to write."

"Wait." My mouth is so dry. "How did I die, Gabriella?"

"Weren't you paying attention?" She giggles. "Sorry. I've developed a sense of humor in my old age. Good way of coping when everything goes wrong and it all comes crashing down on your head. But in your case, nothing's settled yet."

She's sketching again. A calendar page grows around the tip of her pencil. She flips to a drawing of a man at a cashier's cage. Then another page. A baby in a cradle. "The book isn't closed on you, but for now, these are your other boundaries. Forward and back across the slice of time you've carved with your life."

If she's saying I can rise from the dead at some point, I'm all ears. If she's saying I can't ever get past Sally in the cage, then I only have a week left with Amy, from the point in her timeline we shared a midnight call. After that, I won't be able to protect her from Runbad or anyone else.

"I'm saying I've dropped in to see whether we can make the past and the future a bit more fluid."

Sometimes when I chance past the cemetery, Billy picks thoughts out of my head this way. Except his comments aren't so ambiguous. He may mock me, but at least I know what he means.

"Billy?" Gabriella scowls. Grabs my wrist. The weight of her pressing fingers *forces* my gaze from the sketch pad to her endless eyes. "Suppose I'm real," she says. "You can't ignore the possibility."

I give it less than even odds, but yeah, she's right.

"The jinns move you from place to place. You stay put, more or less, and that's why they've always been able to find you later. I'm here to show you how to hide."

"I'm not looking to hide."

"Sure you are. Lie low until you find a way to open your book to a different chapter."

If she's talking self-preservation, I'm not—

"Not just for you."

The bus slows. She releases my wrist.

I manage to break eye contact and turn to the sunlight streaming through the window. We're looking down Loyola Avenue toward downtown New Orleans. "When... when is this?"

"Five days before the game at Snakes."

That wave of nausea? It's getting stronger. "So Amy—"

"She hasn't heard from you since you called early morning yesterday. We're at the beginning of a downhill slide for you two."

Great. A day stolen. This time by a golden-haired demon. Another trickster. A jinn.

"Look at me," she says.

No chance of that happening. Not with those deep, probing—

"I'll tone it down."

So I man up and steal a glance... at an innocent little girl. Blue-eyed, and just blurry enough to suggest the obvious. I need to see about that prescription.

"Or maybe I'm giving you an out," she says, "so you

don't get overwhelmed by too much *real*... to the point of uselessness."

"Who *are* you?"

"The multitude, but let's not get sidetracked."

Gabriella fades a bit more. "Since we're into truth here, I'll tell you what you won't admit to yourself, Michael. Maybe you do want to protect Amy, but mostly you're afraid of losing her."

Deep breath in. "She's my..."

"Everything? Let's go with lifeline."

Something's off. I try to blink through the moisture in my eyes to chase away the illusion that I can see clear through this girl to a passenger across the aisle. Her words have grown almost too soft for me to hear.

"Listen close then," she whispers. "Here's how you can skip to a place you've been before. Just close your eyes and picture it. Or for leaping somewhere new to you, imagine where it is on a map. Forward and back in time are just as easy. Think about whatever you might have been doing that day. Think *hard.* Close your eyes *tight.*"

Poof. Gabriella is gone. Disappeared.

"You aren't dead yet."

"Wait. What?"

"Don't obsess about it."

The bus stops.

Another deep breath.

I stagger in line behind the other passengers, careful to keep my distance... avoiding the touch of anyone who might root around in my head the way she did.

On the sidewalk, the glaring sun sobers me better than a cold shower. I can almost disbelieve the entire Chicago adventure and all that came after. Those hurricanes at my favorite bar and grill can pack a powerful punch.

I almost disbelieve until a woman separates herself from the small pack of friends and family waiting for their loved ones to disembark.

Tight black dress. Red heels. Blonde hair.

Cynthia.

She rushes over and catches me in a lovers' hug before I can react. Nibbles my earlobe. Whispers. "I want that phone. *Now.*"

"Fuck off."

She grips my wrists.

I forget how to breathe. My lungs burn. The sidewalk roils like an angry sea beneath my buckling knees.

"Where is it?" she hisses.

I shut my eyes.

I picture a map.

And on that map, a city in the desert. I always did want to find my way to Vegas someday.

CHAPTER TWENTY-EIGHT

WHAT DOES ANOTHER DAY without Chauncey mean?
Chauncey?
Just wait. Every day he's a no-show, he'll get a stupider name.

My new, stronger self takes his absence in stride, using the time to pass my remaining bad chips during a long session at Snakes. Craps, wheel of fortune, blackjack, clanging slot machines, glitz, glitter, crazy urges. I touch Yosef's tree on my bracelet more than once so my betting won't escalate from conservative to frenzied.

By the end of the day, every counterfeit black in my possession has been exchanged first for reds and greens and later for hundred-dollar bills at the cage. I spend the night in the flat I'm borrowing from Peter. A needy person would have waited in Chauncey's car for him. I don't.

Next morning, I'm back at Eugene's wobbly kitchen table with a kinsman looking across at me and my least favorite dog slobbering on my leg.

Kinsman, I say, cuz lines of genealogy, if not abhorrent behavior, now dictate I'm fifty percent of whatever this man is. Maybe more, depending on my mom's lineage.

I'm counting the money out on the table. *One, two, three,*

four all the way to thirty crinkly Benjamins. They dish 'em out new at the casino. Three thousand total.

Then he grabs the money and starts a recount. *One, two, three, four,* cuz what have I ever been but a liar and a thief?

Dog stomper, too, but the mutt saves himself by stopping the endless slobber and wandering off.

"Good." Eugene leaves the table, goes for a drawer by the sink, and comes back with the last twenty chips.

I fight the urge to count them. Unlike Philippe's place, which typically throws off an aura of relatively harmless drunken recklessness—especially now that I know the man's my dad—this guy's apartment always has a whiff of maniacal rage lurking just beneath the superficial moldiness. Besides, "I don't want those," I say. Even this mild lack of cooperation risks a repeat of the hair-pulling incident, but a girl's gotta take a stand.

Eugene gives me one of the those long, hard stares, cuz he can't possibly believe I'd refuse the spoils of my efforts, let alone insult him this way. "A deal is *a deal,* girly."

"I'm retired."

If looks could kill.

So I slide them into my purse and get the hell out before the man's head explodes and gets me with the shrapnel.

What to do with twenty black chips I don't want? Maybe they've got lower street value than two thousand bucks, but they should pass the wand test, so anybody can walk these over to Snakes and cash them in for the full amount.

Charlie? No, he's not exactly dressed for success. Besides, my friend on the street has always insisted he isn't some *panhandling charity case,* to quote his words. Rumor has it he gets a pension check every month from some long-ago day job. Charlie's pushing sixty, easily, more likely seventy, but he's the picture of health from whiling his days *in God's fresh air*—another of his quotes—and jogging three miles every morning just before dawn. I can verify, having joined him now and then.

He's happy. Why should I mess up his mind with too large an

offering? He really does look like he's doing fine. Bleached hair, deep tan, that perpetual smile.

I'm providing a firsthand account, cuz I just walked past him on the way to the truck stop. No, this doesn't mean I turned weak and wandered into Mike's neighborhood to look for him in his car again. I made a point of detouring away from the parking lot and taking the *northern* route past the cemetery. The one with a row of oaks and, this morning, a pair of blue jays plus an off-the-beaten-path pelican to make my day.

Before long, I sail through the creaky screen door and into the truck stop convenience store where I'm gonna help Charlie on the sly.

Meet Kirsten. She works one of the counters and looks the other way when I'm stealing stuff for Charlie, judging by the fact I've never been busted in this store. She's my age, and cute enough to do well as a waitress, receptionist, model, counterfeit-chip mover... yeah, that last thing's my plan for her. But only in a small way. She likes working an honest job, and I'm the last person who'd want to corrupt somebody. So I'll pretend the two chips I've pulled out of my purse are real.

"Hey, Kirsten."

"Hey, Amy."

"'Sup?"

"Not much."

Our conversations are always deep like this. But I've gotta take this one to a whole new level.

"I need a favor and I'm willing to pay for it," I say.

Kirsten looks left.

Kirsten looks right.

She leans over the counter.

She shakes her head.

"Amy, if this is one of your wild-assed schemes, I can't—"

That's right, folks. My reputation precedes me wherever I go.

"No. Honestly, it isn't. I wanna help Charlie and you know how stubborn he can be."

"Who's Charlie?"

I motion over my shoulder. "You know. The guy sitting on the newspapers, over by the cemetery."

"The one who always wears a Florida Marlins baseball cap with fishing lures sticking out of it?"

"Yeah. Charlie. Here, take these two blacks. Cash them at Snake Eyes. You keep fifty. With the other buck and a half, ask him what he needs every morning and buy it for him out of the store."

She looks doubtful. "*Every* morning?"

"Till you run out."

"Why can't you do it?"

"I don't come out this way often enough, and if my *absent* boyfriend doesn't show pretty soon, I'll be coming around less often than that."

"Total loser, huh?" She's smiling. We've bonded. The deal has been struck.

I'm soon out of there with two chips down and eighteen to go.

How many churches in this town? How many synagogues? Eighteen of 'em are gonna come out a hundred bucks ahead each in their collection platters, donation boxes, candle trays, or wherever the hell else they raise their money. I noticed a Baptist church earlier, over by the Greyhound station. That'll be my next stop.

Forty-five minutes and one collection-box ping later, I'm walking in the bright sunlight, humming a song, and minding my own business—which at the moment happens to be the project of cleansing any and all ill-gotten gains from my purse, leaving myself with just my emergency set of clothes and a remaining poker stake of four hundred dollars or so. That's roughly what I started with before I fell off the righteous path and mixed it up with my closest kin.

And oh, the four hundred? Once this project is completed, I'll be giving the felt one last shot. But if that fails, I'll hit the want ads hard. No more life of crime, and maybe no poker, either.

First, I've gotta wait for this damned Greyhound to clear

away from the street I need to cross. Come on, buddy, cough up your passengers and—

Good, there it goes.

Oh my God. Am I looking at that low-life bitch, Cynthia who snagged my complete loser of an ex-boyfriend and ran off to Haiti with him? Who's she hugging now?

No. It can't be.

Mike? I'm so flat-on-my-ass wounded I can't even think of a different name.

Okay. No problem. It's cool. I'll just pick up this loose tree branch here, cuz somebody has to clean up the litter from yesterday's storm. A hundred people will trip over the lousy thing before the city gets around to taking it away.

And I'll drag it behind me across the street once that truck scoots on by.

There.

Wait. Where's Mike? Cynthia's still standing here, but he's gone.

No problem. Mister *I'm a one-woman man a*nd I can have a little talk later. But for now…

Cynthia doesn't look too happy even *before* she notices me coming her way with a thorny weapon in tow. She's got hands on her hips as if she's pissed at the now-missing Mike as I am. But now, when she turns to find me closing in, her eyes grow wide as saucers.

"Hey, Cynthia."

"What are you dragging behind you there, Amy? It looks bigger than you are."

"Oh, don't worry, hun. I'm sure I can swing it just fine."

But I should have just let it rip without answering, cuz now Cynthia's waving at a cop on a bicycle, and he's heading over— all black helmet, black jacket, and thick black belt, bulging with cuffs, a billy club, and whatever else he might need to take me down.

"What's up, ladies?"

"She's threatening me," Cynthia says in her best southern

twang, coming across vulnerable enough to win any number of fine rewards. Maybe even an Oscar.

"That right, miss?" The cop's dead-eying me now.

"No, I didn't... I... oh hell, yeah. This bitch stole one man already and now she's going after the better one. Can you blame me for getting a little testy?"

"Crime never pays, miss."

Yeah. Like my mom never told me *that* lame cliché.

Come to think of it, she didn't, but I've been picking up stray bits of wisdom on my own lately.

Chapter Twenty-Nine

"Singing in the Rain" blasts from the speakers while fountains shoot water a hundred feet in the air. The monstrous, Italian-themed Bellagio welcomes me with open arms. I'm on the sidewalk, watching from the railing, my heart *pounding* in my chest. But not from the man-made splendor laid out before me.

I've done it. On my own. Jumped from New Orleans to Vegas just by thinking about it. *This* is a gift from a higher power.

If I can do this, I can do anything. I can protect Amy from danger.

I can avoid losing her.

Gabriella was right about my deeper motive, but it isn't a singular one. Paint me at least somewhat unselfish. The urge to free Amy from the trickery of any and all jinns ignites me above all else. I've even closed my mind to the rumors of my own death.

Gabriella told me not to obsess about that. The future's *fluid.* So I've shifted my obsessions. And honestly, I couldn't even breathe if I focused on being dead much longer.

So… where do I head to find Amy now? Seems to be midday, so the odds are good she'll be swapping false chips for real ones at Snakes. In that case, she's positioned herself a mere eyeblink from where I am in this twisty new universe. I don't even need to picture a map. Just closing my eyes and thinking Big Easy should do the trick. I'll meet her and spell out the history of a scam. And if I can't overcome her inevitable disbelief, there's always show-and-tell.

Poof, I've disappeared.

Presto, I'm back again.

I can transport myself, Amy, or whomever you've coined yourself today. Do my powers project? Maybe if I grab your hand, we'll fly together. See, you need to stay away from Snakes five days from now. Steer clear of the gypsy casino a day or two before that, too. Plus the apartment, in case Runbad shows up looking for you.

Or forget flying if magic isn't your thing. There's always my car. We'll lay low somewhere until the scam blows over.

"You can't hide from *me.*"

Oh no. Cynthia *again?*

Whew. The woman standing beside me at the rail isn't her. Close, though. Same sultry blonde look, complete with a slinky black dress and heels an inch too high. But those eyes...

I've seen them before. Two wells of dizzying darkness.

I edge sideways from this hypnotist of a woman and focus on Snakes, shutting my eyes tight to close the deal. But the music still plays. The fountain still roars. I sneak a peek and find her yet at my side.

She spares me by looking away. "I had to alter my appearance a little."

Huh? I'll buy some time. Distract her with conversation. And then shut my eyes *tighter.* Think *harder.* "Wait. Back up. How do we know each other?"

She shrugs, still thankfully staring out in the distance. "We met on the bus. But men don't often bring their little girls here to Vegas, do they? You and this better rendition of me... we do blend in nicely now, right?"

Good God. Gabriella transmogrified herself into a show girl?

A hooker? Should I do a double take? Question my sanity for the thousandth time? I've seen so much of this crap lately I'm taking it in stride. "Why didn't you just send somebody else from the team? With a better sense of blending. This *multitude* of yours."

"*I* am the multitude." More than a small dose of anger in her voice. Wounded pride.

I shut my eyes tight and click my heels together again, but she's burning her X-ray vision straight through my lids. Forcing them open to flay me with her thousand-year gaze.

The earth swims.

And steadies.

She's looking down at her stilettos. "Sorry. I'm working on my... issues."

Great. As if drowning beneath wave upon wave of untrustworthy supernatural beings isn't bad enough, now I'm dealing with a neurotic one.

"Pot calling the kettle black, mister."

Not even close. I'm flat-out crazy. Otherwise why would I imagine myself speaking telepathically to a shape-shifting woman-child who calls herself the multitude?

"Because I'm here to help. Although you do make it hard, Michael. Honestly, I don't like your attitude." But she's got me by the hand like a lover, pulling me from the fountains and along down the sidewalk.

She leads me toward the Roman columns of Caesar's, unmistakable even to a newbie like me. We walk and walk without drawing much closer. Everything is larger than life here. Distances are deceiving. Dreamlike.

"You're awake," she says. "Stop doubting this or we'll never win."

We? Someone who can pick thoughts out of heads like reading a newspaper or transform from a creepy-eyed little pest to a creepy-eyed big pest is more than capable of dealing with tricksters on her own from where I'm standing.

"I've been told not to change the past anymore," she says. "Things turned squirrely last time. And let's just say the slap on the hand was no fun, so I'm officially not touching a thing this go-round."

"Except *my* hand? What's your angle?"

Two barefoot women holding their shoes jostle past us.

Gabriella's eyeing them. Attention deficit? Fine with me if she decides to stalk somebody else.

But no. She squeezes my hand and quickens her pace, click, click, clicking down the sidewalk with me in tow. "Our interests are aligned," click, click. "Amy is Igor Tesfaye's cousin. You wouldn't know him, but he did a small favor for me once."

Sounds Russian. And French. What was the name of Amy's counterfeiter? *Philippe.* My *protect-Amy-from-mobsters* meter starts buzzing.

"Steady," she says. "Igor's a good man. He wouldn't like that his cousin unwittingly paired off with a jinn. So... someone helps me, I help them these days."

I stop in my tracks. Amy hasn't paired off with Runbad. She wouldn't.

Gabriella is swept forward by a throng of tourists, and I'm free to close my eyes... to think Snake Eyes.

Click, click, click. She's back. "Stop doing that, Michael. Do you have any idea how annoying you are?"

She's got my hand again, and we're closing in on an outdoor restaurant. "*I'm* not supposed to reshape the future by changing the past," she says. "But who's to blame me if *you* happen to make a favorable tweak or two, more or less on your own?"

Yeah, right. I'd better just focus on these trendy stone tables and benches. Or grab a newspaper from that machine over there and check the baseball scores. Can't let my thoughts stray to the idea Gabriella's sounding a lot like some high-octane jinn.

"I heard that. Don't make me turn my eyes on you again."

She doesn't need to ask twice. That's why I sit next to her on the same bench and not across.

She removes one heel and then the other, setting them on the table. "See? I'm blending. We're just another couple stopping for lunch."

"Yep. Me and my barefoot buddy. Here's the thing, Gabriella. Those two women we passed? They took their shoes off before the walk, not after."

"Don't mock me. You try learning a custom and see if you follow it perfectly the first time."

This quirky blonde siren is a riot. I'm beginning to like her enough to hear whatever yarn she's planning to spin.

"Worry more about me liking *you.*" She slips a purse from her shoulder, fishes her shades out of it, and fixes them on a classically shaped, albeit supernaturally crafted, nose. She turns to me, and her shielded eyes do me no harm. "A show of good faith, Michael. You see? I could hypnotize you but I won't."

"Swell. So what are we here to talk about?"

"I want to help you figure a few things out. All in the interest of our... alliance."

"Fire away."

"The jinns have been trying to win favor with God for ages," she says, "and the Cupids are a big part of their plan. They match this lonely heart with that one, hoping to better the overall gene pool so they can someday say they've improved the world. Only they're jinns, so the matchups often end badly. Are you hungry?"

"Huh? No, I'm fine."

She grabs a menu from the holder on the table, puzzles over it. Sets it down. The wind blows it away.

I don't laugh or she'll be taking those sunglasses off.

Instead, she watches the menu dip and dive, coming to a stop against the leg of another table. She sighs. Turns back to me. "Two of Peter's customers happen to be sitting in the same card game one day, and it's not the right place to be, for reasons you'll figure out, I'm sure, so he finds a way to get them to leave. Or you do."

Now *she* looks ready to laugh. I got duped by Runbad and we both know it.

"A third person at the table also needs to leave. You've

already done your favors, so he calls her himself, during the game. But Amy doesn't take kindly to his words. She hangs up on him. Remember?"

"I'm not sure, I... wait. Her phone plays the roadrunner beep, and I heard it go off a couple times. *Two* people called her, one after the other."

"Shh," Gabriella says. "Peter thinks only *he* called."

A waitress approaches. "Drinks?"

Gabriella stares at her, and I can almost see the gears turning in her head. She blew it with the heels. She messed up with the menu. Now she's afraid she'll ask for something stupid, and we won't *blend in.*

Might as well bail her out. "Two lemonades," I say.

The waitress scurries away, leaving me and a smiley blonde bombshell in her wake. "I'm beginning to like you a little," Gabriella says. "Anyway, Peter's late for the rodeo, so to speak. He's racing to the casino, stewing. Amy hung up on him. She isn't leaving the table. Everything's ruined. He's lost her forever.*"

"Wait. Why?"

"You'll figure that out, I'm sure. But meanwhile, just after you arrive at the cashier cage, Amy *does* leave. You see her go, and so does Peter. Although she hung up on him, she must have listened to what he told her. He'd asked for a moment alone so he could explain things to her. Out in the parking lot. That must be where she's going."

The drinks arrive. Gabriella sips hers. Smiles. "These jinns... they assume too much. Sloppy. Anyway, are you in good health, Michael?"

"Not if I'm dead."

"Maybe yes, maybe no," she says. "But before time stopped for you, I mean."

"I guess."

"No history in the family of heart attacks or brain aneurisms at too young an age?"

"Beats me. Probably not."

She slides out of the bench and stands. Fits her purse over her shoulder. "Thanks for the lemonade. I liked it."

"Great, but where's your story going?"

"Nowhere. I've told you all I can. Oh, wait. One other thing. That phone in your pocket? I reset it to call zero zero only, back when we were on the bus. Call me a control freak." And she's walking away. Mixing with the crowd. *Blending in.*

I try to chase after her, but she's gone.

CHAPTER THIRTY

I'M ON PHILIPPE'S STOOP again, getting ready to ring the doorbell. What else would I do, stay home—which I no longer have, really—and pine away for *Blahooty?*

Oh, by the way, my missing guy gets a stupider name every day he's gone, just like I promised. He hasn't called in five days—not before I saw him hugging that boyfriend-stealing bitch, Cynthia, and not after.

I'm wallowing in the hurt. For a girl who's been reeling, a brief affair takes on the proportions of forever after the first few days. A throwaway *I love you* becomes a wedding vow. My mind's got a good handle on this, but my stupid heart keeps pumping water into my eyes.

So what better way to cope than to patch up an even more ridiculous relationship as best I can?

Beginning with a question or two.

So, *ring, ring, ring* goes the doorbell.

And of course he doesn't answer.

Ring, ring, ring some more.

Nope.

Pound, pound, pound. This is getting old.

Oh, there he is, peeking out the blinds of the side window, just like last time.

Hi there, Philippe. Look, it's me waving. I'm not the feds coming with a swat team to take you down.

Long pause for him to stow his weaponry, just like last time, and...

He cracks the door open.

"I have a question for you," I say.

"Put your purse down first." He rubs his hand across the bruise on his cheek.

"Oh. Sorry about that. This crazy thing took on a life of its—"

"On the stoop, Candy."

"It's Rebecca today." But I've gotta comply, cuz there's this burning question on my mind, and he won't hear it if he slams the door in my face.

There. My dastardly weapon is stowed, leaning against my leg and threatening to spill what little I have onto the stoop. The stupid, broken latch. This is what I get for thinking the purse I bought at some merchant's stall for twenty bucks was an actual Coach. How far back does my long run of bad judgment stretch?

And what do I hope to accomplish here? He'll laugh in my face. Or spit in it.

I swallow. "Philippe, what did you like most about my mom?"

He stares at me, hand his on cheek.

Stares some more.

I'm ready to turn away.

"Everything," he says.

Everything.

Everything.

"Same here," I choke out.

More staring.

Back and forth.

Me through leaky eyes. I gather my purse and sling it over my shoulder. "Can I crash on your couch for a few days?" That's the second question, now that I've taken the measure of the man.

Philippe opens the door wider and retreats into the house. "I have an extra bedroom."

"That's way too permanent. Your couch is fine."

"Where's your suitcase?"

"All my important stuff's in here." I pat whatever this thing is on my shoulder. It holds my emergency change of clothes, a rabbit's foot my mom gave me the day I left home to drift south, a toothbrush, and a small poker stake. What more does a girl need? Except, "I have some other shoes at this guy's place, but I can't go to his flat anymore. He's coming home from Haiti any day now, and he won't be happy to find me there."

I'm babbling. So grateful for a couch where I can lay my head. My new normal, I guess. "A lot of shoes, actually, plus, you know, more of these sundresses and—"

"I'll send somebody over to get them tomorrow." He heads into the kitchen and returns with the ever-present bottle of vodka in his hand. "Want a snort?"

"It's the middle of the day."

"Fuck that." Philippe lifts the bottle and chugs it down. Then he hands it over, and I'm chugging too, cuz I've been reeling lately.

Him, too, I think.

A few hours later and I'm back outside.

Yep. *Hours.* But Philippe and I didn't drink the whole while. He told me stories.

I learned he's a low-level soldier. The Russian mob's equivalent of a working stiff. He coaxed a smile out of me with his tall tales about this big score and that one, always just beyond his grasp. Those poker chips in the cupboard? They mean a lot to a man like Philippe.

I cooked a fine meal while he talked and I listened—grilled cheese sandwiches. Two each. To soak up the vodka.

So I'm not drunk out of my mind anymore despite the half-bottle of booze we split. Just a tiny bit tipsy. The sidewalk gives a little with each step I take, all squishy beneath my feet. The casino lettering above the red canopy up ahead shows double until I focus really hard.

There. Now it's triple.

The entranceway is hard to get through, what with me first

bumping against a loitering lowlife on the right side and then another on my left.

"This way, sugar." Somebody's pushing me forward, his hand firmly on my butt.

I slap it away. "It's Berecca."

No. I mean Rebecca.

Honestly, I'm fine. Just a little wobble in my step, that's all.

First stop, *only stop,* is gonna be the poker room. I'm a reformed woman now, having steadfastly resisted the lure of Philippe's old stories and ambiguous chips. I didn't even toss a false maybe at my wistful dad. Tonight I've no illegal bones to move at the table games or craps or wherever. Just a small buy-in for a few hands of no limit. So I'm heading past the piano toward the stairs, with a quick glance at the bar to pity anyone who would drink from a glass when chugging straight from a bottle with one's criminal Russian dad is so much—

Cynthia?

That blonde whore is hitting on yet another man. She's sitting on the barstool beside her latest John, a red-nailed paw firmly planted on his knee.

I storm up to her—or stagger probably, from anyone else's perspective. "I'm gonna end you... just give me a second." Cuz I'm running to the bathroom first. Or else I'll heave right here in the bar area.

"End?" she shouts. "Just wait till Sunday."

That makes no sense, and the chill running down my spine from her empty threat doesn't, either, but the main focus at the moment is to puke in a stall. Thankfully my hair's only mid-length. There's nobody to hold it back for me.

Okay, I'm back again.

It's amazing what a quick purge followed by splashes of cold water in the face will accomplish. I'm not seeing triple anymore... in fact, almost not even double. I haven't achieved enough sobriety to punch Cynthia's heart out—that'll have to wait till I return from the card game—but I'm sufficiently un-plastered to make it up the stairs more or less.

Thank God for the bannister.

At the top of the staircase, I trip over the annoyingly loose carpet and burst onto the poker-room scene.

"Here to play?" a floorman asks.

"Uh-huh."

"Chips?"

I fish around in my phony purse and come out with a real poker stake. "I'll take a thousand in reds."

He grabs the money. Does a quick count. Frowns. "There's only four hundred here."

"Whatever."

I'm soon seated at a short-handed game. Me and six tourists, with two seats open. The cards fly, the game flows, and I'm not doing the fold, fold, fold thing I'm famous for. I've ditched the sleep-until-I-get-a-monster-hand strategy that bought me little more than eleven consecutive months of losses. See, there's this guy I used to know as Ricky way back, or Bob, I think maybe. He played a whole different style. And he won the day I saw him do it.

So instead of fold, fold, folding, I'm raise, raise, raising; not only doing a commendable job of remaining upright in a room that keeps swimming but also raking in chips with playing hands I can't even read. Except for one in particular that dances in front of me—not a blurred double but a perfectly sharp single—shouting at me to play as aggressively as possible.

The ace of spades and nine of hearts. A wonderful hand for bluffing if I'm an idiot like Ricky or Bob or whatever my Cynthia-hugging, missing boyfriend happened to christen himself that day. He forced my pocket jacks out *with an unsuited ace-nine bluff.*

So after a woman with spikey hair bets twenty and a man in a cowboy hat raises it to seventy-five, I'm shoving three stacks of reds into the pot. "Raise."

Everybody folds so fast my face is buffeted by the wind of their cards flying into the muck. This foolishness continues for another hour or so until I truly do have a thousand bucks in front of me. Maybe more. My stacks of reds are messy. Uneven. Like me.

I should leave now and sober up.

Gather my wits.

Savor the money I won and consider whether this new style of play is the true ticket to fame and fortune without any risk of Turkish prisons and maggoty food.

Oh my God.

Here's Blahooty entering the room, arm in arm with a blonde cunt I can't even think to rename, other than the term I just used, and my mom would have been washing my mouth out with soap for saying. She always said I should act and speak like a lady, but Mom never crossed paths with the likes of Cynthia, did she?

I won't even look at her, focusing my fury, hurt, and no small dose of puzzlement on Blahooty instead.

"Play nice now, baby," Cynthia says to him.

We wait for the dealers to change, and she's *all over* my man.

Ex-man.

I will not cling.

"Hey, Amy," he says, "small world.

Amy? He cuts me to the quick with that one. No explanation for dumping me. Not even the slightest guilty shrug over all his false endearments. And he's quit the name game, *our one special thing,* like it never existed.

"It's Rebecca." I'm out of my chair or I'll lose it. Slamming my chips into racks so I can go home and cry, cuz I *have* lost it. And what home, exactly? Just a couch and my awkward attempts to bond with a man I can't decide whether to bean with my knockoff purse or help drink to an early grave.

Oh, no. What's *this?* Blahooty is ridiculing my former life of crime by sliding two blacks to me for change.

"Seriously? Are you mocking me?" But I have too goddamn many chips to fit in my racks and allow me to leave with some dignity. So I make change for the bastard, pushing over a couple stacks of the reds that betray me by being too sloppy fat in my moment of darkness.

This isn't ending without a reminder of what he's losing. "What, may I ask, is *your* name today?" I say.

"Um, Ricky?"

Please. Not that. I'll never be able to hear the name again without crying. I grab a fistful of bones to throw, but he isn't worth getting banned over. "You *told me* you were a one-woman man, and I *believed* you. Now you walk in here with some whore on your arm and refer to yourself by the very name you coined the first day we met?"

Yep, I sound ridiculous here, like somebody's worst nightmare of an ex-girlfriend loser, but it's the liquor talking. Really. It is.

"Who are you calling a whore, bitch?" Cynthia lunges out of her seat, spilling her drink all over the table in the process.

Honnnkkkkkkkk.

An air horn? Seriously?

Two musclemen hurry into the room, and not the hoodie kind I might bond with before they start hauling me out to the street for my show of public drunkenness and lost pride.

No, wait. They're dragging *him* away instead.

"You're kidding me, right?" he says. "You clowns wanna toss *me* out of here?"

Of course they do.

Cuz there *is* a God.

Or at least a big angel.

God would have bitch-slapped Cynthia, too, while He was at it.

I look at her, but I'm spent.

"Wait till Sunday," she hisses.

"You can find me at Snake Eyes," I say. "I'll never set foot in this shit hole again."

I know, I know. My mom wouldn't have liked the *s* word, either. *She* was a lady from top to bottom, and I didn't learn enough from her before she died.

I keep waking up for more water. Kudos to Philippe for leaving a glassful on the end table for me at some point overnight.

Of all people, he surely knows what a body needs after too much alcohol. But the act of sitting and reaching for the glass kills me. My head. My *back*. Couch cushions are so unforgiving.

Can't wander off in search of better quarters, though. Not unless it means going out and finding my own place. Philippe's second bedroom would be too much like giving up.

I haven't fallen that far... yet.

I kick the blanket to the floor—another surprisingly kind offering by my dad while I was conked out—and I manage myself upright.

"Can't sleep?" Philippe's in the wicker chair across the room, the nightlight doing just enough to make him seem real. And he's forgone his bed cuz what, he's watching over me?

Totally unnecessary. I'm a self-help kinda gal. But I do like him more now, a little. "What time is it?"

"Almost dawn, I think."

"I need some air. Can I borrow a flashlight?"

"Yeah, okay." A few beats later, he's rummaging in the kitchen. The sound of drawers opening and closing explodes in my head, and the light over the old Formica table blinds me even from a distance.

I escape to the front door, open it, and take a deep breath. Yeah, I slept in my clothes and maybe I reek, but who cares? The false promise of a soon-to-rise sun shrieks my name.

"Here." He comes up behind, pressing a heavy flashlight in my hand. "Want some company?"

"Not for this. But I've got a date on Sunday with somebody a little taller and a whole lot meaner than me. Wanna be my second?"

"Got your back," he says.

So yeah, I like him a little.

I leave alone and head the wrong way. If I'm able to walk anywhere, why would I go *there* to torture myself? Maybe my aimless wander in the flashlight-lit darkness brings me to the old cemetery wall by happenstance. To the parking lot a few blocks beyond where a burned-out streetlamp stands over what's sure to be a truly sordid and gut-wrenching scene.

In fact, my hand's gotta be grabbing the handle and yanking the car door open on its own.

I couldn't possibly be this big a glutton for punishment.

The two of them are inside. My new Things One and Two. Cuddled. Naked.

He lurches up first when I shine the light in their eyes. "Huh!"

Oh, poor baby, I woke you.

"Who?" And *she* doesn't even try feigning modesty, leaving it all out there for me to despise. A pair of hooters way too perfect. And the rest of it.

Who is the right question, bitch. I'm gonna be your worst nightmare. But we'll wait till our Sunday playdate. My skin crawls at the thought of *any* contact with your bare flesh in this ugly scene. Not even by my fists or the heel of my shoe.

Him, on the other hand... I have words for him. But I'm all over the place, not sure what to say that won't come out whiney and broken. I'm unsure of his name in this broken game of ours, clueless whether to cry, beat him senseless with the flashlight in my hand, or hit *myself* with it, not in the head but the chest. "Damn you, Ricky!" My heart's the problem here, spilling emotions out of my mouth like I'm the star in one of my mom's damned soap operas.

"Who?" First her and now him with these profound questions. And he's covering up like, what, he thinks I'm gonna clobber him in the nuts with the flashlight? I should.

Nah, he isn't worth the effort. "We're done, asshole. Next time we meet, I don't know you." There. That should cut him down a peg. But still...

"Wait! What are you talking about? I don't—"

Okay, fine. I need this. And so do you, *Ricky*. "Bastard." I let the flashlight fly. Right against his knee.

That had to hurt.

Almost as bad as my heart.

I'm out of there.

CHAPTER THIRTY-ONE

GABRIELLA'S GONE. COULDN'T FIND her. So I'm back at our table in the outdoor café behind Caesar's... *stuck* at our table, to put it more accurately. Nobody gave me a user's manual for this time/space jumping thing. Close my eyes? Think about where I wanna be? Not working.

From where I'm sitting, they're *all* control freaks. Runbad, Cynthia, Freddie, Gabriella... at least *she* admitted her nature. They take delight in messing with the lives of us ordinary humans. Or in my case, my almost life. I'm neither here nor there, am I?

I can't click my ruby slippers and fly to Amy. Gabriella took that option away, gluing me here in Vegas with only one option available—the phone in my pocket with a single number to call.

According to Runbad, zero zero gets me Amy at the poker game in Snakes. She'll be sitting there hating me, because she caught me with Cynthia in the backseat of my car.

I didn't cheat on her at the time. From my perspective, our relationship hadn't started yet. But any excuses catch in my throat. In the first place, she'd never believe me. Besides, I had no business sleeping with some blonde bimbo I'd only just met. Seeing myself through Amy's eyes makes me small, no matter the angle.

I never want to be small in her eyes again. Not for fear of my embarrassment but because she's got too much hurt in there already. Anyone alone with Amy can see it when she lets her guard down. She can't be dragged down further by the likes of me.

So Gabriella wants me to call Amy now, and I must.

To say I'm sorry.

To say good-bye.

Gabriella owes some guy named Igor Tesfaye a favor, and here it is. His niece will cut ties with the poison also known as me and maybe find somebody worthier.

I owe the same favor.

A perky blonde waitress comes by with a fresh drink. "It's happy hour," she says.

"Even for lemonade?"

"Yep!" She flashes a winning smile. "Here's to good health."

Wait.

Wow.

Here's to good health. Gabriella wouldn't tell me much directly, but she sure was good at dropping clues. Did I have a history of heart problems in my family? Brain aneurisms at an early age? Nope. And I'd been taking good care of myself.

But I died? *Maybe yes, maybe no,* she said.

Time to consider the affirmative. At least until I start hyperventilating. Then I'll stick my head in the sand again.

I died, and that means something happened. Healthy people my age don't keel over for no reason.

Maybe the *when* will tell me the *how.* I hope so, because the timing puzzle is easy to solve. Runbad spelled it out for me the day he drew a line at the cashier's cage, separating the past from the future. Sally's wand chirped, she said something to me, and poof. Next thing I know, I'm at the Riverwalk hours later in my newborn, time-traveling, zombie existence.

If I'm healthy at the cage, which I was, we're talking external forces taking me down, man-made or otherwise. And maybe widespread. So let's imagine something big happened, as opposed to a ceiling tile taking me out. That would explain why Runbad wanted a couple people to leave the game. They were assigned to him as part of his Cupid role. He couldn't match them up with their soul mates if they were shot up, blown to smithereens, drowned in a flood, or otherwise indisposed.

A catastrophe of some sort might also explain why Cynthia wanted my phone. If something big's gonna happen, and I don't call Amy before zero hour, she doesn't leave the table.

Then Cynthia has Runbad all to herself with no competition. Hey, she ran off to Haiti with the guy, snatching him away from Amy once already. Why not make it permanent?

I'm reaching for the phone in my pocket. Fumbling to get it out, because my hand's shaking so badly.

Wait.

Would a jinn do such a thing? Murder by willful neglect? I wish Freddie had told me more about them. All I know is this. If my deduction is right that something massive happened at Snakes, Runbad had the opportunity to save numerous people.

He only went after the two from his work assignment… and Amy, because he has a thing for her. If a bomb went off, everyone else in the vicinity died.

Runbad didn't lift a finger.

And now, in my new head-*out*-of-the-sand mode, I know the real reason to call Amy. No need to go through the math in my head any longer. Runbad's phone call to her at the game didn't work. She hung up on him. I was there. Sitting right beside her.

I remember.

She took a *second* call.

Maybe from *me?*

And then she left.

I wrestle the phone out of my pocket and punch the number.

CHAPTER THIRTY-TWO

CALL ME AMY. CUZ the name game gets old when there's no one to play it with.

Sure, Philippe's standing right next to me at the entrance to Snakes, but he has no sense of humor. If I call him Sammy, the name will fly over his head, ricochet against the door, and smack me in the face with a reminder not to fall head-over-heels without a feeling-out period when a Mike, Bob, Stewart, Henry, or whoever strays into my life.

The next time a man comes along, I'm not gonna throw myself at him. People go on three dates before the first kiss for a reason. Time doesn't merely heal—which I sure could use right now—it also reveals.

My mom never shared that little nugget. I had to figure it out on my own. And sadly, I've never been a quick study when it comes to love.

Mike brushed past us a moment ago and headed inside without a word, like I don't exist. And that's fine. I thought he was special, but my reads haven't been good lately. Not since my mom killed herself.

There, I admitted it.

So she's a memory, Mike's out of the picture, too, in a different way, but this Russian gangster lurking beside me? The guy who followed me all the way over here, lagging about a half block behind, thinking I wouldn't notice? He has my back. And I trust him now, even though I didn't when we first met. Maybe that's the way relationships are supposed to work. A cautious approach at the beginning.

Duh. Of course that's the way they're supposed to work.

Even in the case of this surly, balding Russian, I need to give the test drive more time. Still, the first few spins around the block are looking good. He might've been late to the table when it came to family values with my mom, but here he is for me. Not that I'm looking for company at the moment. "Listen, Philippe, I get it. You caught me in a moment of weakness when I asked you to be my second, and now you're here to back me up. But I don't need that."

"Maybe I'm just heading to the same joint you are," he says.

"Well, good, cuz I don't think this playmate of mine is gonna show. Besides, I can fight my own battles."

He shrugs. "I'm just here to move chips. My helper quit on me."

I push through the door. "Blackjack's off to the left."

Philippe follows me in and keeps on coming, even though I turn *right*. He's got my back whether I want it or not.

And I do keep liking him more and more.

We weave down the aisles past table games and slots designed to suck up every last dime, and into the poker room, where the odds should favor me, at least a little. But Phillipe? "You'd be better off spraying those bones somewhere else," I say. "How about betting on red over at the roulette wheel?"

"Poker." He matches me step for step until he stops dead in his tracks, so suddenly I pull up, too. We're at the entrance to the poker room, and sitting at table four are none other than Yosef and Hans.

With all else going on, I'd completely forgotten. It's the day before Memorial Day. Spiritual cleansing must be complete. God, Yosef looks about twenty-pounds heavier. Bulky. When he and Hans said they were buying lined hoodies, I didn't take it to mean they'd be packing their sweatshirts with body fat from overeating at whatever spiritual retreat they headed off to.

Regardless, they're ready to play cards, and I'm smiling wide enough to split my face. Thanks to Philippe first and now my two best friends, my world is a little less broken.

We buy chips at the cage, Philippe throwing caution to the wind as he swaps a few blacks for reds. I should school him on discretion and etiquette when spraying bad bones, but he's yet to strike me as the listening type. A Russian gangster still alive at age sixty-five or whatever knows it all.

I find the most worrisome friends.

And family.

The floorman ushers us to the same table where we're to sit side-by-side in seats one and two, right next to my best hoodie buddies in seats three and four. Mike's in seat six, potentially making the whole scenario such a nightmare I might otherwise leave. But not now. Nope, not with my friends and family surrounding me like a cocoon. Except...

The glare I'm getting from Hans is anything but warm. He's sitting to my immediate left, close enough for me to hear his sharp whisper as if it were the roar of a lion. "We *told* you not to come."

The shock of his anger wells my eyes. I've been an emotional wreck lately for so many reasons, and now somebody I adore is treating me like the plague? "Just f-for a little while." I barely manage not to burst out blubbering.

As for Yosef, he doesn't say a word. Just sits in his chair staring at some point in the distance.

The air has thickened with far too much tension. I'm ready to get up, wish Philippe well, and leave, but the dealer's already dishing out the cards. I *still* oughta just fold without looking and hit the road, but what if I've got something really good down there?

It's a sickness, I know. The twelve-step process is shouting my name.

But just a little peak at these two cards and I'll be on my way.

Ace queen. That's solid. Anything better than ace ten always gets my heart pumping a little. Besides, maybe I need to just lose myself in the action right now.

Some Asian guy with a Guns N' Roses sweatshirt bets two dollars, and I make it eight.

Fold, fold, fold, fold, and...

"Make it thirty."

Okay. Three guesses who just did that to me again. I'm folding for sure, cuz I just don't want to deal with Mike even one little bit today, but first, it's time to show with my death rays exactly what I think of him.

Hey Mike, I'm staring in the general direction of your soul, except you don't have one, do you? So you can go ahead and take all the time in the world glancing around those TV screens hanging down from the ceiling *everywhere,* because the electronics salesman who walked in here one day did a killer job of a presentation. Go ahead and do that, but I'm still staring. Do you see any pain in my eyes? Nope. Not even a little, cuz I've moved on.

Oh, you're ignoring me to study Philippe now are you? He'd kick your butt if I asked, but like I told *him,* I can fight my own battles, thank you.

Here. See these two blacks in my hand now? You changed them for my reds the night before last. Want em back? Maybe I'll just toss them in the pot here, and scare you out of it.

Hans and Yosef catching your eye now? Well they're in my doghouse at the moment for not wanting me here, but they've got my back, too.

Oh go ahead and ogle the woman to your left now. She's just another tourist in a poker game. Easy prey for you I'm sure, if you're looking for some backseat company tonight.

Enough. I'm gonna bust out crying for sure if I keep channeling my pain this way. And yep, I am hurting. "Fold."

But I'm not done. I can't stop myself from mixing it up. Call me the opposite of passive-aggressive, I guess. The seat to Mike's left is empty. I motion toward it, the dealer nods okay, and I'm on my way over to sit right beside the man who said he loved me more than once, less than two weeks ago. For no good reason that I can fathom.

"Tell me you didn't have something stupid like ace nine off-suit." Yep, I'm begging now. We had fun with this hand, Mike. You had fun with *me*. I'm still here.

"Right," he says, and his eyes are dead.

"I'm a sucker for dark-haired strangers. Why not let guys like you win a pot now and then?" I've gotta leave. I'm bantering with this guy for what... the hope he'll change his mind about dumping me? So pathetic.

"Thanks, Mom," he says.

Before I go, he can have his unlucky blacks back. I've got a new aversion against poker chips of that denomination. Philippe may have found a small piece of my heart, but reminders of a counterfeit scheme that could have destroyed my life aren't high on my list. "Change please?" I slide the blacks in his direction, batting my eyes and smiling the way Cynthia might, but he doesn't get the sarcasm.

He pushes two stacks of reds to me. "Lucky chips."

Okay, time to let him have it. "I doubt that. You're one of those guys who live out of their cars while chasing the dream. Vegas, the World Series of Poker, and so on. What's so lucky about a wasted life?"

Got him with that one. Those damnably magnetic, blue eyes widen for a moment.

"It's a nice car," he says. "The backseat's comfy."

While we're fencing back and forth, hands are dealt and folded. His and mine. Hand after hand. Yosef's, too. And Hans's. They've been folding since I sat down. I won't need to teach them my playing strategy. They've nailed it. Only Philippe goes at it against the tourist and the rock band fan, flinging enough chips around to drag a pot or two. Everybody else is either card dead or too caught up in the drama of the moment.

"I didn't mean that the way it sounded," Mike says.

Honestly, I don't know how it sounded. Was he suggesting

I'd ever crawl into a space previously occupied by Cynthia? After she left stains behind from her disgusting nakedness?

I'm fussing with my hair now, to stall till I can think of a halfway decent retort.

Gotta be one in here somewhere.

Okay, how about, "Like you'd ever find anything but trash in your backseat." Wow. Dug deep for that one and came up with a gem.

And now for the lethal blow. To let him know the name game is over. Cuz *we're* over. "I'm Amy."

"Mike." He stabs my heart yet again.

Beep-beep... kapow. My phone to the rescue. Anything for a distraction from this. I fish it out of my purse. "Hello?"

"Amy! It's me. Listen, you gotta leave. Now! Meet me in the parking lot and I'll explain everything."

Seriously? First this mess with Mike and now Peter's back in town from Haiti to torment me? "I kicked you out of my life once already. Don't make me do it again." And I hang up on the bastard.

Beep-beep... kapow.

I'm cursing the redial feature now. Peter doesn't know when to quit.

Except... that's not his caller ID.

I know this number. Wrote it down. It's Mike's from when he called me at dawn. And again at midnight a thousand years ago. *Mike,* who happens to be sitting next to me. "Hello?"

"Courtney! I'm using the wrong name so you know it's me. *Do not* hang up. Please! You're sitting there hating me, and I'm right next to you at the table, completely oblivious to what's been happening. Yeah, go ahead and gape at me now. I remember that part."

Does vodka have a lag effect, returning its victims to drunkenness a day or two after the fact? I know this man's voice on the phone, but he's right at my elbow, *not* on the phone. Looking at me in utter confusion, probably cuz I'm staring the hell out of him.

"I told you I've been time traveling, Courtney. How else could I be in two places at once? Now listen. You've gotta get up from the table and get the hell out of the casino *right now*. Wish me well or whatever and get out. Find the cops. Something bad is gonna happen after *I* leave the table, so you've gotta go first. *Move.*"

Cops. With Philippe vulnerably sitting here with hundreds in illegal chips? "No, I can't go anywhere near them."

Am I floating? I can't feel the seat under my butt or the floor beneath my feet. What's the word for audio hallucination? I think that just happened to me. I'm fumbling my chips into a rack and rising from the table, cuz I need some air. And not because Mike told me to leave. *That* was just a voice in my head, ending in static. Never real. Not for a second.

So I'm standing in the entrance to the poker room now, and I have no recollection of how I got here. Staggered like a zombie, more than likely. I'm watching the game left behind, watching forever. Long enough for Mike to rack his chips and peel to the cage. The Asian leaves for a smoke or something. His chips are still on the table. The tourist takes off, leaving her chips behind, as well. Odd.

Dealers are doing their shift-change thing all around the room. Table four's dealer leaves without a replacement... probably since the game is breaking up. Here comes Philippe, heading in my direction, leaving only Hans and Yosef behind. "You okay?" he says.

"Yeah, I, uh... honestly, I'm not sure."

We're moving now. He's hurrying me toward the exit doors.

"Bad vibe over those two," he says.

Huh? I slow.

"Come on," he says.

But I can't. Something popped into my head so petrifying I can't move. "You... uh... Philippe." I grab his hand and squeeze. "My playdate. I think she's outside. Could you go check for me? Tall blonde. Heels too high. Mean eyes. Red dress probably."

"Got it covered." He's on the way to the door.

But I'm still frozen to the carpet, cuz my mind cannot comprehend the crazy fit of mad deduction sending chills up and down my spine. *Lined hoodies. A loved one killed by an American bomb. Paradise.* How could I have missed all the random clues they'd been throwing at me almost from the day we met?

I free one foot, lifting it high. Then the other. Now I'm running, *running,* back to table four, where Hans and Yosef sit with their heads bowed. My panting breath must be somebody else's. I've left my body behind in the dust I'm moving so fast.

I shoulder into a floorman and hurry on by.

"Watch where you're going," he snarls at my back. "Where's the fire?"

Finally, I reach them. "No!" My voice only a squeak.

Their heads are still down. For final prayers? Hans looks up and gapes at me. Yosef's reaction comes slower. Just a gradual slump deeper into his chair.

I collapse into the seat on his left. The position of power in Texas Hold 'em, but I'm a wreck.

Hans is the tougher of the two. That's been obvious from day one. I cannot win against him. But this one? He's in love with me. I've known that. The parallel to my own downhill slide since the death of a loved one—the collapse into head-over-heels romance in the hope of somehow refilling an empty well—I recognized his malady the day he gave the tree to me.

"Yosef." I'm able to muster little more than a whisper.

He doesn't respond. Just sits there, head bowed, his fist clutched around the detonator.

"Yosef, you called me your little sister, remember? Do you seriously want them to be scraping pieces of me off the walls?" Tears warm my cheeks, but I haven't lost it. I'm putting all I've got into as firm a*nd stern* a tone as I can muster. This is lecture-from-Mom time.

The lives of anyone within a hundred feet are at stake.

All in at table four.

"Leave us," Hans hisses.

I ignore him, especially avoiding his eyes. If I look into them and break down, I lose. *Everyone within the blast range loses.* I'm shivering so hard my teeth chatter, but I plow on. "Yosef, look at my bracelet. The tree. *Strength.* Know what that means in this scenario?"

He shakes his head. Does his shift out of a catatonic state provide a ray of hope? Maybe not. I don't know what the tree *means* in this scenario if he asks.

Think, Amy.

Come up with something.

Think, Courtney. Be the amazing, fire-breathing vixen you'd hoped Mike/Ricky/Bob originally imagined you to be.

"Yosef... I know they killed Elsa and most of you, but if you do this thing, *nobody* will remember her the right way. Dozens of other Elsas will die. Just look around at them all."

"Amy." Hans has had enough. The rage plain in his voice. "Get the fuck—"

But I know the magic words for stalling a bully. Learned them in my criminal days. "Back away, Hans," I shriek. "Just back the *fuck* away and let me speak to my big brother."

Every eye in the poker room is probably on us now. *Three down-and-out gamblers,* they must be thinking. Arguing about shrunken bankrolls, lousy luck. And that's good. Because I'm goddamned sure if anyone smells the danger and starts panicking, Yosef will, too.

Holy God, that would be bad.

Please, Mother. What would you do to fix this? What do I say to this broken man?

No answer. It's on me. And I better speak fast before Hans recovers from the shock of learning I can be three parts witch when I need to be.

"You can do this, but you won't, Yosef. Tell them *that,* and you'll memorialize her while shaming them. Otherwise..."

Yosef rises from his chair.

He gazes at me.

Long.

Hard.

He looks past me to Hans.

"Do it," Hans says. "Now."

I close my eyes. It's over. Will it hurt? Is there a heaven? I've no right to think I've ever earned one.

One beat.

Two.

Three.

Nothing happens.

I open my eyes in time to see Yosef climb onto the table. He raises his hooded sweatshirt over his head. Lifts it off. Revealing what anyone can see is a suicide vest. Wires. Explosives.

Yep. We're done for.

People *are* panicking now. Shouts, screams from all around.

I shut my eyes again.

"I can do this!" Yosef shouts. "But I won't."

Dare I sneak a peek?

He's removing the vest. Lowering it to the table. Gently. Cuz that damn thing is *loaded.*

How long do I sit here like this? Staring. Listening to Hans cry. To Yosef cry. Minutes? Hours?

A swat team ten million strong descends on us. Me shivering. Hans and Yosef raising their arms.

The cops drag Yosef off the table. Pull Hans out of his chair. And cuff my hands behind my back, *tight,* so painfully tight before they haul me out of there.

But worse than the physical pain is the black cloud of loss swallowing me up. I don't know what it is. A piece of my life sliced away? Like dreaming I met someone and fell in love only to awaken to emptiness? Cuz if this mysterious lover with a thousand names was only a dream, I'll *never* fill the hole in my heart? Something like that, only much, much worse.

I can't stop crying as they lead me away.

CHAPTER THIRTY-THREE

I'VE GOTTEN TO KNOW a guy named Charlie. He lives on a pile of cardboard and newspapers along the way to the truck stop where I shower in the mornings. Charlie wears a sideways baseball cap with fishing lures sticking out of it. A raggedy man but sharp as a tack. Coolest guy I've met in a while.

This morning, I've walked the three blocks out of my favorite parking lot, and here he is, camped out between sidewalk and street. "Hey, Charlie."

"Back at ya, Mike." He flashes a gap-tooth smile.

Next move is scripted by habit. I try handing him a buck.

He waves me off. "I'm already provided for, son."

"Don't call me son."

We've been lobbing the ball back and forth like this for weeks. Our secret handshake. But I'm gonna throw him a curve today. "Why not stick it in your pocket and save it for a rainy day?"

"You mean like Philippe?"

"Good one. You're quick."

"Gotta be or I'll get trampled down here."

I don't read the papers much. Anything worth knowing usually comes to me through osmosis. Lately, though, Charlie's been filling in the gaps. A month has gone by since the day of the *Snake Eyes Three,* but he still comes across the occasional juicy story. Like this one…

After the Three get dragged out of the casino, the cops and feds go to work. They interview me and the other eyewitnesses—my fifteen minutes of fame for playing a while at the same table as them—they raid a few apartments, chase some new leads, and they come up with another culprit. A discount arms dealer who sold the suicide vest for a couple thousand bucks. So, backslaps all around for that score.

Meanwhile, off to the side, the FBI gets a tip about a counterfeiter, and they swoop in on somebody's humble abode a *second* time. Man named Philippe with suspected ties to organized crime. Sure enough, they find a stash of phony poker chips in a kitchen cabinet. Two hundred seventeen thousand dollars total. Another big score.

Except… the chips aren't phony. They're real. He's been buying them for years and saving them for his estranged daughter.

So he's in the clear, right? Not even close. The IRS swoops in and takes every last chip away, because poor Philippe can't provide proof he ever paid taxes on the money he's been using to buy them. The tax bill plus penalties eat up the whole stash.

And the final twist to the tale? Philippe's estranged daughter is *her.* Ringleader of the Snake Eyes Three. Amy or something. The press took to crowning her the *Many-Named Goddess,* because of all the IDs the feds found in her purse that day. Story goes she called herself Amy when they arrested her, but she's been switching to a different name every morning. Take that with a grain of salt, though. How could anything but speculation leak out of whatever black site she's stashed away in?

"Hey, before you go." Charlie rummages beneath his papers and comes up with a handful of yellow ribbons. "Take a few. In case you pass some trees today."

I've been seeing more and more ribbons tied around trunks lately. Charlie, too, apparently.

"Thanks, man." I grab one, shove it into the sleeve with my new netbook, and head on down to the truck stop.

Yellow ribbons. Yeah, that's the thing. The Snake Eyes Three started out as terrorists, but they're folk heroes now. Word is they counted coup that day in Snakes—something the Plains Indians took pride in a hundred fifty years ago. Instead of killing, they gained prestige by *touching* an enemy and escaping unharmed.

Except these three didn't come out unscathed at all. The two men have already been charged with felonies. As for this chick, Amy, the local DA swears that if the feds get stupid and let her go, she'll do six months minimum for the misdemeanor of possessing those fake IDs. Three years if he can prove she's a distributor. He's hoping he can.

Crazy. This fool needs to tone down the rhetoric. His message isn't sitting well with the yellow-ribbon contingent.

Our numbers are growing. This Many-Named Goddess? She resonates. Charlie often tells another story to anyone who'll listen. He claims to know her and insists her name *is* Amy. Met her mother, too, maybe ten years back when he took his cardboard and newspapers up to Missouri for a little vacation. Amy and her mom squatted right next to him out there on the sidewalk for a whole summer. The mother was way down on her luck at the time.

Flash forward to a couple years ago. Amy's an adult now, not the tough sixteen-year-old kid he knew. She comes down to visit him here in New Orleans and decides to hang around. Plays some cards at Snakes for a while. She's a poker player, like me. But then one day last June, she gets word her mom died.

Amy dies a little, too. Her eyes go blank. She can hardly function. Charlie makes room on his newspapers for her. So she lives on the street for a week or two before she rouses herself and kicks her butt back into action.

Can't hold her down, Charlie tells everyone. *She'll get out. Wait and see.*

Cool story. I don't believe half of it, but tall tales do have a habit of spreading. I've posted this one on my blog to give it some legs. If the feds and that DA don't release Amy soon, we commoners will be storming the bastille.

I mean, look at *me*. Here I was trying to chase a Vegas dream but almost as destitute as she was. Maybe not camped out on the sidewalk, but living out of one's car is only half a step higher up the ladder. She overcame all that. Made a statement people might remember for fifty years. So what do they do? They lock her away and swallow the key.

Meanwhile, I've made it to the truck stop. Been paying extra to store my netbook in this locker, but I've gotta protect the stories.

Damn, these showers are cold this morning. See, that's what I'm talking about. We don't have it easy, we homeless ones. Or the mentally challenged with imaginary friends. Our stories are interesting, sometimes inspiring, and we need to be heard.

I hop the hell out, my hair barely wet. Towel off, dress, and fetch the netbook. Then off I go through the store's perpetually squeaky screen door and into the clammy morning air of the Big Easy. Destination Snake Eyes to make one kind of statement— *Raise*—so I don't have to worry about the next meal when devoting most of my time to a rewarding if underpaid new calling.

A few blocks down, and I'm next to the cemetery. Voices rise from across the whitewashed wall, spiraling up from the crosses, stone vases, towering angels, and plump baby nymphs keeping guard. The loudest words hitch a ride on shimmers of southern heat, floating over to find me.

You know her.

Not really, Billy. We've had this argument before. I played cards with her and her cronies *one time,* ten minutes, tops, the morning of the event. That's it.

You know her.

Get off my back.

I quicken my pace and get clear of the graveyard. Snakes is the ticket. Been running good ever since Memorial Day. Enough to buy this cheap netbook and put a dent in the money owed some friends I'm winning back.

Or maybe I should just head to the Riverwalk and grab some bench for a while. The sun might burn a chronic afterimage out of my head.

Some version of post-traumatic shock is messing with my sleep, and it's gotta go, man.

I am *not* slipping back into lunacy.

The photo, the photo, the photo.

Good God. Billy's imaginary resting place is blocks behind me now and I'm still hearing his voice.

Where am I? Lately, when I put my body on automatic and let my mind wander, whatever navigator I've got in my head has been going on the fritz.

Guess I'm still straddling the edge of the French Quarter.

Yeah. Some party beads in the gutter, meaning I'm nearing the tourists, but just enough rust and decay all around to tell me I'm still a few blocks away.

I could cross this street for the shortest route to Snakes, but duty calls first. My morning blog entry. A woman named Victoria who lives inside a viaduct shared a chunk of her life story with me. So I'm detouring around the corner in search of the hotspot I found near here before.

To be honest, it's mostly the tree calling my name at the moment. I saw a huge yellow ribbon, way bigger than Charlie's, tied to its trunk yesterday. The ribbon drew plenty of pilgrims who left flowers and wreaths behind. Photos, too.

Down this block, I think.

Nope.

Half a block farther.

There it is. A monstrous old thing with roots probably stretching all the way across the street. Maybe even under that run-down two-flat over there. Billy claims it's Philippe's place. I doubt that. Would an Old Man Coffee who squirrels his life savings into racks of poker chips invest in an Internet connection? To what end?

Billy and I have been talking too much lately. After the event at Snake Eyes—a near miss by me and dozens of others who could have died—post-traumatic holes in my memory opened wide, and he dived right in.

I'll scour him out again. After I find a way to take control during the dreams I've been having, he's next on the list. But first, I need to ask Amy some questions. For my readers.

The dreams started three days ago. Maybe four. Me on a bench looking out at the river with the Many-Named Goddess herself, this drop-dead gorgeous redhead with crafty eyes. I look at her, address her by the weirdest name—Alaska—and she says, *What should I call you today?*

So one day, I'm Rufus, and another I'm Herbert, and another Dilly—yeah, that's right—because she says she's a little bit mad at me but she can't remember why.

I can't, either. Patches of my memory are missing. Not a whole lot. Just things that happened at Snakes during Memorial Day weekend and maybe a little before.

I lower to the ground and lean into the tree. My head against the bark. Reopen my eyes after a few beats, but I'm no better off. Still a tad too fuzzy.

Some of these flowers are pricey. Dozens of roses. Red, yellow, white. But it's the picture I'm after. A surveillance shot somebody cut out of a newspaper and taped to the trunk. We didn't get any rain last night, so maybe it's still hanging.

There it is. Peeling some but still clinging to the bark for dear life. A casino shot. Amy's looking straight across the table, and that means she must be staring right at me. I remember our positioning at the time but not much else before all hell broke loose.

Am I bluffing you out of a hand? Pushing you around like some tourist? You don't come across like the push-around type. Not in the pictures and not in the stories.

Why do I keep dreaming about you, Amy?

Every morning, I wake up a little more in love.

But don't tell Billy. He thinks I'm crazy enough already.

Time to refocus. The tree makes a nice backrest down here on the ground. I open my netbook and get into the blog. Picked up a handful of new followers this morning. We're hundreds strong and growing.

In the next dream, I'll ask Amy about her mother. That's a story we all want to hear.

CHAPTER THIRTY-FOUR

I'VE BEEN INTERROGATED EVERY which way for weeks. Not always gently. The kid-glove types are nowhere to be found, and Guantanamo threats are scaring the daylights out of me. Am I destined for the third-world prison cells and maggoty meals I'd previously and naively considered a possibility only if I'd gotten caught passing bad chips in Turkey?

The new Things in my life are FBI special agents, numbering four or five, plus a couple CIA types. On top of that, throw in some random profilers, coercers, good cops, bad cops, counselors, and even a priest. If Hans, Yosef, and I are part of a larger cell, they need to know names. People's lives are in danger. So tell us, you piece of garbage.

They took away my bracelet with the little tree-of-strength charm, but I can picture it when I shut my eyes. I wrap my hand around the tree in my mind's eye and squeeze so often it's getting tarnished.

I've got holes in my memory, so they send in a shrink. Friendly guy, compared to the others. *PTSD*, he calls it. *Try to remember,* he says, *cuz we need names.*

The Thing count is growing, well into double digits. Not a single one of them gives me so much as a pat on the back for saving the lives of the people in the casino who would have otherwise been regarded as poor souls at wakes and funerals throughout Greater New Orleans. I'm thought of as *in on it*, and no doubt reviled throughout the land, or so the Things would have me believe.

But then one day, the mood changes. I start meeting friendlier Things.

Fewer Things.

Things who will listen to my stories, even though I'm a poker player and a liar and a piece of garbage.

Cuz I'm not anymore?

I don't get it, but who am I to question my sudden good fortune?

I tell them again *I* wasn't the one wearing the suicide vest, and they hear me. I say again it wasn't my fault *an entire network* of security cameras went bad, spoiling every frame with weird double images. They sympathize over the fact their lip readers couldn't confirm I talked Yosef down rather than shout encouragement to blow everybody to kingdom come the way a piece of garbage might do.

I explain again how the thousand dollars they photographed me giving Hans and Yosef was an innocent act without sinister motive. They tell me what a generous young lady I am.

Seriously?

Only later do I learn how a political breeze blowing in my favor gusted to hurricane force the day a copycat walked into a crowded Israeli marketplace, locked and loaded, shouted the magic words—*I can do this! But I won't*—and surrendered.

Another in Germany the next day.

Two cells are taken down by these acts. *Counting coup,* the press calls it.

Only later do I learn I started a movement when I talked Yosef down.

Little old me.

And only later do I learn a *Many-Named Goddess* march in Washington drew a crowd ten thousand strong.

They bring me newspapers to read, so it's later now, and I've learned.

Yay for politics. I've been innocent all along, and they finally agree. The Things hand back my belongings—sans a bunch of fake IDs, which the DA now says he'll look the other way on—drive me by van from somewhere off the grid to somewhere back on, take my blindfold off... and I'm free.

Breathing the riverside air like the finest of wines, right outside Snakes.

Which is still in one piece.

What now?

Where do I go?

Well, let's see. There's a stolen flat in the Quarter, but my ex-boyfriend's certainly back from Haiti by now.

How about some extra newspapers next to Charlie? Nah, the sidewalk beneath gets hard in a hurry, and the sun *bakes*.

Or door number three.

So I'm walking and walking toward the worst part of town. Not that I need protection. The horde of paparazzi trailing behind would send anyone running, even the most hardened mugger. Those flashing lights, shouted questions, microphones in my face till I swat them away. And to think I once wanted to be a celebrity because they seem overly pampered. Now I know the dark side of it.

I walk fast with head lowered. These people won't get any answers out of me. Not yet, anyway. My mom once said, if the milk is free, why buy the cow? This came during a boy-crazy phase in my teenage years, but like much of her advice, the little saying is just as relevant today.

My long march ends at the doorstep of a recently-rendered-penniless Russian—the poster child for either filing one's tax returns promptly or secretly opening offshore accounts. A juicy story the press already knows. But they don't go away.

I shoo the most aggressive ones off the stoop with the meanest stare I can conjure. "Private property," I hiss.

And then comes the ritual.

Ring, ring, ring.

Wait, wait, wait.

Pound, pound, pound.

Wait, wait, wait.

Philippe peers through the blinds off to the side. The man's been through hell, I'm sure. Responding doesn't come easy. Especially with a crowd of paparazzi trampling his lawn. He opens the door a crack. Looks me up and down. Then beyond at the others. "What do they want?" he says.

"My life story. I'm thinking they'll pay to hear it."

He sneers. "Yeah? For ten cents?"

At first, his attitude puts me off. But then I recognize his mockery as a defense mechanism for down-and-outers like him and me. Why would anyone pay for *our* story?

"I've kinda got a specific number in mind, Philippe. Two hundred seventeen thousand dollars."

We're staring back and forth now, neither one of us cracking a smile, like two cats who can't decide whether to groom each other or start clawing.

"Playdate, my ass," he says.

"Quit bitching, Philippe. Maybe I saved your life. And by the way, counterfeit chips *my* ass."

He's grinning now. Opens the door wider and leads me into the house, retreating into the kitchen.

We're soon at the table again like old times, only he's got a glass of milk in front of him instead of the booze. "Eugene says it's healthier," he says.

"Well, duh."

Out of nowhere, a shadow passes over me. The partial fragment of a bittersweet memory, like from a dream I might have had. This has been happening a lot lately.

Maybe Philippe has a clue. "The times I came over here, did I ever mention anyone? A friend, maybe?"

"You mean Hans and Yosef?"

"No, somebody else."

He shrugs.

The mood lifts as suddenly as it came.

I place a black poker chip beside his milk glass. The last one in my purse. Before the little bomb-scare incident stole a month from my life and ten years from my expectancy, I'd sprayed all the other supposedly faulty bones into every church collection box I could find.

I arch my brows. How to put the question gently? "This fucking thing's real?"

Philippe spreads his hands, this balding old Russian. He has more of a grandfatherly look than a dad. A curmudgeon like from some Dickens novel. Must've robbed the cradle when he bedded my mom, for sure. "You were spiraling," he says. "Needed an adventure. Besides, you wouldn't have touched a single chip if I told you the truth."

He's right, of course.

"Pride. Just like your mom."

"Yeah, yeah. So now you're broke?"

"Always was," he says. "Those chips were for you."

"I can find my own way."

He doesn't respond but I know he's biting his tongue. There's an eight-hundred-pound elephant in the room.

"Not like my mom, Philippe. A better way." Finally, I'm able to admit she had issues. Life lessons have come down hard on me lately. I need to choose my role models with better care while still holding loved ones dear. The balancing act has always been tricky, but maybe I'm nailing it now.

"Did they rough you up in there?" he asks.

"Somewhat."

"Waterboard?"

"A little."

"What did you tell them?"

Philippe's pretending to be casual, but he isn't fooling me. "Nothing about counterfeit bones if that's what you're asking."

He scowls. "You think I don't trust my own daughter?"

"You shouldn't. I used to lie for a living."

"Just like your..." His gaze flies a thousand miles away. "And now?"

"I don't think I can anymore."

Philippe comes around the table and musses my hair. I can tell he wants to hug me, but neither one of us is a hugger. "I would have taken you places," he says. "Paris. Marrakesh."

"Can I crash on your couch for a few days?"

"*Mi casa es su casa.*"

I hug him for that, and he hugs back.

We're in the living room a minute later and I'm looking into an empty closet. "Don't tell me the IRS carted all my stuff away."

"Stuff?"

"Yeah. The clothing and things I left at my ex's. You said you'd send somebody over. I wrote the address down for you."

He looks away. "I'll send somebody tomorrow if I can."

Oh, crap. Philippe doesn't have somebody anymore. Hoodies don't grow on trees. "No problem. I'll walk over and get it."

"I'll come, too."

This man standing here in his raggedy T-shirt and his faded jeans. He wants to be there for me, and I should hug him again. But if Peter's at the flat—and why shouldn't he have returned after a whole month?—if he's back, I should deal with him on my own.

"Not this time. Maybe we'll take a walk later, okay? If you don't mind a crowd following us around."

I notice the key to the flat on an end table beside the couch. Must have left it there the day Philippe and I drank and drank. And resting beside it, a second key?

Philippe follows my gaze. "So you won't scare the shit out of me ringing the doorbell no more."

Those two keys. Sitting there for a month. Waiting for me.

So many hugs in one day. I release him after a moment and head out the door.

Six blocks this way, twelve that. So good to walk after being cooped up like a bird with broken wings. And this baking sun? Intoxicating.

The ranks of my followers thin. They aren't marathoners like me.

Nine more blocks into the heart of the French Quarter and the little flat where I once brought... who? I'm halfway up the stairs when the sense of déjà vu rolls over me again. But the moment passes just as quickly.

I fit the key in the lock, open the door, and there's all my stuff in a pile on the floor.

"Welcome back." Peter steps out of the bedroom. His look is the same. Crew cut, muscle shirt, jeans. A cigarette dangles from his lips. A man I once loved who ran off with a whore named Cynthia. Leaving me as if I were... a piece of garbage.

"I... I just want my things."

He comes up to me, crowding my space.

I back up a step, but he grabs me by the wrist, fast, and...

A movie plays behind my eyes. Not my life flashing by, but a portion of somebody's I now remember. *Mike.* His return warms me like a fire. I've discovered the colors that were hiding from me, the musical notes an octave higher than where I'd been stuck. And I learn the most amazing secrets. But they're mixed with so much deceit and foul intention I need to wrap my arms around myself to suppress a shiver. Wormholes, jinns, time running forward, time in reverse, higher-ups who sign away lives with pen to scroll, a little girl with bottomless eyes, and scams... despicable scams. Everything is stirred into a bouillabaisse of alternate reality and poured down my throat till I need to retch.

The show ends after a dozen forevers. I'm on the couch panting.

Peter sits too close and crowds me again.

The physical world looks the same. This apartment with light filtering through blinds left partially open just so, the way I've always liked. Peter with his tattoos and crooked smile. But one of two possibilities has opened my eyes far wider than ever before. Either a new dimension or two has been revealed or I've gone crazier than Mike. One way or the other, nothing will ever be the same again.

Still, this dream Peter just gave me, or whatever it was... what I witnessed in this funhouse mirror of a reality show didn't fill in every blank. The genie scam must have had a beginning, an inciting event, but all I've seen is a loop from Snakes to the gypsy casino and back. I pass chips to Mike, he passes them to me, and then on and on forever. "How did this start?" I ask.

He takes a long drag from his cigarette. Puffs it out. Wry grin on his face now. "I get a call from upstairs. They're bitching about my work ethic, because I'd neglected two people and now they're about to die in an explosion before I can match them up with their soul mates or whatever."

A shrug. Another drag on his smoke. "I do my job, and maybe they won't die, but it's too late now. *Big deal,* I say. *Plenty more where they came from.*"

Oh, good God! I've gotta stop him right there. "Peter?"

"Uh-huh?"

"I slept with you back before I met Mike."

He leers. "More than once."

"Ew."

"Wait, Amy. Hear me out. This girl, Gabriella, comes along and tells me, *you're there, too.* I'm like, *oh, crap, I've gotta do something.* See? That's the real me, Amy. A hero."

"A hero." I don't know what more I can say to this... wart. Or to myself for letting him into my bed once upon a time. Let him talk till he's done and hopefully goes away, I suppose.

Peter grinds his cigarette butt into a coaster. Looks at me. Then away. "Anyway, this girl, Gabriella? She says, *Call Amy on the phone and warn her, you dummy.* So I do. Except you hang up on me. Then I race over to the casino only to see you walking out. Before the kaboom. Must have listened even though you hung up."

"But I didn't," I say.

He shrugs. "Things get twisty because of all that happens after. But I'm thinking you're fine and that's that. Time to hit the road."

That's that. He hasn't lifted a finger to try saving anyone else in the casino. I'm almost ready to heave, but he's too caught up in his tale to notice.

"But, see, the story's just getting started," he says, "because

Gabriella hits me up with this great plan. She says she's thrown some guy named Mike into this other dimension that shares a few entry points with ours. Squirrels him away just in the nick of time to avoid the blast. And now *I* can kill two birds with one stone. Save the Asian and tourist to keep from getting fired, and chuck my whole crazy life as a jinn by running the genie scam on Mike. I can become human and he gets to be… this other thing."

He pulls another cigarette out of his pocket. "You mind?" Lights up before I can tell him where to shove it. Takes a fresh drag. Blows it out. "When everything's said and done, though, I guess Gabriella scammed *me*, didn't she? I'm still a jinn, and I struck out with you. Unless…"

"Unless I give you a second chance with me?" The urge to heave is back with a vengeance. "Peter?"

"Uh-huh."

"Never come near me again."

He raises his hands. "Whoa there. This isn't on me. I cut a bad deal, that's all. These bosses with their scrolls and sign-offs and shit. I never should have had to tell you the whole story."

"You'd come back to me with Mike lost in limbo, with everyone else dead, and never say a word how you could have prevented it? You'd just live a lie?"

"Pot calling the kettle," he says.

I can't even look at him.

"So that's it then?" he says.

"The door's over there."

He stands. Takes a few steps. Stops. "This is my place. Why don't *you* leave."

"You have no place anymore. You're just another jinn made of smoke and fire." I paid really good attention when he played that movie.

And now we're done. For good. Except… "Wait."

"I'm listening."

"Go restore Mike's memory. You owe me that much."

"Bite me, Amy."

And he's gone.

CHAPTER THIRTY-FIVE

A HOMELESS MAN NAMED Simon told me his story today. Bad luck, worse luck, and then the truly awful things started happening. But he hasn't quit on us. He wants to be mayor. I signed his petition, giving the other six names some company. His story will get out there if I can find the hotspot, but my bearings are off this morning.

The sounds of commerce are more distant than they should be, and lacking in their usual bustle. In fact, the elbow-to-elbow, touristy streets of the French Quarter are nowhere in sight. I must have turned the wrong corner somewhere past the cemetery.

Everything in my immediate surroundings hints at ruin. Wrought-iron balconies bend toward inevitable collapse. Paint peels from crumbly brick walls. Discarded party beads litter the gutter. A sour breeze offers no respite from the heat.

Somebody angles toward me from across the street. Jeans and a muscle shirt, average height, close-cropped hair. Stocky. Maybe thirty or so. He slows, takes a drag from a cigarette, eyes me, and keeps on coming.

Ex-military, judging by the crew cut. A panhandler now, or a drunk. Either way, a man with a story. But his smirk says grifter.

No matter. I'll shake his hand and hear whatever tale he wants to spin.

"Name's Peter," the man says. Whatever his story, give him credit for a firm handshake.

"Mike."

I notice a woman leaning against the wall of a building not ten feet away. Tall blonde. Killer figure. How did I miss her? She's smoking away with one hand and gives me one of those finger waves with the other.

Neither says another word, so I move on. I've run into these types before. Either they're playing with less of a deck than I am or they sized me up for some scam but thought better of it.

The dream I had last night echoes in my head as I move on down the sidewalk. Echoes and fades, leaving me with the emptiness false memories often trail in their wake. Like I've forgotten a color or a flavor or a song. A dream about the love of my life, and she doesn't exist. Now *that's* a bad beat.

Haven't felt much like poker these past few days, but I head to Snakes, anyway. Sometimes the lights and clamor fill a hole when I walk inside. This time, though, not so much. I find a seat in a game and play with half a heart, listening to the banter of some guy from Texas. His name's Isaac. A salesman with a ton of stale jokes.

But he stops yammering before getting to another old punchline, and he stares off to the side.

A poker room always carries the steady white noise of chips clicking, players murmuring, and the occasional shout of joy or frustration. Sometimes anger. But the sound right now in this place? It morphs into something a bit off. A combination of louder murmur and fewer clicks.

I follow Isaac's gaze.

Wow. There she is. The Many-Named Goddess herself, wearing her signature spaghetti-strap sundress, just like in her newspaper pictures. She brightens the room with her celebrity.

The Goddess brushes a stray bang from her forehead.

So odd. I almost remember something.

But I don't.

She's standing at the entrance, scanning the games until our eyes meet.

Now she's walking toward my table, but there's no open seat. Wait. She's heading right at *me*?

I swallow.

In my defense, a goddess will do that to any mere mortal. Yet when she stops in front of me and I look into those gray-green eyes, I find a little girl in there…and I almost imagine she's as lonely as me. See, that's the thing. Strip away the names—Amy or Mike. Forget the labels—homeless or magnificent. We're all flesh and blood behind our masks.

"I've been loving your blog," she says.

"So you're the one."

She smiles, even though the joke's an old one. And now she's sporting dimples to die for. "I'm Patricia. What should I call *you* today?"

A name from an almost-forgotten dream pops into my head. "I'm Dilly."

Her grin widens for a moment, but she looks past me at the games, and it falters. "I can't do this scene anymore, Dilly. Let's have lunch somewhere different, and I'll tell you my story."

"Now you're talking." I fumble my chips into a rack and head to the cage so fast Patricia has trouble keeping up with me.

EPILOGUE

A LOCAL COLLEGE ASKED me to give their commencement address next month.

Me.

Amy.

How cool is that?

How amazing is that?

I'm picky about these engagements. You'll never find me in a conference room motivating a bunch of suits. But give me a school. Give me a youth center.

When addressing a group, my two messages are simple.

Grass roots wisdom like my mom used to share.

First, you haven't truly lived until you spend a few days on a pile of cardboard and newspapers. So do that sometime.

If you're lucky, maybe Mike will ask to hear your story, and all his many readers will learn about you.

Next, what's the least you need for making do? Call that your floor, but be careful. If you build one too high, you'll be afraid to take risks. That brings us back to the cardboard and newspapers, doesn't it? Not everyone who hears this second thing gets it. But some do.

I'll never know how much my life story would have sold for. I gave it to Mike for free. He blogged it in installments, and by the time he was finished, his followers were legion. Mike writes a syndicated column now, so we do have a little bit of money to live on. Too much, actually. The afternoon I got scared of forgetting my mom cuz we were rising too high above our floor, Mike wiped my tears away. He reminded me what I did the last time I had too many bones in my purse.

So I've been buying black chips at Snakes lately and spraying them all over town—in the collection boxes of churches and synagogues, and into the hands of reliable truck-stop cashiers to take care of guys like Charlie when they get low on the essentials.

My mom is rolling over in her grave. She had so many stories to tell about what she'd do if she ever had a nickel to spare. I wish Mike could have met her and written them down. Maybe she and I wouldn't have been invisible the summer we spent on the sidewalk.

See, that's what my man does. He takes the homeless, the disenfranchised, the forgotten, and he casts them in the light of day.

When a toy company asked to do my action figure, I almost said no. The chip count would have been more than I could spray. More importantly, I've been trying to *fade.* Anyone who once was invisible does miss it sometimes. But Philippe's two-flat had gone into foreclosure and he needed a new home.

He's my dad, though, and pride runs deep in our family. So I did say no. Philippe can crash on our couch for a few days anytime he wants. Mike and I have taken to squatting in the missing Peter's flat again, and there's always room for one more.

As for Charlie, he's still on the sidewalk and happy as a clam. Lately, he's been talking about a vacation up north maybe, to see who he might meet.

Hans and Yosef? Who wouldn't wonder about them? Although they didn't kill anyone, they certainly came packing—a serious crime no matter how one looks at it. They get a shot at parole five years from now. Meanwhile, Hans said in a letter that Yosef still calls me little sister. I suppose that's the reason stalkers in black sedans have joined the ranks of paparazzi to snap my picture now and again. No matter. I've learned to ignore the background noise and focus on helping Mike.

I scout stories for him when he's feeling fine, and I cover for him when the crazies take hold. He's my everything and I try to be his. So we awaken every day happy, and we go to bed the same way.

Mike will always be a little nuts in a beautiful way.

And me? I'm the Many-Named Goddess. A terrorist, folk hero, thief, and a liar. The daughter of a grifter... and the apple doesn't fall far from the tree.

Believe our stories if you want.

Or not.

But thank you for listening. You've helped make us visible. And human.

Ciao.

Or as my dad would say in the motherland, *see ya*. Cuz my keyboard doesn't have any of those weird Russian letters.

ACKNOWLEDGMENTS

IN LATE 2014, AFTER finishing work on a novel that hasn't been published yet, I set pen and paper aside and stepped away from writing to pursue other interests. A fanatical exercise regime swallowed three or four hours each day. An online poker addiction helped keep me occupied. So did my job. And my family.

Somewhere along the line, a general story concept began percolating in my brain. A struggling poker player is shadowed by a shady drifter named Runbad. Maybe one or the other of those two has Las Vegas aspirations. Perhaps a supernatural element will come into play.

By late 2015, I had written just a single scene, a mere 1,500 words. In those few pages, my player, Mike, gets scammed by a female con artist in a New Orleans poker game. And then what? I didn't know.

Not much interesting happened in my life after that. More exercise. More online poker, more job, more family. No writing.

Then, one day in the dead of winter, my long-time critique partner, Mia Jo Celeste, emailed. She'd completed a draft of a new novel and wanted to know whether we could exchange chapters for critiques. I was all over that idea—anything to kick my writing into gear—but I cautioned her that only a single scene in my novel had been drafted. Entire chapters? We're probably talking a snail's pace, Mia.

Yet, somehow, four months later, Faulty Bones was written and ready to go. So how about that?

Throughout the critique process, Mia's suggestions were right on point. But beyond the technical aspects of her assistance, something started channeling the minute she got in touch. No way did this novel come from the brain of J. M. Fraser. I'm thinking Mars maybe. Or Venus.

Thanks, Mia.

I also want to acknowledge a fine novelist, Helen Johannes. Once my story picked up steam, I sought her out for additional critique assistance. Do you find Mike and Amy likeable? Helen helped with that. Did you make it through the first half dozen chapters without getting totally confused? Yep, Helen again.

Next is the awesome creative genius Elle J Rossi. She took this entire crazy novel and painted its pure essence on the cover of the book. Whether or not you like my story, you'll stare mesmerized at that artwork.

And Amy Stumbo Knupp. She copy edited this novel and made some amazing catches. Errors and inconsistencies I wouldn't have caught in a thousand years. But that wasn't her main contribution. *Faulty Bones* would still be under the mattress if not for Amy's enthusiasm and encouragement.

I also thank Carolyn Fraser for beta reading my novel, and having faith that one day, her dad might produce something worth publishing.

Thanks to Eric Arsiniega for designing two eye-catching websites for me.

Thanks to Amy Atwell and Author E.M.S. for digital and print formatting as well as awesome patience in dealing with me during a busy time of the year.

Thanks to Yvette Graff for beta reading all three of my novels and loving two of them, including this one!

Thanks to Kelly Brandstatter for bubbling over with excitement and ideas when I told her how this novel could be a step toward helping a forgotten people.

ABOUT THE AUTHOR

J.M. FRASER is a businessman and writer. He empty-nests (not counting three or four cats) with his better half, Mary, in the suburban prairies west of Milwaukee. When not doing whatever it is that they do, they visit their two grown daughters, Carolyn and Natalie, as often as they can. The apple doesn't fall far from the tree. One day, each of these wildly creative young women will produce an amazing book.